Bitter Betrayal

Meaghan Pierce

Pierced Soul Publishing

Editing by Comma Sutra Editorial

Cover Design by Books and Moods

For all the women who want to feel dainty, delicate, and desirable

Chapter One

She obviously had a death wish.

It wasn't pulling into the parking lot of Reign, one of Philly's most popular nightclubs, in the middle of the day that was the problem so much as she was walking into the lion's den. And the lions might be hungry.

She parked behind a Jaguar that was angled between a Range Rover and an Escalade. Apparently they liked their cars black and expensive. The building looked deserted in the light of day, two unassuming stories of faded red brick and blacked-out windows. But at night, even in the sticky, sweltering heat of August, the line of people clamoring to get in would wrap around the side of the building.

It was stupid coming here—in broad daylight, no less—but she'd racked her brain trying to think of any other way to help rescue them. The truth was, she was powerless in her world. She had no other options.

Cutting the engine, she climbed out of the borrowed beat-up Toyota, pushing her sunglasses up on her head when they fogged in the temperature change. Sweat beaded between her shoulder blades as she crossed the parking lot. Summer had Philadelphia by the throat, and it wasn't prepared to let go.

Fist raised to knock, she paused, suddenly unsure if this was the right decision. Betraying her family, even to save innocent lives, would come at a cost. Was she willing to pay it? Shaking the doubt from her mind, she pounded the flat of her fist on the door. She wouldn't be able to live with herself otherwise.

Nothing. Frowning, she pounded again. Someone was obviously here, so why the hell weren't they answering? Her eyes darted across the parking lot toward the street. If her father found out she was here, the Callahan brothers would be the least of her worries because the consequences would be swift and severe.

She reached up to pound one more time when the door suddenly swung in, and she jolted. She had to step back and still crane her neck to see the man framed in the doorway.

He towered over her, at least a foot taller than she was. Muscled arms crossed over his broad chest, a patchwork of tattoos disappearing under the sleeves of his shirt. Brogan Callahan.

The cool blast from the air conditioning was nothing compared to his icy stare. His gaze raked down her body, lingering on the generous swell of hips her mother had been trying to diet off her for years.

"Aidan isn't here," Brogan sneered.

Knowing the youngest Callahan brother's reputation for never sleeping with the same woman twice, her eyes narrowed. "I'm not here to see Aidan. I'm here to see Declan."

"We're busy, and Declan is married. I promise he's not interested."

Bristling when he moved to slam the door in her face, she leapt forward to wedge herself against it, arm shooting out to keep it from closing. She silently cursed herself when his eyes dropped to the small tattoo on her wrist, his hand moving to rest on the butt of his gun.

"We're even less interested in inviting a Giordano in," he said through gritted teeth.

"I promise I have something you're going to want to hear." He stared at her, unmoving. "I wouldn't be here, incurring my father's wrath, if it wasn't important."

His eyes narrowed on her face, his head tilted ever so slightly as if he was trying to place her in his memory.

"Well? Are you going to let me in or not?"

He studied her for a moment more, blue eyes piercing. "No. But wait here."

He motioned for her to step back, then disappeared inside. She could feel the sweat dripping down her back, annoyed he hadn't at least let her wait inside out of this damned heat.

As the minutes ticked by, she pushed her sunglasses back into place. Edging into the shade when the sun peeked over the building and slanted across the parking lot, she wondered if he was fucking with her. He probably had no intention of coming back, let alone bringing his brothers.

She didn't recognize the cars driving by on the street, but that didn't mean they didn't recognize her. The idea of pissing off her father with nothing to show for it had anxiety settling in her chest. Maybe this was a mistake after all.

Just as she turned to leave, the door opened again. Another cooling blast of air conditioning wrapped around her as each brother filed out, eyeing her with suspicion.

For generations, the Callahan family had sat on the throne of Philadelphia's underground of organized crime. Declan, recently married, had taken over the Callahan syndicate when his father died unexpectedly two years prior. His method of control over the city differed from his father's, but was no less effective.

People listened when money talked, and Declan had pumped a lot of money into hands all over the city. From the lowest of foot soldiers to the highest of politicians. He might dress like a businessman in perfectly tailored suits and polished shoes, but people knew not to fuck with him unless you were prepared to pay his price.

"This is a step up from your usual line of communication. People who operate outside their patterns make me suspicious," Declan said.

So they recognized her. She wasn't sure if that made her feel better or worse. "This is too important to write down and risk it falling into the wrong hands."

"Okay, then. Enlighten us." Declan somehow managed to look both bored and intrigued.

"Can we go somewhere more private?" Her eyes swept the parking lot, a chill pricking her skin despite the heat. This felt too exposed.

"No."

Her gaze shifted to Brogan, who eyed her with curiosity—and maybe a hint of disdain. The third Callahan brother had to be the muscle, if not the brains, behind the operation, what with his tree-trunk arms and deep scowl. You'd never imagine he was related to Declan if they didn't share those same Callahan blue eyes.

She blew out a breath. Here goes nothing. "My father's trafficking women."

She hadn't expected to blurt it out quite so frankly, but none of the four men even seemed fazed by it. Finn, the second oldest and Declan's right hand, even offered a sardonic chuckle while the two exchanged a look.

"And why would you share that with us?" Finn shoved

his hands into his pockets as if brushing her off, but his eyes were sharp. She imagined he never missed a detail.

"Because everyone in this city knows you don't tolerate moving girls."

"Then that makes your father a pretty stupid guy," Aidan replied.

She tensed. There was no love lost between them, but he was still her father. Except riling her is exactly what they wanted, so instead she calmly asked, "Do you want the information or not?"

Brogan leaned over to whisper something to Declan and whatever he said had Declan's gaze snapping to her, jaw clenched. When a car passed by on the road, slowing ever so slightly, Declan flicked a glance at Finn before turning to face her again.

"Let's take this inside."

She had to fight against indignation at Brogan's rough grasp on her upper arm. He led her through the empty club that looked alien without its crush of bodies and swirl of neon lights and down a set of concrete steps. She was doing the right thing here, and she didn't appreciate being manhandled.

When the door closed behind them, her heart thudded in her chest. Suddenly, this seemed like a very stupid idea. Being alone in a soundproof basement with four of Philadelphia's most powerful and dangerous men ranked pretty low on her list of good life choices. But desperate times and all that.

Brogan jerked her to a halt outside a small room, deftly patting her down for weapons. He made quick work of it, didn't let his hands linger, something that definitely should not—did not—disappoint her. He pulled her phone and keys out of her back pocket, passing them over his shoulder to

Finn, who slid them into a metal box hanging on the wall outside the door.

Brogan gave her a light shove into the room, pointing to a chair set in the middle of the floor. She sat in it only because the idea of being forced into it if she insisted on standing seemed worse than doing so of her own accord.

They faced her in a half circle, and she clenched her hands in her lap. Either this would be fine or she would never leave this basement again.

"So your father wants to declare war against me."

The blood rushed through her ears as her heartbeat quickened. That was a dangerous way to put it. "I didn't say that."

"You said he's trafficking girls in my city. Our position has been made abundantly clear on that front. The last men who tried ended up floating in the river. What would you call it?"

She met Declan's gaze with her head high. "An error in judgment." Aidan snorted, but she ignored him. "I only know about one shipment. How many can there be?"

"Dozens."

Her gaze found Brogan's, and she shook her head. "No. That's impossible. He wouldn't—"

"He would and he is," Finn interrupted. "So why don't you start at the beginning."

Gripping her elbows, she sucked in a sharp breath. She'd been naive to think this was the only one, that she happened to overhear his first and only attempt to traffic women. Dozens. The thought made her sick.

She dug her fingernails into her elbows to anchor herself. This was the point of no return. "In three days, they're supposed to pick up a group of women from a house east of the city and"—she swallowed against the nausea that threatened to choke her—"deliver them to buyers."

"Deliver them where?"

She froze. She hadn't heard of a drop-off point. Only an address her father had read to confirm pickup.

"Give me a break. She doesn't know anything." Aidan rolled his eyes. "She's just a bitch trying to get one over on us or get back at her dad or whatever the fuck. It's probably not even legit."

"My name is Libby," she snapped. "And I would think at this point I'd have earned a little trust, all things considered. I did warn you about the bounty on your wife's head after all," she added, eyeing Declan.

She watched Finn lean over to mumble to Declan, speaking in hushed whispers, and she let her gaze drift to Brogan. He hadn't moved or spoken since taking his place beside his brothers. His eyes were locked on her in a way that made her blood hum.

"She stays here until we can check this out."

"You can't keep me here." She started to rise but thought better of it when Brogan tensed.

"I already have you here," Declan replied. "And here is where you're going to stay until my men confirm this isn't a trap."

Libby looked from Declan to Brogan and back again. "Why would I come here, at considerable personal risk, just to lure you into a trap?"

"So you're doing this out of the kindness of your heart?"

"I'm doing this because I know what it's like to be a prisoner," Libby spat at Aidan. "And no one deserves that. I came here because you're the only people in the city who can and will stop this."

"That still doesn't explain why I should let you go."

"Because," she said through clenched teeth, "I'm supposed to attend a party my father is throwing tonight, and if I don't show up, that will make him pretty suspicious."

She forced herself to remain perfectly still when Declan

pinned her with an icy stare. She could tell he didn't trust her, and the feeling was mutual. But she only needed him to believe her enough to take this seriously and do what she could not—save these women from a fate worse than death.

"Fine," Declan said. "Give us the address of this house, and Aidan will show you out."

Declan silenced Aidan's protests with a look so deadly she had to fight the urge to bolt. There was trouble in Callahan paradise.

"What happens when you go into a situation like this?" she wondered, scribbling the address she'd memorized on the paper Brogan handed her.

"What do you mean?"

She glanced at Finn. "Are there...survivors?"

Finn's brow shot up, and he cocked his head ever so slightly. "Not generally. Dead men can't take details back to anyone."

"Why?" Declan wondered. "Is there someone you want us to spare in exchange for this information?"

She flicked a glance at Brogan, who watched her intently. She likely knew the men who'd be caught in Callahan crosshairs. They had families, wives and kids, maybe. And still, their fate would be better than the women they trans- ported like cattle. A quick, clean death was better than a slow, torturous one. This was the cost. Turns out she was willing to pay it.

She shook her head, rising before Aidan had the chance to yank her out of the chair. "No. There's no one."

Shrugging off Aidan's grip when he shoved her toward the stairs and up, she crossed the club on shaky legs. Growing up around death didn't prepare you to be the cause of it. She wouldn't be the one to pull the trigger, but the result would be the same. Now she'd have to live with the consequences.

"If it were up to me, you'd be tied down to that chair right now, hoping none of our men died," Aidan gritted out as he pushed her toward the door, tossing her keys so violently they nearly hit her in the face.

"Good thing saner heads than yours are in charge."

Pushing her sunglasses back onto her nose, she stepped out into the heat. She started across the lot toward her car, forcing herself to not look back when she heard the door open and close behind her, the scrape of shoes on pavement as someone followed her out. Had they changed their mind about letting her go?

Quickening her pace, she lunged for her car door, hissing as the hot metal burned her skin. She used her shirt to open it, catching movement out of the corner of her eye.

"What are you doing?" she asked as Brogan rounded the hood of her car and stopped to watch her, eyes dipping down to the exposed skin of her stomach and back up to her face.

"You forgot your phone."

When he held it out over the hood of the car, she snatched it.

"And I've got orders to follow you home, make sure you don't give dear old dad any warnings."

"You can't do that." If someone saw she was being followed home by a Callahan, she'd be dead in twenty-four hours. Or less. Panic clawed at her. "I'm not going to tell anyone. I swear."

"I believe you." If he was as startled by his words as she was, he didn't show it. "But orders are orders. Don't worry," he added, tone softening as if he could sense her fear. "I'll make sure no one sees me."

She checked the time on her phone before shoving it into her pocket. "The house won't be empty at this time of day. Not with a party tonight." He turned to go. "But...maybe you'll blend in."

She swore she saw his lips twitch in a barely contained

smile before he stepped back and folded his large frame behind the wheel of the Jag. It wasn't the car that would stand out—it was his hulking tattooed frame behind the wheel.

She'd feel a lot better about this whole thing if he let her leave without an escort, but she didn't seem to have much choice. Climbing behind the wheel, she cranked the engine, grunting when the warm blast of air hit her in the face.

Cutting down the fan until the air cooled, she backed out of the parking lot, fingers tight on the steering wheel, watching in her rearview as he pulled out behind her and followed at a distance.

Chapter Two

As they circled away from the club, Brogan couldn't help but wonder why this mysterious woman seemed so intent on helping them. First the warning about the bounty Evie's own sister had put on Evie's head a few months ago. Now this.

Someone more cynical might think Libby had other intentions, but he wasn't so sure. What had she said back at the club? *I know what it's like to be a prisoner.* Whatever her reasons, every time she defied her father she put herself in danger. Tony Giordano wasn't one to suffer snitches or strong women. Libby appeared to be both.

Brogan slowed to a crawl when she pulled into the driveway in front of a house built to look like an Italian villa. She maneuvered around a caterer's van parked beside a gaudy gold fountain and pulled in behind a red Mercedes. She popped the trunk and pulled a trio of shopping bags from the luxury car. So she'd borrowed the beat-up Toyota. Clever girl.

To her credit, she didn't so much as glance in his direction as she made her way around the front of the house, allowing herself to be seen by the people carting boxes to and from the door. But even from this distance, he could see the tension in her shoulders as she jogged up a set of wide stone steps to the front porch and disappeared inside.

He pretended to check his phone while he waited a bit to see if she came back out or someone else pulled up. He didn't want to hang around too long and make people suspicious. The longer he sat, the better chance of someone recognizing him, but he wanted to be sure she wasn't fucking with them.

I believe you, he'd said to her back at the club, and he'd been telling the truth. From the moment she opened her damn mouth with its full top lip and biting sarcasm, he was intrigued. Something about her called to him.

Lust, sure. She was exactly the type he went for. All soft curves and generous thighs and an ass you could really hold on to. But he wasn't one to think with his dick, which made this pull he felt all the more concerning. There was absolutely no way he could get himself tangled up with an Italian, let alone one of Giordano's own kids. It wouldn't end well.

He waited a few minutes more, checking that the app he'd added to her phone pinged properly before pulling away from the curb. If she left the house to go anywhere, they'd know it. And that was as close as he could ever allow himself to get to her.

Libby glimpsed the Jag through the front window and heard the low growl of the engine as it sped away. He'd kept his distance as promised, and she'd done her best to take the long way home, avoiding the neighborhoods where most of her father's loyal men lived with their families.

The house was a flurry of activity, with maids cleaning every available surface and catering staff taking over the kitchen to get ready for tonight's party. If she looked hard enough, she'd find her mother among it all, happily barking out orders, perfectly manicured nails pointing and directing the chaos.

Her father was out. Thank God. He hated the expense of throwing parties but indulged his wife's love of hosting them to shut her up about his extramarital activities. They were impossible to ignore, though. Libby had more half siblings than she could count at this point.

She climbed the stairs to her bedroom and shut out the noise below. Setting the shopping bags on the edge of her bed, she sank down next to them. If anyone asked where she'd been today, she'd given herself an alibi. Some frivolous shopping, lunch with a girlfriend.

Borrowing Connie's car was a last-minute decision. It didn't stand out as much as her Mercedes did, and flying under the radar was the whole point. She just had to hope that the woman who'd raised her since diapers didn't mention it to anyone.

Libby might be a Giordano, but that didn't mean she'd escape punishment if her father found out what she'd really been up to today. She knew all too well how he liked to punish and work out his rage with his fists. She also knew the people who double-crossed him tended to disappear forever.

Careful to appear the perfect daughter, Libby satisfied herself with quiet rebellions. The college classes she took online that her parents didn't know about, the money she hoarded in a secret bank account, the methodical campaign she waged against her father for years to send her little sister to a real university.

Libby was willing to put up with it all. Until DiMarco. The first time she met DiMarco had been when her father brought him over for dinner. There was something about him even

13

then that made her uneasy. He always stared at her a little too long or hugged her a little too tight.

A few years older than her father, there was something sinister about DiMarco. He hid it well under polite smiles and a charming Italian accent, but the way she always found his eyes on her from across the room was unnerving. He reminded her of a predator stalking prey.

DiMarco did nothing without a reason, including manipulating his way up the Mafia's ranks until he was sitting at her father's right hand and whispering in his ear. Tony Giordano was by no means a saint, but Andrea DiMarco encouraged him to indulge the darkest parts of himself. She suspected even her mother noticed from the way she seemed more comfortable when Tony was gone than when he was home.

The entire family felt the lurking presence of their father's closest adviser, except for her sister, Teresa, who was safely away at school. Pulling her phone out, Libby crossed to the window and took a photo of the busy driveway below, sending it to her sister.

Wish I didn't have to endure another boring party without you. Love you.

They were five years apart but had always been close. Bonded by their mutual love of the color pink and their misfortune in being born daughters in a world that prized sons. In Tony's world, women were only good for two things. Fucking and making babies.

Libby might be the oldest at twenty-seven and smarter than both her brothers combined, but she was not the heir. She was a woman, a commodity, an ornament at her father's beck and call until he found her useful. A pretty Mafia princess meant to be traded at precisely the right moment for her father's political gain. It was simply her dumb luck that moment hadn't arrived yet.

She turned at a knock on the door. "Come in," she said

when neither of her parents barged through it. They never waited for permission.

Connie poked her head around the door. "I thought I saw you come up here. Your mother would like to see you in the library."

"Already? The party doesn't start for hours."

Connie gave her a pained smile. "I'm afraid so. Best get it over with quick."

Libby gave Connie's arm a light squeeze on her way out the door and found her mother in the small library at the front of the house that was purely for show. No one read much except for Teresa. Teresa had been slowly working her way through all the books on the shelves since her tenth birthday.

"Oh, Elizabeth, there you are," Anna Giordano said, as if she didn't just summon her daughter from the other side of the house.

Libby fought hard not to roll her eyes. "Connie said you needed to see me?"

"Yes, I just spoke with your father."

Libby's stomach tightened, and she swayed a little on her feet. Had he found out about what she'd done already?

"He'd like you to wear something special to the party tonight."

"Oh." The grip of anxiety eased ever so slightly. "Did he say why?"

Anna pinned her daughter with a disappointed frown. "Does he need to say why, Elizabeth? Honestly, you've been acting so strange lately."

"Have I?"

"Mmm," Anna replied. "Spending more time out with your friends than you do at home and now the attitude. Your father doesn't approve, and frankly, neither do I. If you want to keep your privileges, you'll do as you're told and wear something appropriate to the party tonight. Do try and make it flattering," she added, dropping her eyes to Libby's hips and stomach.

"Of course, Mother," Libby agreed sweetly, though she was seething inside. "Anything else?"

"Watch your tone, Elizabeth. This party is critical to your father, and I promised him you'd be on your best behavior. Keep your mouth shut and play your part, and we'll all have a good time. You can go."

Dismissed, Libby climbed the stairs. She eased her bedroom door closed though she wanted to slam it, picked up the nearest breakable object, and heaved it at the wall. Satisfied at the explosion of glass and the drip of perfume down the paint, she sank down onto the floor and leaned her head against the door.

She knew what it was like to be a prisoner. Escaping her own bonds seemed all but impossible. Which is why she'd done everything in her power to get Teresa out.

Chapter Three

L ibby smoothed the front of her dress, studying herself in the mirror. It was exactly the kind of thing her mother would approve of. Not too tight, not too revealing, not too flashy. She hated everything about it.

Not the dress. The dress was fine, if a bit boring. She hated the pretending. Pretending she cared, pretending to smile, pretending she wasn't screaming inside her carefully constructed gilded cage.

She opened her bedroom door to the sound of soft music and the clinking of glasses. This was one of those parties meant to show off money and power. Her father was joined by captains and their wives, along with a few businessmen who knew what her father was and didn't care as long as the money was good. And him.

She glimpsed DiMarco as she came down the stairs and veered sharply to the left before she caught his eye. Anyone who didn't know him, didn't sense the darkness in him, might call him distinguished with his graying beard and hair he wore a little long but swept off his face. He was always impeccably dressed in a suit and tie, unusual for Mafia ranks.

It was all window dressing to cover up the monster underneath.

Grabbing a glass of bubbly off a passing tray, she took a bolstering drink, plastered on a smile, and made the rounds with guests. She congratulated the Rossinis, who were pregnant. Again. That had to be baby number seven. Or was it eight?

The Marinos had recently sent their youngest daughter to college. That information actually interested her, and she hoped more girls followed in Teresa's footsteps out of this life and into a world of possibilities. She could hardly begrudge them their freedom.

Wife after wife droned on endlessly about their house, their kids, or their husbands until Libby thought her brain would leak out of her ears. She was trying to figure out how she could slip away unnoticed when she caught her mother approaching out of the corner of her eye. Damn.

"Elizabeth. There you are."

The tightness in her mother's tone made her wary. "Were you looking for me?"

"Your father is about to make an announcement."

In an uncharacteristically rude gesture, her mother dragged her to the front of the room, where her father stood with DiMarco. Something was wrong. She could tell by her mother's tight grip on her arm and the strained smile on her face.

"Mother, what is—"

"Quiet," Anne snapped.

"Thank you all for coming tonight," Tony began, waiting for the room to still. "I wanted to celebrate the close of a very lucrative deal tonight."

Money and power. Did the people in this room know where their money was really coming from? Did they care?

"But I also want to celebrate something else."

He turned to Libby with his glass raised, a smile on his face but a warning glint in his eye. Her stomach dropped. This couldn't be happening.

"Tonight, we're also celebrating the engagement of my daughter, Elizabeth, to the man I trust most in the world. Andrea DiMarco."

No, no, no. All the air was siphoned from the room. She would have doubled over at the excruciating pain in her chest if not for her mother's vise grip on her arm. She had to get out of here.

"Smile." Anne's whisper was harsh in her ear as the people behind them began to clap.

"I won't marry him." She could tell she said it loud enough for people to hear when the clapping faltered.

"Shut up," Anne hissed as her father closed the space between them.

"This is not up for debate, Elizabeth."

She shook off her mother's grip, rubbing her hand across the marks Anne's fingernails left on her skin. Chin ticking up, Libby summoned the strength to meet her father's dark and dangerous gaze even if her knees were shaking.

"I will not marry that man."

It happened so fast that she didn't have time to brace herself before her father brought the back of his hand across her cheek. Stars exploded across her vision as her head snapped back, and the metallic tang of blood coated her tongue. People behind them gasped, but no one rushed to her defense. Not even her mother.

"You don't have a choice," her father snarled.

Libby shuddered at the truth of those five simple words.

Tony adjusted the ring on his pinky and wiped her blood from it before turning to his wife. "Anne, clean her up and bring her back here. She's being rude to our guests."

As her mother dragged her out of the room, Libby's gaze

drifted to DiMarco and the sickening grin that spread across his face. She stumbled into the powder room while her mother slapped on the lights and closed the door with a deafening click.

"I told you to keep your mouth shut," Anne said, opening and slamming drawers.

"You wanted me to just stand there while he promised me to that…that monster? He's old enough to be my father, for fuck's sake!"

Anne rounded on her daughter. "You watch your mouth, or I'll…" Her eyes dropped to the cut on her daughter's lip, which was already swelling.

"You'll what?" Libby snapped. "Hit me? Do your worst, *Mother*." She spat the last word and watched her mother's face drain of color.

Anne threw a hand towel at her daughter. "You made this mess. Now clean it up. If you're not back in five minutes, you won't like what happens next."

When Anne slammed the door behind her, Libby gripped the sink, head hung between her shoulders. Tears burned her eyes, but she willed them away. Crying would only ruin her makeup. Taking a shaky breath, she looked up at her own reflection.

Her father's ring had caught her lower lip and split it open. Blood trickled in a thin line down her chin. She wet the towel and dabbed at it, wincing. The bleeding had stopped, but it was tender.

Rinsing the blood down the sink, she turned her head and examined her cheek. It was red from her father's hand, but at least her ears had stopped ringing. There'd be a nice bruise there by morning.

When someone knocked softly on the door, she jerked, fingers gripping the edge of the sink. "I'll be out in just a minute."

The door cracked open anyway, and she jumped back, heart leaping into her throat. She took a steadying breath when she recognized Connie.

"Oh, Libby," Connie whispered. "He's never hit you in the face before."

And there it was. The ugly truth of her life in a single sentence. Her father dealt with disobedience and disrespect with his hands, and she'd taken the brunt of it off her sister their entire lives. Tonight it was made abundantly clear that no one was willing to help her.

Libby let Connie fix her up as best she could in silence and then made her way back to the party simply because she had no other choice. More than a few people had left since she'd been hauled off to make herself presentable, but the ones that remained refused to make eye contact.

Conversation stalled when DiMarco spotted her in the doorway and made his way across the room. Stopping in front of her, he stood menacingly close, and when he leaned down to brush his lips against hers, she turned her head so his lips met her cheek instead.

"I've been looking forward to making you mine for years," he whispered. "You'll be fun to break."

She fought hard not to recoil when he wrapped an arm around her waist and people stepped forward to congratulate them. She caught her father's eye across the room, and the look he gave her was a challenge. Cross me and suffer the consequences.

When DiMarco's phone signaled, she tried to step away, but his fingers flexed on her waist, holding her tighter. "Not so fast, Elizabeth. Or should I call you Libby?"

"I'd prefer you didn't speak to me at all."

His smile was quick and cold and made her shiver.

"Oh, how I do love a challenge. If you'll excuse me." He held her hand in a vise-like grip to bring it to his lips, and her stomach turned when he brushed a kiss against her knuckles. "Wait here for me, darling."

When he finally let go, she sank down onto the edge of the nearest chair before her legs gave out. He whispered something in her father's ear, and they strode out together.

The party moved on around her. People either ignored her completely or sent her pitying glances—and a few smug ones. She felt like an idiot for not seeing this coming, for not being able to guess exactly what her father had been plotting with DiMarco. Or what DiMarco had been planning all along.

Either way, she couldn't go through with it. She'd rather be dead.

"Elizabeth." Libby looked up into her mother's weary face. "Your father said you can go to bed."

She looked around at the nearly empty room and sighed, pushing to her feet. Eyeing the front door as she stepped out of the living room, she briefly considered making a run for it. Except where would she go?

Turning toward the stairs, she gripped the banister, pausing when she heard voices coming from her father's office. Glancing over her shoulder to make sure no one was watching her, she slid into the shadows and crept along the wall toward the door, holding her breath.

"The buyers are worried the Callahans might be onto us. We need to move them sooner."

"When?" her father asked.

"Tomorrow night," DiMarco replied. "I've changed the auction to the warehouse on 5th. Bigger space. More privacy."

There was a pause, and her father's response was clipped. "You've changed it?"

"What I mean to say is," DiMarco quickly recovered, "we can and should change it. On your orders."

She could hear papers rustling, the click of a pen.

"Fine. Do it. If the Callahans get wind of this, it'll be war. And wars are expensive."

Tiptoeing around the shaft of light coming from the crack in the door, Libby silently made her way up the stairs and into her room, locking the door behind her. The timeline had just shifted up by two days. She had to warn them. Hopefully she'd be able to get away long enough tomorrow to leave them a message.

Chapter Four

By the time the sun rose the following morning, Brogan had already been awake for over an hour. Unable to sleep, he'd quickly checked security cameras near the address Libby had given them and pulled up maps to try and figure out where they might be taking the girls.

Now that he had a location, he'd even attempted to break the cipher DiMarco used on the documents Evie had stolen for them a few months ago. Having a thief in the family was definitely going to come in handy. Even if this time it had given them nothing but more questions.

Still unable to make sense of the jumble of letters and numbers, he abandoned his bank of computers for some target practice, jogging down from the third floor to the basement. Previously used for storage, Declan had convinced their father to finish the basement that ran the length and width of the house maybe six years ago now.

Declan had been given free rein to renovate it how he saw fit, and they ended up with a generous living area that boasted two pinball machines, a pool table, and a dartboard.

They built a bar in the far corner, complete with a collection of high-end liquors, beer on tap, and a full fridge.

Leather couches in a rich chocolate brown were arranged in front of an enormous fireplace and wall-mounted TV. And the stone patio with an outdoor kitchen proved a perfect investment in the family gatherings they often threw when the weather was nice.

Declan had recently talked about turning one of the storage areas into a secure panic room after what happened to Evie. Brogan knew Declan still blamed himself for leaving her alone when she'd been attacked a few months earlier.

His brother didn't like to talk about it, but Brogan knew it had shaken him. Even if Declan ultimately killed Peter, he imagined his brother would always torture himself with what-ifs.

Flipping the switch at the bottom of the stairs, Brogan crossed to the bar and pulled a bottle of water out of the fridge. Turning down the hallway to his left, he walked away from the living area toward his favorite part of the basement reno, the large gym with professional-grade equipment and the soundproof, two-lane shooting range.

Passing the gym, he stepped into the range, reaching into the cabinet on the far wall for a paper target and a pair of headphones. He fixed the target to the hooks and pressed the button to send it flying to the back of the range. Flicking the safety off, he leveled his weapon at the target and unloaded the clip.

He hadn't been able to stop thinking about Libby since she knocked on the door of their club yesterday. He couldn't figure out why she would betray her own family by sharing their plans, asking if they'd leave any survivors. Until he caught a glimpse of a healing bruise on her ribs in the parking lot.

He didn't understand this desire that burned in his gut to

end whoever hurt her, but it was all he wanted. Declan wouldn't like it, but Brogan would be at that ambush if only to put a bullet in as many of Giordano's men as possible. And if he was the one to end whoever hurt her, then all the better.

He pressed the button to bring the target back to the booth, admiring his cluster of shots at center mass. He'd never had an opportunity to be anything other than a good shot. His father put a gun in his hand when Brogan was barely five and taught him to expertly shoot everything from a BB gun to a semi-automatic assault rifle, though he preferred a 9mm.

He pinned another target, sending it back before reloading. He inhaled long and deep, letting his heartbeat slow as he took aim. Squeeze the trigger, lead the target, focus. His father's words echoed in his head.

The kickback as bullets exploded out of the muzzle hummed up his arm, a physical reminder of the power he wielded over life and death. He brought the paper back, nodding in approval at the tighter cluster on this one, and wrote the date on both with a Sharpie, folding them neatly and placing them in a box marked with his name.

He used the supplies in the bottom drawer of the cabinet to disassemble and clean his weapon. Another thing his father taught him. A soldier is only ever as good as his tools. That's why he was really fucking pissed that he couldn't crack DiMarco's code and figure out the extent of his trafficking.

Brogan's skill with tech had come naturally, born from a love of video games and a desire to know how things worked. He'd taught himself to code at thirteen, and by sixteen he was building computers from scratch.

It wasn't until he'd nearly gotten his ass beat for hacking into a video game server for cheat codes that Declan had the good sense to realize how handy it would be to have someone who could hack into secured databases and get them almost anything they might want or need.

Since then, he'd perfected his skill and accessed some of the world's most sensitive information undetected with just a few strokes of his keyboard. Well, except for that one time he almost got caught by Interpol when trying to get dirt on a buyer who stiffed them on payment. He'd barely gotten out before they picked up his breadcrumbs.

Weapon clean and reassembled, he tucked it into the holster on the inside of his waistband and tidied up the table at the back of the range. He could hear movement as he reached the top of the stairs. Scenting bacon in the air, he made his way back to the kitchen to see if he could talk Marta out of a few pieces.

He found the housekeeper at the stove, flipping bacon with one hand and ladling waffle batter with the other, her graying hair bundled up on top of her head. If his mother were still alive, they'd be about the same age. When he saw Evie sitting at the island stirring sugar and cream into a cup of coffee, he frowned. It wasn't like her to be up this early. Unless she'd had a nightmare.

As he crossed the kitchen, he studied his sister-in-law. Her face was pale, her eyes tired, with a hint of dark shadows she'd tried to hide with makeup. The nightmares had eased up in the weeks since she and Declan had officially tied the knot. But he knew she still had them occasionally, her screams echoing through the halls until Declan woke her and soothed her back to sleep.

Her smile when she saw him in the doorway was genuine, his mother's emerald flashing on her finger when she lifted her mug to take a sip.

"You're up early," he said, crossing to the pot and pouring himself a cup, drinking it black where he stood.

"Couldn't sleep. And you?"

"Practicing my shooting downstairs." Brogan grinned when Marta handed him a small plate with a few pieces of bacon on it. "Declan up?"

Evie glanced at the ceiling. "He was in the shower when I came down."

Brogan munched on a piece of bacon, nodding. "He tell you what happened?"

"He did. You believe her," she said after a long study.

He shrugged. "I do."

"He does too. He's wary, but he believes her."

"I believe who?"

Evie's smile warmed when Declan appeared in the door-way, and that was nice to see too. He watched his brother cross the kitchen, stopping in front of his wife and tilting her chin up with his fingertip. He brushed a quick kiss across her lips, then another one, and murmured something against her cheek that had her laughing.

"I'm going to hurl if you two don't get a room."

"It's sweet," Marta insisted, scolding Brogan with a pointed look. "Now go in and sit down, and I'll bring this in."

They crossed into the dining room while Marta loaded everything onto a tray and waited until she left again to continue their conversation.

"Any luck figuring out where the drop-off location might be?" Declan glanced at Evie when Brogan shook his head.

"Knowing what I know about men like DiMarco, they'll keep their auction location far away from wherever they're keeping the girls. That way, if one gets burned, you don't have to burn the other." Evie leaned back in her chair. "So if the house is on the east side, expect the auction to be on the west."

"A warehouse? Lots of quiet places to meet out there."

"Probably." Evie agreed. "How much time do you have?"

"Two days. Assuming this Giordano girl isn't fucking with us."

"Libby," Brogan said. "Her name is Libby, and she isn't fucking with us."

"How do you know that?"

Brogan shrugged. "I just do, and I'm going."

"You're absolutely not going. I need you here monitoring security cameras to make sure we don't get ambushed and no one slips past us."

Brogan ignored the way Evie had stopped eating to study him and focused on his brother. "All I have to do is pull them up, and anyone can watch a camera feed. I'm the best shot in the family. The best way to make sure no one gets away is to have me there."

"And if I say no?"

"Then I'll go anyway, and we'll have to fight about it later."

Declan cut off a bite of waffle, chewing it thoughtfully. "Fine. Finn and I are meeting with the men we handpicked for this one in about thirty minutes. Finn thinks two dozen should be enough, and I agree."

"Cait and I are going to set up the safe house today. There's an empty rental property we can use. Should be enough beds if Brogan's theory of groups of ten holds. We've got people organizing food and supplies. Then we'll have to figure out what to do with them."

"Cash and new identities?" Brogan suggested.

"Whatever keeps them from going to the cops," Declan replied. "The last thing I need is my name in the papers beside the bust of a sex trafficking ring." Declan checked his watch and tossed his napkin on the table. "Let's head to the club early, then. You can explain your stupid idea to Finn before the others arrive."

"Brogan," Evie said when they both rose to leave, "don't get your ass killed, or I'll never forgive you."

"What about me?" Declan wondered.

"Are you going into the line of fire against the advice of your lovely wife?"

Brogan's lips twitched into a grin.

"No."

"Then you're fine. But, you know, be safe!" Evie called as they retreated, and Brogan chuckled.

Chapter Five

"That is the dumbest thing I've ever heard." Finn stood in the center of Declan's office at the club with his arms crossed, a scowl painted on his face. "If you want to shoot things, I'm sure you'll get the chance to kill some Italians before Giordano is firmly back in his place. Or dead. Preferably the latter."

"This isn't...that's not what this is about. It's just...something I have to do," Brogan insisted.

Finn looked to Declan, who lifted a shoulder. "And if we say no, you'll only do it anyway."

"Yes, but I'd rather not be in the dog house like Aidan is, so I'm asking."

"You're not really asking," Finn muttered.

"Close enough," Brogan replied.

"If you die, I'll never hear the end of it from Cait."

Brogan rolled his eyes. "What is it with the women in this family?"

"They like you for reasons we cannot fathom." Declan slapped Brogan on the shoulder as his phone rang. "Helen."

Declan shot a glance at Brogan while his assistant spoke in his ear and frowned. "Hang on."

He put the phone on speaker. "Open and read it. The Giordano girl dropped off another note," Declan explained as paper rustled across the line.

"Time changed. Tonight. Found drop-off address." Declan scribbled it down when Helen rattled it off. As Evie predicted, it was on the west side and in a fairly secluded area. "Helen. Burn that."

Declan hung up without waiting for an answer. "Giordano's going to know he's got a traitor if we intercept after a change like that."

Finn looked at Brogan. "How confident are we that your girl is flying under the radar?"

"She's not my girl."

"We might never get a chance like this again," Finn added.

Declan studied Brogan for a long moment. "If Giordano wants a war, I want to be the one to take the first shot."

"Then we'll take it," Brogan replied, meeting his brother's gaze.

When the lights flickered on in the main area of the basement, Brogan turned, voices echoing through the stone and concrete.

"Let's get started," Declan said.

Declan and Finn walked the group of men through what they knew, though Brogan noted they didn't share how they knew it. The tension in the room was thick. They were just as eager to put Giordano back in his place as he was.

Now that they knew the drop-off location, they could tailor their plan to match. Two groups of men would sit on the house, one front and one back, to make sure no one tried to make a run for it, and two more on the warehouse. Declan didn't want to take out the buyers, but he wanted to know their names.

Then they'd place three more groups on the most likely routes from the house to the drop-off just in case one of their tails got made or they got wind of an ambush. The goal was to take them by surprise and avoid a firefight in a neighborhood full of people who might call the cops.

Not that Giordano's men would make it out alive. Brogan would make sure of it.

They answered questions, assigned teams, and sent everyone home with strict instructions to reconvene at eight o'clock. They wanted to be in position as night fell.

Brogan spent the afternoon carefully choosing his equipment so one of the McBride boys could run surveillance from the back of the truck while he was handling the ambush and extraction. Danny McBride got a crash course in monitoring video feeds and strict instructions not to push any buttons so he didn't fuck anything up.

By dusk, they were loaded into plain black SUVs and off to their respective locations. On the drive, Brogan finally gave in to the one thing he'd been talking himself out of doing all day and pulled up the video feed of Declan's restaurant where Libby had dropped off the note this morning.

Her hair was down, shielding most of her face from the camera, but when she turned to go after handing the note to the hostess, he paused the frame on her face. He could have easily written the shadow on her cheek off as a trick of the light if not for the hostess's reaction.

Then he noticed a dark spot on her lip and zoomed in. It was grainy, but he'd bet money that she had a split lip and a bruised cheek, like someone had backhanded her between the time she left the club and the next morning when she showed up at the restaurant.

The possibility filled him with rage. Rage he could channel. He hoped to Christ the bastard who bruised her was there, because he wanted to make them pay.

They pulled into their spot at the front of the house as street lamps blinked on and waited. The mood in the truck was somber, everyone silent and alert.

"Movement at the warehouse," a voice squawked through his earpiece. "Buyers arriving."

Brogan trained his gaze on the house, constantly scanning for movement. It took forty-five minutes before he noticed a curtain twitch in the upstairs window, revealing a quick sliver of light before going black again.

"Heads up," he said into his mic.

No sooner had he spoken than a white panel van pulled into the driveway, waiting for the garage door to open before easing inside and closing the door again.

"We've got a car on the other side of the house loading up two girls. Do we follow?"

"Yes," Brogan replied. "We've got a van on this side, so they could be handlers or house madams."

After a few minutes, the garage door opened again, and the van backed slowly out and down the driveway into the street, turning left. Brogan waited until they turned the corner to follow.

"Where are they, Danny?" Brogan asked, fingers drumming impatiently on the steering wheel as he reached the end of the street and didn't see the van. "Danny!"

"Hang on. There! Two streets over and going west, northwest."

Brogan cycled through the map in his head. "Colin, they're headed your way. I'm going to take a shortcut and come up right behind them. Be ready for my signal."

Brogan sped up the cross street and cut back toward the direction they saw the van turn while Danny muttered directions from the backseat. If he was right, they'd take one more left turn and dump out just behind them on an isolated road with only a couple houses.

He slowed at the stop sign. The road was empty to the right, but he could make out the glow of taillights to the left. He turned, gunning it as he shouted for Colin to move.

He screeched to a halt behind the van while Colin's SUV blocked it from the front. Men poured from their vehicles and surrounded the van, guns drawn. Brogan launched himself from the front seat and yanked open the van's back door to terrified screams and shouts.

There were three men and eight women in the back of the van by his count. Two men immediately dropped their weapons, hands raised, but the third reached for a girl, pulling her back against him as a shield and holding a gun to her head. She started to sob.

"Liam," Brogan said, voice calmer than he felt. "Get these women into the trucks. Quickly."

He trained his gun on the lone asshole with the hostage while his men helped the women out and piled them into the waiting SUVs.

"Now her," Brogan said, glancing at the girl the prick still held tight against him. She was young, too young. Barely eighteen if she was a day.

"You can have the bitch if you let me go."

Brogan swiveled his arm and shot one of Giordano's surrendered men in the chest before training his gun back on the coward who shielded himself with a woman.

"You're not leaving this van alive. If you give me the girl, I'll kill you faster."

The man held Brogan's gaze as if trying to gauge his sincerity. Brogan wasn't sure he was going to make the right decision until he suddenly shoved the girl forward and then lunged, weapon drawn.

Brogan caught the girl with one arm, swinging her out of the line of fire, and took aim at the bastard, dropping him to the floor where he lay with dead, staring eyes.

"You're okay," Brogan soothed when the girl collapsed against him, trembling with sobs. "We're going to take you somewhere safe. I promise."

"What about this one, boss?" Liam asked, indicating the last man inside the van, hands still raised.

"Kill him," Brogan said simply before leading the girl to the truck and helping her into the back.

They rode in tandem to the safe house while Liam took the van to McGee's to be cleaned. It was late when they pulled in, and the neighborhood was quiet, but he still had both trucks pull into the garage and wait for the doors to close before letting the girls out.

He kept the men out while Evie, Cait, and a few other syndicate wives brought the girls into the house and showed them to their rooms. It was after midnight when Evie stepped into the garage, scrubbing her hands over her face and sinking down onto the wooden steps that led inside.

"Christ, Brogan. They're all beat up, starving, terrified. I know Declan doesn't want to keep them too long, but we can't just send them out into the world like this. They need time."

"We have a few days before we need to make any moves," Brogan assured her.

"Yeah," Evie replied, looking up at him with eyes brimming with tears. "But how many more of them are there?"

Chapter Six

It took two days before any of the women opened up to Evie and Cait, and three more days before they began sharing their names and stories. Declan and Finn didn't seem all that happy about how much time their wives spent at the safe house, but none of them could deny that it seemed to be working. The more they trusted the Callahan women and their kindness, the more they talked.

Just not to him. Or any men. That first night, Cait and Evie decided not to let any men inside until they thought the women were a little steadier. Which meant every bit of information Brogan had was secondhand through his sisters-in-law.

They relayed as much as they could remember when they came home to eat and crash for a few hours, but he had questions only the victims could answer. He was willing to give them time, but the longer they delayed, the more time Giordano had to cover his tracks and start rounding up more girls. Assuming he didn't have some already. Either way, the bastard wouldn't lay low for long.

Brogan looked at the list of names Evie gave him when she came in at nearly two in the morning. There were only eight, and, according to Cait, the two women they'd seen ushered out the front door weren't handlers trying to disappear but more victims. Victims that slipped through their fingers when the tail car and cameras lost them after they made it onto the highway.

He brought up the PPD missing persons database and ran a search on each name. Nothing. He frowned, bringing up the FBI's database to run a wider search. Still nothing. Had they given fake names, or did no one care enough to report them missing? The woman they'd held the longest had been there nearly six weeks. No one missed her?

He didn't expect any results, but he ran their names through an international database just to be sure. Still coming up empty, he pivoted into verifying their identities. Several of them had arrest records for minor things like drugs or petty theft. Probably how the Italians lured them in. A few more had suspended driver's licenses, some tickets, a couple DUIs.

He made notes on Evie's list, jotting down a few questions he wanted to ask. They had to let him in the house sometime. He saw nothing concerning in their past, nothing that put the syndicate at risk or led him to believe they might double-cross them. They all appeared to be victims who ended up in the wrong place at the wrong time.

"Did you find anything on them?"

Brogan looked up to see Evie carrying a large sandwich and a Sprite. She set both on the desk in front of him and glanced at his bank of computer screens.

"You don't have to bribe me with food, you know. I now have a familial obligation to help you."

She smiled, pressing a hand to her heart. "I'm touched. Marta made me eat and mentioned she hadn't seen you since breakfast. I figured you were hungry. So?"

He pointed to the paper where he'd scribbled his notes and took a bite of the sandwich while she scanned it.

"Not a single missing persons report?"

"Not unless they gave us fake names."

She sank down onto the edge of the desk. "They said no one would miss them, but I'd hoped…" She sighed. "We're going to lay out their options for them today. Ask them what they want to do."

"So Declan finally decided what he wanted to offer them?"

Evie ran a hand over her curls, the corner of her mouth lifting into a half grin. "After some convincing. In exchange for not going to the cops, they can either get cash and new identities they can start fresh with, or they can stay and work for the syndicate."

Brogan's eyebrows shot up. That second one was absolutely his sister-in-law's idea.

"How the hell did you talk Declan into that?"

"I'm very persuasive."

"Please." He grimaced. "I'm eating."

"I'm only making that offer to a couple of them, and after a long, heated debate—"

"That you won."

"Declan agreed to trust my judgment on this. They're sharp, and this will make them loyal, give them something they're missing."

"Family."

She relaxed, but her smile was sad. "Exactly. Once we ask them, I think you'll be okay to come talk to them. I know you have questions. Tomorrow, I think."

"Tomorrow," he agreed. "And Evie? Get some sleep. You look like hell," he added, laughing when she gave him the finger before disappearing.

Finally, he'd get his questions answered and hopefully be able to take down Giordano's little unauthorized side business. But those women wouldn't be able to answer the question that really plagued him. What would happen to Libby Giordano now that she'd helped them?

Chapter Seven

When her bedroom door flew open, Libby blinked against the murky gray light that filtered through the sheer curtains. It took a minute for her mother's shrill voice to register through the haze, but her last sentence snapped her fully awake.

"What did you say?" Libby demanded.

Anne whirled on her daughter, face pale, eyes wild. "I said, what the fuck were you doing with the Callahans?!"

The swear word falling from her mother's lips was as frightening as her accusation, and Libby shivered. Anne Giordano never swore. Libby watched her mother cross the room and yank open dresser drawers, pulling things out of them and throwing them to the floor.

"What are you doing?" Libby jumped out of bed and moved to her mother's side.

"I'm looking for evidence that my daughter, my own flesh and blood, is a traitor." Anne's voice caught on a choked sob, and Libby stumbled back a step.

It had been days since she warned the Callahans, and even though she had no way of knowing if they'd gotten her hastily scribbled note, her father's venomous mood was enough of an answer. Something had happened, and he wasn't pleased about it.

But if her mother was digging through her dresser for evidence, that meant they didn't have any. Right? Maybe she could play the whole thing off, convince her father he was wrong. What did she have to lose? She slid her hand up to cup her throat. Only everything.

She took a steadying breath and fought to keep her voice even. "What are you talking about, Mother? I've never even met the Callahans."

Anne's eyes narrowed, brimming with tears. "Your father isn't so sure. He wants to see you in his office. Get dressed. Now," she spat before storming out of the room and slamming the door behind her.

Tears pricked Libby's eyes, and fear burned in her belly as she stripped out of her pajamas, grappling for the jeans she'd tossed at the foot of her bed the night before and struggling to button them with trembling fingers.

She whipped a shirt over her head, quickly sweeping her hair back into a tight tail while her heart lodged in her throat. Rubbing her sweaty palms on her thighs, Libby reached for her phone on top of the dresser and sent a quick text to her sister.

I love you.

A single tear fell onto the screen, and she wiped it away, shoving her phone into her pocket. She hadn't heard from Teresa in what felt like forever, but she wanted to leave her with something good. Just in case.

Her feet dragged like lead down the stairs, and at the bottom, she turned right toward her father's office, steeling herself before stepping into the doorway. It was empty, which only made the knots in her belly twist tighter.

"Not here," Anne said from behind her, making her jump. "He wants you to meet him at the bar."

Libby closed her eyes, swallowing hard. She'd heard stories about the back room at her father's bar and what he and his men did behind closed doors to anyone they considered enemies. She turned and met her mother's stony glare.

"He sent a car." Anne pointed with one long, perfectly polished finger at the man who waited by the front door.

"Mother, you don't really think I—"

"Just go, Elizabeth. And think long and hard about the truth on the way."

The man—she didn't recognize him—had a scar down his left cheek and refused to meet her eyes as he held the car door open for her, closing it softly behind. It was as if he wanted to pretend she wasn't there, that he wasn't doing this task for his boss. And that made it worse, his apprehension and nerves.

The ride was eternal, and when they finally arrived, she reached for the door handle, squeezing her fingers together to keep them from trembling. The man led her to the door, holding it open for her but not following her inside.

"Hello, Elizabeth."

DiMarco stepped into the light and stalked toward her. Libby shrank back against the door when he stopped so close she could feel his breath against her cheek.

"You've been busy, it seems," he murmured. "I wonder... are you fucking one of them?"

He reached up to touch her cheek, and she flinched. With a wicked gleam in his eye, he took a step back, and she willed her breathing to slow.

Turning on his heel, he motioned over his shoulder. "This way."

She followed him past a long, scarred bar and tables stacked with chairs, down a narrow hallway to a back room with a thick wooden door. He pushed it in and motioned for her to go ahead of him.

This room was smaller than the one at Reign, with only a single overhead light that cast eerie shadows on the walls. The room was empty save for her father, who stood in a corner, arms crossed over his chest.

"I don't know what you think—"

"Quiet," DiMarco interrupted, and Libby spun to face him.

He closed the door behind him and hung his jacket on a peg on the wall. Libby took a step back when he moved closer.

"Carla Russo told her husband that she thought she saw you standing in the parking lot of Reign. Is that true?"

"The Callahan nightclub?"

"Don't play dumb, Elizabeth," her father said. "Were you there or not?"

Her eyes never left DiMarco's when she tipped her chin up in defiance. "I don't know what you're talking about. I didn't—"

The blow to her face rocked her back on her heels, stars shooting across her vision. She shook her head to clear it, tasting blood for the second time in a week. She ran her tongue across the split in her lip DiMarco had reopened while he adjusted the ring on his finger.

"Lying will make this so much worse."

"Why don't you tell me what you think I did," Libby said, following DiMarco with her eyes as he circled her.

DiMarco reached up to grip her ponytail, jerking her head back so she fell back against him, smiling when she yelped. "I think you warned those bastards about our new business venture. Which is really none of your concern." He spun her to face him, holding her tight against his body. "Is it?"

"I never said it was," she gritted out, blinking against the pain that radiated along her jaw. "I'm not the only blonde in Philadelphia."

This time when he hit her, she stumbled back a step and braced herself on the wall. She flicked a glance at her father, who only glared, refusing to speak up for her. He wanted blood for this. Apparently it didn't matter whose.

"I said this would be worse if you lie," DiMarco growled.

Libby's eyes snapped back to DiMarco's face. "I'm not lying! I don't know who Carla saw, but it wasn't me."

When he lunged for her, she danced out of the way, which seemed to loosen the control he had on his anger, the veins in his neck bulging as he stalked her across the room.

"Someone warned the Callahans about my…our shipment, and now that shipment is gone."

Libby couldn't ignore the relief that bloomed in her chest at those words. They were free, safe. Thank God.

"I'm sorry, but that someone wasn't me."

She glanced away from DiMarco to catch her father's eye, to plead with him to let her go, giving DiMarco enough time to reach out and grip the end of her ponytail. She cried out as he yanked her forward by her hair, her body colliding with his. Fear lanced through her at the deadly look in his eyes.

"There's just one problem, Elizabeth. I don't believe you."

He slammed his fist into her stomach, and she dropped to the floor, gasping for breath as she tried to crawl away from him. But he gripped her ponytail again, yanking her up onto her knees. Another backhand to the face made her vision go blurry, and she sank to all fours, tears gathering in her eyes.

"Please," she whispered.

"Please, what?" DiMarco kicked her hard in the stomach, and she wheezed, crumpling to the floor as pain sliced through her.

"I didn't—"

He kicked her again, and she coughed, tasting blood,

warm and sticky, on her tongue. She watched her father stand silently in the corner while DiMarco used his fists and feet to punish her, laughing when she tried to curl into a ball to protect herself. Libby could hear nothing but the ringing in her own ears, feel the cuts from where his ring sliced her flesh.

Tears streaming down her face, body on fire from the blows, she wondered for the first time what happened when you died. Then her world went black.

Chapter Eight

L aptop tucked under one arm, Brogan knocked on the garage door of the safe house and heard a flurry of activity on the other side. Chairs scraping against the floor, dishes clattering into the sink, and the murmur of voices.

"Boy," Cait said when she opened the door, "you sure know how to clear a room."

Brogan frowned, and she chuckled, motioning him inside. "They went upstairs to get dressed. Some of them are more nervous than others, but they all remember you."

"Me? Why?" He settled at the table and flipped open his laptop.

"Because you were the first person they saw in weeks who wasn't trying to hurt them. You're a hero."

"I'm not a hero."

"You are to them." She squeezed his shoulder, then smacked it. "So try not to look so"—she wiggled her fingers at his eyebrows—"broody."

His frown deepened as he watched her carry the last of the breakfast dishes into the kitchen and hand them to one of the O'Sullivan wives. He didn't want to be anyone's hero. He tried the hero gig once, and it hadn't worked out so well for the damsel.

The stairs creaked, and he looked over and saw a pair of eyes peeking at him over the banister. She didn't look scared; she looked...like she was sizing him up. He sat back and waited until she finally descended the rest of the way and took the seat across from him at the table.

"I was trying to decide if you really were as big as I remember you or if I'd built you up that way in my mind."

He quirked a brow. "And?"

"You're as big as I remember you." Her eyes dropped to his biceps. "You must bench press small trees or something."

Her serious expression melted into a small smile when he huffed out a laugh.

"I'm Mackenzie, by the way."

He recognized her from her mugshot. Most recently, she'd done six months for petty theft but seemed like she'd been trying to get her life together since crossing the river from New Jersey.

"Brogan. How long were you there?"

Her smile fell, and she leaned her elbows on the table. "Since they kidnapped me, you mean?"

"Yes."

"Six weeks? Maybe seven."

"So you were there the longest."

"Yeah. I was."

He looked up at the deadpan tone of her voice. "I'm going to try not to ask too many questions about that."

She shrugged. "I figure whatever you ask is going to be less invasive than the cops. And, historically, they aren't that interested in solving shit like this for people like me." She waved a hand at him. "Ask away."

"What were you doing when they grabbed you?"

She shifted in her chair, color blooming on her cheeks. "They didn't grab me."

He looked up from his laptop, eyebrows lifted in surprise. "You went willingly?"

"Well, I didn't go willingly for *this*. I answered an ad on the internet for a housekeeper. I had just gotten out of jail and was trying to get by without stealing stuff for a damn minute, and I got stolen instead."

She chuckled, but there was no humor in it. "They lured me right to that house. It seemed so normal. How was I supposed to know?" she murmured, more to herself than to him.

"How many were there?"

Her eyes shifted back to his face. "Always three. If there were ever any more than that, you knew they were there to… sample the merchandise."

Anger bit into him, but he smoothed it down. "Did you ever see"—he brought up a picture of DiMarco on the screen and turned his laptop around to face her—"this man?"

She leaned forward, eyes narrowed, but ultimately shook her head. "No. They were all younger guys."

"Did you ever hear them talking about other girls?"

"They complained that their cut of the money from 'all us bitches'," she began, making air quotes, "wasn't as much as they thought it should be. So I would assume they had more than just us. But there were only ever ten of us in the house."

"Do you know why they only put eight of you in the van? And took these two out the front?" He flipped to the clearest picture he had of the two women who'd been loaded into the car.

"No. We never spent any time with them. The rest of us got to eat together and shared rooms, but those two were always separate from us. I only saw them once when they were brought in. Together," she added before Brogan could ask. "I don't even know their names."

He typed up notes while she watched him intently, drumming her fingers on the tabletop. When he looked up, she didn't look away.

"Is Evie's offer for real?"

"Which offer is that?"

"To stay and work for you guys."

Brogan sat back and studied her. He could see why Evie made an offer to Mackenzie. She was level-headed and matter-of-fact, but under that, he sensed a desire to belong. Evie's instincts were on point.

"It is."

"What would we even do?"

He shrugged. "That's for Declan to decide."

Mackenzie nodded, picking at her fingernails. "He's in charge?"

"He is. Spit it out," he added when she started worrying the hole in the knee of her jeans.

"Is this another trick? A worse one where you pretend to help us only to..." She cleared her throat.

"It's not a trick, Mackenzie. You can either take the money and go—wherever you want—or you can stay and commit yourself to the syndicate. You get to choose."

Mackenzie blew out a shaky breath, nodding slowly. "Can I go now?" she asked after a beat.

"Yeah." She pushed to her feet. "Send someone else down."

He met with each woman in turn and asked them the same questions. Mackenzie was the oldest at twenty-six, but the youngest was barely eighteen. They'd all been lured directly to the house somehow, most with a fake ad for a housekeeper. None of them recognized DiMarco, and none of them knew who the two mysterious women were.

He didn't have anything more than when he'd started except for the dead look in their eyes and the way some of them jumped at the slightest noise seared into his brain. They all wanted the cash and new identities, promising not to go to the cops. They wanted it to be over and to get the fuck out of Philadelphia. He was happy to oblige them.

The other woman Evie had made an offer to, Grace, declined to stay. She wanted to head west and see if she could connect with the grandmother she hadn't seen since she was a girl. Only Mackenzie lingered, undecided, at the base of the stairs.

"You don't have to decide right now," he told her as he stood, scooping his laptop off the table.

"Everyone will be gone in a few days, though, right? You won't let me stay here forever."

"I'll make sure my brother gives you as much time as you need."

"Your brother? So you're not just one of them, you're like, *one* of them."

"I don't know what that means, but…yes?"

She followed him to the door. "Hey," she said, studying him for a long moment when he paused. "Thank you. I have no idea where they were taking us, and I'm really glad I didn't have to find out."

Before he could respond, she turned and went back into the house, closing the door behind her with a soft click. He stared after her, wondering how many more women like her were out there, how many more they'd have to rescue before this was all said and done.

Chapter Nine

Libby jolted awake when her head hit something hard. It took a minute for everything to come into focus, and when it did, her body screamed with pain until she gasped. Everything hurt so much that she almost willed herself to pass out again. The sound of an engine rumbled under her ear, her cheek pressed against the cool metal of what she guessed was a van.

They took a sharp turn, and she rolled, groaning when something pressed against a cut on her side. If they were going to kill her, they needed to get it over with because this was agony.

"Hurry up, Tommy. I think she's waking up."

She squeezed her eyes shut, swallowing another groan when the van took a turn too fast and pain vibrated through her hip and down her leg. Were they going to dump her body somewhere remote where no one would ever find her? Tears burned at the corners of her eyes.

The van jerked to a stop, and she heard the grind of a door sliding open, a wave of hot air rolling over her before rough hands gave her a shove. She fell to the ground, hitting a patch of gravel with a yelp and rolling down a grassy hill.

She didn't move, didn't breathe, while voices argued somewhere above her in a whisper. A crack echoed in the air —a tree branch snapping?—before she could open her eyes, and pain exploded in her side seconds later.

"If they want you, they can have you. Traitorous bitch."

Doors slammed, and gravel peppered her face as the vehicle sped away. Holding her breath, she waited to see if they would come back to make sure she was dead. When they didn't, she opened her eyes.

Pain reverberated through her skull at the bright light from the sun, but she forced herself to take stock of her surroundings. All she could see were thick green treetops. No cars drove by, but she could hear the distant sound of a dog barking. Was this a neighborhood? Or maybe a park?

She would not lay there and slowly succumb to whatever wounds that bastard had inflicted on her. Gritting her teeth against the pain, she rolled onto her hands and knees, breathing through the wave of nausea that washed over her.

A ditch. They'd rolled her into a ditch like garbage. Her own father stood by and did nothing while… She shook her head gently, pushing that from her mind. She couldn't think about that now. She had to find help.

Ignoring the pain that twisted through her with each movement, she crawled until her fingers hit asphalt. A road. No. She looked up at a wrought iron gate hung between two stone pillars. A driveway.

She used the mailbox to pull herself to her feet, swaying when her vision blurred. Every step was torture, and sweat broke out on her forehead, but she limped toward the gate, collapsing against it. The metal was hot, but it barely registered through the haze in her brain.

She could just make out the outline of a house beyond the

winding drive that snaked through a thick grove of trees and disappeared. She rolled, slumping back against the gate. What now? She couldn't get through, and even if she could, there was no telling how long the driveway was. She'd never make it.

The tears came then, and she let them, turning her face up to the sun as they spilled down her cheeks. She was going to die here at the end of some stranger's driveway, covered in bruises and blood. Would she end up on the news? Would her father pay? She fucking hoped so.

Her legs wobbled, and she started to slide to the ground when she noticed a silver call box. A choked sob escaped her lips, and she stumbled toward it, gripping it tightly while she punched random buttons with shaking fingers.

"You know," a female voice said through the speaker, "pranks aren't f— Oh my God."

"Please," Libby croaked. "Help me."

"Stay right there. We're coming. Brogan!" the woman screamed before the speaker went silent.

Libby frowned, but it only made her face hurt. Why would Brogan be here? When the gate swung in silently, she whimpered, steeling herself to push away from the box and stagger toward the entrance.

She looked up when footsteps pounded against the pavement and saw Brogan burst through the trees, his blurry form sprinting toward her. She took another step, swaying on her feet as the world spun.

Brogan reached Libby in time to catch her before she fell, her eyes rolling back in her head seconds before she dropped. Scooping her up, he turned and ran back up the driveway with her in his arms.

Evie met him at the door, eyes wide and full of disbelief.

"Doc is on his way. And I called Declan. He's bringing Finn. Jesus. Shit," she said when Brogan carried Libby in and up the stairs. "Who is that?"

"It's Libby," Brogan said through clenched teeth.

Evie stopped short on the stairs before jogging to catch up with him again.

"You don't think… Who would do that to her?"

"A dead man," he spat, waiting impatiently for Evie to open the door to one of the guest rooms.

He laid Libby gently down on the bed and stepped back, taking stock of her for the first time. She had a new bruise across her face that had swollen around her eye and already turned an ugly, mottled purple.

The split on her lip was fresh, and she had cuts and bruises down her arms. Blood dotted the t-shirt she wore, and he clenched his fists at the thought of what lay under the fabric. Whoever had done this was going to pay. He was going to squeeze every last drop of pain from them before he killed them. Slowly. Very slowly.

He heard Declan and Finn on the stairs shortly before they burst into the room.

"Fucking Christ," Declan swore, moving to the side of the bed. "What the hell happened?"

"I don't know. But I'm going to find out." Brogan's tone was deadly.

"I don't like that they dumped her at Glenmore House."

Brogan's head snapped up, and he glared at Finn. "That's the part about this you don't like?"

"You know what I mean. The message is clear, and it's not a good one."

"She's your mess." Declan nodded at Finn. "You clean it up."

"Everyone out," Evie said, voice clipped as she led the doctor in.

Declan paused to press a kiss to his wife's forehead before casting one last glance at the bed and following Finn into the hallway.

"I'm not leaving." Brogan crossed his arms over his chest, looking from Libby to Evie and back again.

Evie blew out a breath before moving to stand next to him, laying a hand on his arm. "Brogan, Doc is going to have to take her clothes off to get a look at her. She deserves privacy, and you'll feel better if you stay busy. Go work your magic and find the bastards who did this."

He clenched his jaw. "When I do, I'm going to kill them."

Evie gave a curt nod. "And not a soul in this family will stop you."

After a long minute, Brogan let his arms drop to his side and turned from the bed. He stopped next to the doctor, who was laying instruments and portable machines out on a table by the door.

"Take care of her."

The doctor inclined his head. "I'm going to do my best."

With one last glance over his shoulder, Brogan disappeared into the hallway and climbed the stairs to the third floor two at a time. Before he could have his revenge, he needed names, and he wouldn't stop until he found them.

Chapter Ten

Voices teased the edge of her consciousness. A man's voice, more than one, angry but muffled, like she was listening to them underwater. Maybe it was her father deciding the slowest, most painful way for her to die.

She lied about warning the Callahans and would continue to lie until her dying breath. It's not like the truth would save her from her fate anyway. The voices raised in shouts and she jumped, gripping the sheets between her fingers.

Libby struggled against the weight of fatigue, letting the sensations wash over her one by one. The room was cool and quiet. She didn't hear the beeping of machines, and the fabric under her fingers was soft, so she probably wasn't at a hospital.

Her mouth was dry, and she swallowed thickly, dragging her tongue over her lower lip to moisten it and flinching when it hit the newly opened cut. A noise rose from the recesses of the room that was filled with the faint scent of vanilla.

When her eyes fluttered open, it took her a minute to adjust to the darkness. Thick curtains covered the windows, a thin halo of light peeking out from the top and bottom. The room was bigger than the one she had at home. Although, all things considered, she was as good as homeless now.

She tried to sit up, groaning as the room spun, and then sunk back against the pillows. If she had to die here—wherever the fuck here was—at least the pillows were soft.

"You're awake."

Libby's eyes shot open at the unfamiliar voice from across the room. When the woman moved to stand by the side of the bed, Libby could barely make out her silhouette in the dark.

"Are you going to kill me?" she wondered, voice hoarse.

The woman snorted. "Are you okay if I open the curtains?"

Libby nodded, and the woman crossed the room and tugged back the curtains on a pair of floor-to-ceiling windows, bathing the room with light. She blinked against the brightness as the woman moved to her bedside again.

"You're still a little worse for wear, but better than when you got here."

"Where is here?" Libby rasped.

"You're at Glenmore House."

It took a minute for the whole of it to come flooding back. The beating, passing out, waking up in the van and being shoved out of it, and then Brogan was there, sprinting toward her. They'd left her with the Callahans. That couldn't be good.

Libby's gaze drifted back to the woman's face. She recognized her from a picture in the paper announcing the wedding of one of Philadelphia's most eligible bachelors.

"You're Evie Callahan."

Evie crossed her arms over her chest. "I am. Doc says there's no internal bleeding. We were worried about a concussion, but since you were coherent when we woke you, Doc said you were fine. You needed a few stitches here." Evie gestured to her own hairline. "But I talked the doc into doing it without shaving your head." Libby's hand flew to her hair. "You're welcome."

"How long have I been out?"

"About three days."

"Who—" Shouting erupted from the hall.

Evie rolled her eyes and stalked to the door, yanking it open. "Will you three give it a fucking rest? Our guest is awake. Rachel," she added to a uniformed maid who passed by the doorway, "ask Marta to call the doctor."

Libby gingerly pushed herself up against the pillows, inhaling slow, deep breaths until her head stopped spinning. Brogan, Declan, and Finn filed into the room to stand at the end of the bed.

Declan was the first to break the silence. "Do you know who did this to you?"

"Yes." She cleared her throat. "Andrea DiMarco. My father's right hand."

"And your father didn't stop him?" Finn asked.

The grief that swamped her was unexpected, and she swallowed around the sob that lodged in her throat. "My father watched."

"He fucking what?" Brogan demanded.

Her eyes drifted to Brogan, who stood beside his brothers with his hands balled into fists at his sides. No one looked happy, but Brogan seemed enraged. She couldn't decide if he was angry at her for being dumped on their doorstep or her father for letting this happen.

"Someone saw me talking to you outside Reign, and word got back to my father."

"So he knows you warned us? And did this"—Brogan gestured to her, voice tight—"as punishment?"

Libby nodded, pain lancing through her skull at the movement. "He suspects I did, but I denied it. This is just his favorite way to find out information."

"Why wouldn't you tell him?" Declan wondered.

"Because if he knew for sure I betrayed him, he would only kill me slower."

"His own daughter?" Evie sounded horrified.

"Daughters don't get the same grace as sons." Libby's words sounded bitter even to her own ears. "I expect he thinks I'm dead, in any case."

"They did shoot you."

"They what?" her hands flew to her stomach.

"They missed. Mostly." Finn nodded to her chest. "It grazed your left side."

So her father had given orders to kill her. Or DiMarco had, and her father agreed. They were one and the same at this point. She dropped her head back against the pillows, suddenly exhausted.

"I can't stay here."

A knock sounded on the door, and it opened a crack. An older gentleman with graying hair and kind eyes poked his head around the door.

"Marta said it was fine to come up," he said in a lilting Irish brogue. "You look a little steadier," he said when his eyes landed on Libby. "Might we have the room?"

"We'll discuss this more later," Declan assured her.

Taking Evie's hand, Declan crossed to the door, sharing a quick, whispered word with the doctor before slipping out, Finn on his heels. Only Brogan remained, unmoving, at the foot of the bed.

The doctor moved to the side of the bed and rummaged in his bag for a stethoscope. "You likely don't remember me as you were unconscious or sleeping the other times I came. But you can call me Doc since everyone else does. You all right if he stays?" he nodded in Brogan's direction.

She flicked a glance at Brogan and cleared her throat. "Yeah, he's fine."

He draped the stethoscope around his neck and gave her a kind smile. "How's the head? Fuzzy yet? Bit clearer?"

She relaxed back against the pillows. "It's better now."

"I imagine you're tired after all that. Let me check a few things, and we'll see what we see."

He listened to her heart and lungs, nodding in approval as he jotted notes down on a pad he pulled out of his bag. He shone a light into her eyes, frowning at her hiss of pain, and made another note. She expected more pain when he gently prodded the wound on her head, but there was only a dull ache.

"That'll scar," he said, snapping off the gloves he'd pulled on, "since Evie wouldn't let me shave your head, but I imagine no one will notice with all that hair." He smiled. "Your eyes are nice and clear. Focused."

He set his stethoscope back into his bag. "I didn't find any internal bleeding or broken ribs with the portable X, but I wouldn't mind having you come down to my office sooner rather than later for a proper exam."

She nodded. Reaching for a bottle of pills on the bedside table, he shook one out into his palm and held it out to her, offering her the glass of water that sat on the table.

"These pain pills should last you a while so long as you aren't about abusing them. You should be okay to shower now if you think you can stand. But I might recommend a nice hot bath instead." He gestured to her head. "Baths can also help with the bruising."

She stared at the pill before popping it into her mouth as he rose, stuffing his supplies back into the satchel he carried.

"It's a horrible thing what you went through, but you strike me as a strong woman, and the Callahans"—he shot a look at Brogan over his shoulder—"would never let something like this go unanswered. You're in good hands here, miss."

"Thank you."

He slipped out quietly, and she was alone with Brogan. She set the glass down next to the pills, refusing to make eye contact as he came around the side of the bed and sank down onto the edge.

"Thank you."

"What for?"

"For catching me."

She dragged her eyes to his face, studying the square cut of his jaw that was hidden under a layer of stubble. She liked him better clean-shaven. His arms, thick with muscles, rested on his thighs, and she had to grip the sheets to keep herself from reaching out and tracing the lines of his tattoos. She met his gaze, mesmerized by the sharp blue of his eyes, eyes that were filled with concern.

"You okay?"

"Yeah," she lied.

He studied her for a moment, brows knit together, and her fingers itched to smooth the crease between them. She gripped the blanket instead.

"I'm exhausted, Brogan."

"Then you should rest." Brogan pushed off the edge of the bed and crossed to the door. "Libby? They're going to pay for this," he promised before closing the door gently behind him.

Alone, her eyes drifted closed. Good. She wanted them to pay.

Chapter Eleven

W hen Brogan checked on Libby the next morning and found her still sleeping, he tucked the questions he had for her away and went in search of breakfast instead, stopping short when he found his entire family seated around the dining room table.

"Did I miss my invitation?" he wondered, piling his plate with food from the serving dishes on the sideboard and taking a seat beside Finn.

"We were just talking about the girls at the safe house. Most of them have left already. The rest are excited to leave as soon as their documents are good to go. Mackenzie decided to stay. She's going to share an apartment with a couple of single syndicate girls."

"We were also talking about Libby," Evie admitted, jolting when Cait pinched her arm. "Ow! He's not stupid."

"Thanks for the vote of confidence," Brogan replied around a mouthful of toast. "What about Libby?"

"Giordano didn't lay low for as long as I was anticipating."

"Which means he's stupid. Like I said," Aidan added.

"Which means," Declan corrected, "he's gotten too bold, and I want him out. Stupid or not, he can't get away with blatantly defying me. Otherwise my word and my authority mean nothing."

"Then let me kill DiMarco."

"It isn't that simple."

"The hell it isn't," Brogan shot back at Finn. "He's trafficking Christ knows how many women, beating them, raping them, and whatever other fucked up things he's doing. All with Giordano's blessing."

"It isn't that simple because DiMarco is a public figure," Declan explained. "If he turns up dead in an alley or floating in the river or even straight up disappears one day, people are going to notice, they're going to talk, and the cops are going to get involved."

Declan shifted in his chair. "I have clout in this city, but not that much clout. I don't need the cops breathing down our necks. I have to protect the syndicate from all sides here."

Brogan shoved his plate away, his appetite suddenly gone. All he wanted was revenge, and he didn't appreciate Declan getting in his way by making so much fucking sense.

"So what, then? They get away with it while we play political games?"

"If you weren't so pissed off, you'd see the possibility right in front of you," his uncle Sean replied.

Brogan caught Declan glancing up at the ceiling and shook his head. "No."

"Why not?"

"Hasn't she been through enough? She's already helped us out once." Brogan glanced at Evie. "Twice, actually."

"She isn't safe while they breathe, Brogan." Evie's tone was somber. "You know that's true."

"I repeat," Brogan said through clenched teeth, "let me kill DiMarco."

"I will," Declan promised. "He's yours. But we have to do it my way."

"The slow way," Brogan murmured.

"The smart way," Finn corrected. "Strategy is key here."

"Fine. But I don't see how Libby can help with that. She's not on the inside anymore."

"No, but she knows her father, and she knows DiMarco. She knows how they operate, where their strategic locations are. I bet she can give us more than you think."

Brogan leveled his gaze at Declan. "And what makes you think she'll say yes? They may be ruthless fucks, but they're still her family."

Declan leaned forward, resting his elbows on the table. "Right now they think she's dead. They wouldn't have left her at my door if they intended her to survive, and I've given them no reason to think otherwise. Once they find out that's not true, they'll want her. My protection will simply come with certain…conditions."

"So you're going to blackmail her."

"We're going to persuade her," Finn insisted.

"If you weren't thinking with your dick right now, you'd see the beauty in it," Aidan said.

When Brogan shoved to his feet, Aidan did the same, and though Brogan was several inches taller than his brother and broader too, Brogan knew Aidan could hold his own in a fistfight.

"Sit down, Aidan," Declan commanded, waiting for Aidan to slowly sink back into his chair. "Brogan, this is the offer. She can take it, or she can spend her life on the run. The choice is hers. I guess the question here is, whose side are you on?"

"That's a cheap shot," Brogan spat while Cait sucked in a breath. "I always have and always will have this family's back. So fuck you for questioning my loyalty."

Without another word, Brogan stormed out of the dining room and took the stairs two at a time to his lair. He could see the merit in Declan's plan; he could even acknowledge that using whatever knowledge Libby had to take down her father was their best shot at doing this without drawing the attention of the cops. That didn't mean he liked it.

The Callahan syndicate had a way of chewing people up and spitting them out when they were no longer useful—women especially. He'd seen it before. He'd witnessed the consequences of that exploitation. And they'd been a deadly, unstoppable force.

He needed some fucking air. Throwing what he needed to finish the last of the new identities for the girls at the safe house into a bag, he slammed out of the house, tore out of the driveway, and decided to drive until he felt like stopping.

Chapter Twelve

When Libby woke again, bright sunlight slanted into the room through the curtains she'd neglected to close. She pushed herself slowly up in bed, waiting for her head to spin, but she felt steadier this time, if a little sore.

Easing the blankets back, she swung her legs out and gingerly set her feet on the floor. Someone had stripped off the jeans and shirt she'd left her father's house in because she was dressed in a pair of leggings and a tank top she didn't recognize. She found herself mortified that the entire house had probably seen her naked.

Rising, she gripped the bedpost to steady herself, satisfied when she only swayed the tiniest bit. The carpet was soft and thick under her feet as she crossed to the bathroom, and when she flipped on the light, she nearly groaned at the free-standing tub sitting on a dais at one end of the room. The thing was easily big enough for two people.

She ran the water until it steamed before plugging the drain and letting it fill. Moving in front of the mirror over the vanity, she scanned her body from head to waist. Her left eye was black and puffy, which explained the dull ache that pulsed behind her brow.

Someone had cleaned the blood off her face, but it was still matted in her hair around the wound in her head where DiMarco's boot connected with her skull. The cut on her lip where he backhanded her at the bar was scabbed over for the second time in a week.

Libby winced at the quick stab of pain as she eased her tank up and off. She ran her fingers over the cuts and bruises that dotted her abdomen, her arms, her chest. Most of those had come from when she laid in the fetal position on the floor while he kicked the shit out of her and her father did nothing.

When the tub finished filling, she stepped out of her leggings and lowered herself into the punishingly hot water. Leaning back against the side of the tub, she let the water undo the tension in her muscles, the tightness in her side.

She'd known DiMarco and her father were capable of cruelty. She'd experienced her father's anger often enough, and she sensed it in DiMarco. But she could've lived a lifetime without proof that her father didn't care if she lived or died. Or worse, that he wanted her dead.

The fact that he believed she was dead played to her favor. She was free. Maybe she could grab Teresa from school, and they could disappear. She didn't want to leave her sister behind and unprotected if she could help it. Teresa might not want to go, but Libby would convince her. She had to.

As she lathered a cloth with soap, smoothing it over her skin, she plotted. She'd give it a few more days, a week at the most, until she was steady on her feet and could think without the constant dull ache that hummed through her body.

Libby didn't want to rely on this temporary kindness from the Callahans for too long, but they owed her. Their precious queen might be dead if not for her warning about the bounty a few months ago, and she was prepared to leverage that debt for as much as she possibly could.

A little seed money to get her out of the city and set up somewhere new wouldn't hurt. She had enough money in her secret bank account to last a few months if they lived carefully—if she could figure out how to access it without her phone or laptop.

Rinsing the soap from her skin, she used the spray nozzle and the shampoo to carefully wash her hair. The doctor hadn't said anything about not getting her stitches wet, but she imagined submerging her head in a tub full of soapy water wasn't the best idea.

She let the warm water run over her hair until it ran clear, unplugging the drain and watching the murky water swirl away. After rinsing the tub clean, she wrapped herself in the fluffiest towel she'd ever touched and crossed into the bedroom, the air conditioning raising the hair on her arms. Admittedly she hadn't really thought the clean clothes part all the way through.

Just as she turned to go back into the bathroom to rinse out her clothes in the sink, she caught sight of a couple of shopping bags on the bench at the foot of the bed. Perching on the bench, she opened the bag closest to her and pulled out a note.

If it doesn't fit or you don't like it, let me know. I can exchange it for whatever you like. -Evie

Setting the note aside, Libby dumped the contents of both bags onto the bench, eyes wide. Evie had gone shopping for her? Jeans, tops, underwear, a couple bras. Libby was dumbfounded that anyone would do this for her. The act of kindness made her uncomfortable, but she shook it off. It was simply a down payment on the debt they owed. That was all.

To keep her hands busy, she folded and arranged the pile of clothes. When she finished, she had three pairs of jeans, one pair of leggings, six tops, and enough underwear and socks to change them each twice a day and still have extras. Plus the clothes she'd left in a heap on the bathroom floor.

Stacking them in neat piles on the bench—no need to use the closet or chest of drawers if she wasn't going to be here that long—she selected a pair of dark wash jeans and a red t-shirt. Pulling both on over a mismatched set of cotton underwear, she combed her thick, damp hair with her fingers and hung the towel in the bathroom to dry.

Crossing to the door, she eyed the bed and its rumpled sheets. Maybe she could convince the maid to give her a fresh set so she could remake the bed. The idea of crawling into a bed where she'd laid bloody and unconscious for several days after scrubbing herself clean did not appeal.

Cracking the door open, Libby peeked out into the hallway, straining her ears for any sound of movement. Though, considering the size of her room alone, this place had to be a palace. The idea that she might be able to hear someone else in another part of the house seemed laughable.

Unsure exactly how to procure some food, she stepped out into the hallway and closed the door behind her. She went left but only found more bedrooms. Rounding back, she passed her room and continued until she found the stairs.

They were wide and shallow and fanned out at the bottom, covered in the same expensive antique carpet as the hallway. The carved banisters gleamed. She wasn't worried about going down the stairs so much as she was concerned about getting back up them.

Annoyed with that thought, she pushed it out of her mind. Her only options were to brave the stairs or sit in her room and hope someone remembered to feed her. The latter seemed too mortifying to comprehend, so instead she gripped the railing and took one step at a time.

At the bottom, she resisted the urge to explore and headed

toward the faint smell of coffee coming from the back of the house. She passed a living area that looked well used, a powder room that was bigger than the bathroom she had at home, and a formal dining room with a huge table scattered with dishes.

Apparently, she'd missed breakfast. Or, more accurately, hadn't been invited. Maybe she could sneak some leftovers out of the fridge without running into anyone.

The hallway opened into a beautiful kitchen with gleaming white marble countertops and navy cabinets. Two women in uniforms dashed her hopes of being able to go unnoticed. The older of the two, her hair shot with gray and laugh lines around her eyes and mouth, loaded plates into a big dishwasher while the younger carted dishes back and forth from the dining room.

A bowl of fruit was set on the table in the breakfast nook tucked against a bay window at the back of the room, but Libby didn't think she'd be able to grab an apple unnoticed. Too busy debating what to do, she didn't hear Evie come up behind her.

"Need something?"

Libby spun, reaching out to grip the doorway at the sudden onslaught of dizziness. "Sorry, I was, ah, just…I was hungry."

"I'm sure you are. The most we could get in you was broth and nothing since yesterday. We can make you a plate."

Evie crossed into the kitchen without waiting for a reply and greeted each woman by name. Libby tried to imagine her mother knowing the staff's name, let alone using it in such a friendly tone. It seemed foreign.

When Evie reached for the refrigerator door, the older woman shooed her away. Instead of looking angry, Evie just smiled and whispered to the woman, gesturing at Libby standing in the doorway like an idiot. The cook nodded, and, satisfied, Evie moved past Libby into the hallway.

"Marta is going to throw together a plate for you."

"You don't have to go to that much trouble. I can just take an apple or a bowl of cereal up to my room or something."

"Don't be ridiculous. You haven't had real food in days. I'm sure you're starving." Evie led her away from the dining room and into a family room, sinking down into the rich leather of one of the couches and gesturing to Libby to do the same. "Looks like the clothes I picked up fit. I'm glad. Doc had to cut the ones you came in wearing with scissors to examine you."

Libby gripped her hands in front of her, annoyance teasing the edges of her patience. "You don't have to pretend to like me," she snapped.

Evie cocked her head, studying Libby from across the room. "Politeness and liking you are not the same thing. Do I like you? I'm not sure yet. Do I trust you? I'm not sure about that either. Will I be polite to you? For now."

Libby set her jaw as Evie leaned back, tucking her feet up.

"What I really want to know is why you helped us."

"It doesn't matter."

"Doesn't it?" Evie wondered. "Oh, for fuck's sake, I'm not going to bite. Sit down."

Evie flicked a hand at the other couches and chairs in the room, and Libby perched on the edge of one as Marta came in carrying a tray piled high with pancakes, bacon and scrambled eggs, a bowl of fresh fruit, and a cup of hot coffee and set it in the middle of the glass coffee table.

"I made the eggs fresh but wasn't sure how you liked them."

"Oh, ah," Libby sputtered. "Scrambled is fine. Thank you."

"Thanks, Marta," Evie said as the woman turned to leave.

"I promise none of it's poisoned." When Libby still didn't move, Evie leaned forward and plucked a grape off the tray, popping it into her mouth.

Unable to ignore her gnawing hunger, Libby added cream and sugar to her coffee, barely stirring them through before taking a deep drink. She sighed as the caffeine slid through her, uncomfortably aware that Evie stared at her in the silence punctuated only by the scrape of the fork against the china plate.

Libby spooned up a bite of egg, chewing slowly. God, they were good. "I know what it's like to be a prisoner," she finally said. "What it's like to be at the mercy of my father. When I found out about those women, I couldn't do nothing."

"So you put your own life at risk to save strangers?"

Libby shrugged. "I'd do it again."

"Yes," Evie agreed. "I imagine you would. What do you want to do next?"

Libby swallowed her mouthful of pancake. "Next?"

"When you leave here."

She wondered exactly how much she should tell Evie, knowing it would certainly get back to Declan. She needed their help to get out of here, but that didn't mean she required their permission. In the end, she kept it vague.

"I'm going to leave. Start over somewhere."

Evie nodded slowly. "And if there was another option?"

Libby frowned. "What other option is there?"

At a noise in the hallway, they both looked up to see Declan stride in. Dressed in a dark, perfectly tailored suit and white button-down, he smiled when he spotted Evie on the couch and crossed the room to lean down for a kiss. Libby couldn't remember ever seeing her parents be openly affectionate with one another.

When he pulled away, he spotted Libby on the opposite couch, his expression changing, and he moved to sit on the armrest closest to his wife, placing himself between the two women.

"You look"—his eyes scanned the dark bruises on her face —"rested."

"I was just about to invite her to join us for dinner tonight," Evie said, reaching forward to pop another grape into her mouth.

Declan shared a long look with his wife over his shoulder, and Libby got the distinct impression they were having a conversation only they could understand. Declan nodded and turned back to face her.

"That's a great idea. I'm heading to the office." He stood and leaned down to press a kiss to his wife's forehead. "Try and behave yourself today."

"I'll see what I can do."

He left as quickly as he came, and Libby finished eating in the silence that followed, setting her empty plate on the coffee table. She was hungrier than she realized.

"I don't think dinner is a good idea." She wanted to avoid a Callahan firing squad if she could help it.

"I think it's the perfect time to make your case."

Libby's brows shot up. "Make my case?"

"I imagine you'll need some help with your plan to start over."

Libby didn't like the implication that she needed to beg for help, but she said nothing. For now.

"Excuse me," Marta said from the doorway. "Do you need anything else?"

Libby shook her head when Evie sent her a questioning look. "No, thank you, Marta. Oh," Evie added when Marta bent to retrieve the breakfast tray. "Actually, can you have Rachel change the sheets in Libby's room?"

"It's already being taken care of, ma'am."

Evie smiled. "What would we do without you?"

When Marta was gone, Libby rose from her spot on the couch and crossed to the door. "Thanks for breakfast."

"You're welcome. Libby," Evie said before Libby could disappear into the hallway. "Dinner's at seven."

Libby nodded, making her way carefully back up the stairs and closing her bedroom door once Rachel finished changing the sheets, carting off the stained ones. She hoped they burned them.

She crossed to a door she hadn't noticed before that led out onto a small Juliet balcony and stepped out. Standing in the doorway, the cool air at her back, she took a deep breath and let the sun and the summer air warm her face. She wasn't going to be anyone's prisoner anymore.

She would do whatever it took to control her own destiny. Even if it meant making her case to the Callahans.

Chapter Thirteen

Brogan looped circles around Philadelphia, but his anger wouldn't ebb. He drove toward the Main Line on back roads and through deserted streets, pushing the Jag as fast as he dared and taking corners at speeds that would typically have his adrenaline pumping. But none of it penetrated the haze of outrage that had settled around him.

He knew Declan was right about DiMarco, but the bruises on Libby's face, the cuts on her arms and torso, the haunted look in her eyes gnawed at him. He should have turned her away the day she banged on the door of the club and never given her a second thought.

If he had, she wouldn't be in the state she was in. He wouldn't crave the satisfying feeling of blood on his hands, and his own fucking brother wouldn't be questioning his loyalty to the family he'd sacrificed everything for.

And if all of that felt a little too close to home, he shoved it down and ignored it. There was no sense in dredging up the past and reliving something he'd rather forget. Making the turn onto his street, he slowed, taking the winding curves through the tree-lined road at a reasonable speed.

He passed the spot where his father had plowed into a tree during an ice storm two years earlier. Another moment when his entire world had been turned upside down. But at least that one hadn't been his fault.

He stopped in front of the house without turning into the drive. Beyond those trees stood the three stories of stone and glass that made up Glenmore House. His family had lived there for generations, surviving market crashes and wars and overzealous cops. They'd continue to survive, probably out of sheer stubbornness.

Not ready to run into Libby or Declan, he drove past the house and pulled up to Finn's gate instead, punching in the code. He parked in the circular drive behind Cait's SUV and climbed out.

Bypassing the house, he followed the path through the landscaping they had redone last summer to the pool in the back, grateful that their three-year-old, Evan, wasn't splashing around in it. Not that he didn't love his nephew, but he needed the punishing pace of swimming laps to clear his head.

He stripped down, keeping his boxers on in case someone came out and jumped into the deep end, letting his body sink to the bottom before kicking back up to the surface and running a hand through his close-cropped hair. The water was warm, thanks to the sun and the heater they ran so Cait could enjoy early morning swims before Evan woke up.

He pushed off from the side, his powerful kicks propelling him through the water as his arms sliced through the surface. He tried to push Libby's face from his mind, focusing on the water that swirled around him, on the rhythm of his breaths.

But she was there with her stick-straight hair the color of wheat, deep brown eyes, and perfect hips. He turned for another lap, and her face was replaced by another's. He pictured strawberry blonde hair and freckles sprinkled across her nose and cheeks. That was the face that haunted his nightmares. The woman he would have done anything for but couldn't protect in the end.

When he turned his head to take a breath, he noticed a pair of legs at the edge of the pool. He slowed his pace, coming to a stop at the far wall in the shallow end, leaning back against the tile as he caught his breath.

Finn walked around to where he rested and crouched down, wordlessly handing him a beer. Brogan took a swig, squinting against the late afternoon sun while Finn lazily cranked the umbrella on one of the tables that circled the pool.

Once the umbrella unfurled, Brogan moved into the small slice of shade it cast over the pool and watched Finn sit and take a slow pull from his own beer.

"Want to talk about it?"

Scowling, Brogan set his beer on the side of the pool, watching the condensation soak into the stone. "Talk about what?"

Finn rolled his eyes and took another drink. "This hard-on you have for DiMarco."

"So you're saying he doesn't deserve a bullet between the eyes?"

Finn twirled the bottle around on the table. "That's not at all what I'm saying. And you know it. What's really bothering you?"

Brogan shrugged. "I just want to get the bastard. Because he'll do a whole lot more damage until someone does."

Realization dawned in Finn's eyes, and he leaned forward to rest his elbows on his knees. "This is nothing like what happened to Samantha."

"Isn't it?" Brogan took an angry swig of his beer. "Because it feels exactly the same to me."

"No." Finn shook his head. "It isn't. And you have to

forgive yourself for that before it eats you alive. There was nothing you could have done differently then, and now you'll get your chance. You're not the only one who wants to see that bastard pay."

"But I—"

Brogan was interrupted by his nephew's squealing, running jump as he leapt into the pool and bobbed up to the surface, sputtering and excited. Turning, Brogan waited for Evan to doggy paddle his way over.

"We interrupted something," Cait said, rounding the pool and leaning down to press a quick kiss to Finn's lips before settling into the chair opposite his.

"No," Finn assured her, "perfect timing. In fact, while we have a built-in swim buddy, we should make good use of this alone time." Finn waggled his eyebrows and made Cait laugh.

"They're changing the sheets in our room right now, and I don't want to interrupt them."

"Woman," Finn said, pushing to his feet and holding out a hand to his wife, "there are six bedrooms in this house, and they all have locking doors."

Cait's gaze shifted to Brogan, and she raised her eyebrows, tilting her head in a silent question. When he nodded, she jumped up and followed Finn inside with a grin.

"Where they goin'?" Evan wondered as Cait's laughter faded.

"They're going inside to…play," Brogan decided.

"I want to play!"

Brogan chuckled. "Not for several more years, kid. Hey," he said when Evan frowned. "How high do you think I can throw you?"

A grin spread over the boy's face. "This high!" he said, spreading his little arms out as wide as they would go.

"Yeah? Let's find out. Make sure you hold your breath when you go in the water, okay?"

Once Evan nodded, Brogan gripped his nephew by the waist, lifted him out of the water, and sent him shrieking through the air. He landed with a splash. When he bobbed to the surface, laughing and gasping for breath, he paddled back toward Brogan.

"Again!"

Brogan tired of the game long before Evan did, but he convinced the kid to play on the gently sloping walk-in entrance with a bucket of toys he dug out from a bin at the edge of the patio. The boy made for a good distraction.

He was sitting on the side, feet dangling in the water, nursing the last of his beer, when he heard Cait and Finn approach.

"Hey kid, your mom and dad are coming."

Evan's whole body perked up, ears straining, and when he heard his father's laughter, his face lit up. He jumped up, running toward the sliding glass door just as Finn slid it open.

Finn tossed Evan in the air while Cait made her way over to Brogan and leaned down to cup his face in her hands, giving him a loud kiss on the lips. "You're the best brother *ever*," she assured him with a wink.

Finn laughed while he hooked Evan under one arm and let him dangle upside down. "Declan called a family meeting over dinner. Thirty minutes."

Brogan glanced at the trees that shielded Finn's property from Glenmore House. In the winter, you could see the outline of the house through the branches and catch the sunlight glinting off the windows in the afternoons. Turning away from the house, he met Finn's gaze.

"Thirty minutes," he replied.

Chapter Fourteen

L ibby looked up when Brogan stepped into the doorway of the family room, where everyone had gathered before dinner. She'd been hoping to talk to him all day. She felt like he might be the only Callahan who'd be on her side about leaving.

But he barely made eye contact as he entered, gaze flickering over her for the barest of moments. Maybe she was wrong about him, and he'd be just like all the rest. She'd practiced her speech. They might be intimidating, but they owed her, and Declan always made sure his debts were paid.

Rachel announced dinner, and they all filed into the dining room, settling into what felt like assigned seats while she hung back to get the lay of the land. A mistake, since the only empty chair was directly between Brogan and Aidan.

Great. The brother who was hell-bent on ignoring her and the one who'd been staring daggers at her since she'd come downstairs. Perfect. She reluctantly took her seat between them.

They passed platters around and served themselves, something that never happened at home, where everything was served on covered plates by stiff maids, like some ridiculous choreographed show. The food smelled good and looked even better. Real food, too, not catered to whatever diet her mother might be on that tasted like cardboard.

The biggest difference that struck her was the conversation. It ebbed and flowed around her. The easy teasing and inside jokes and catching each other up on current events and gossip. Her house was a tomb by comparison, her father preferring to eat in near-total silence. Unless he asked you a question, of course.

"Not hungry?" Brogan asked when he noticed she wasn't eating. She nearly dropped her fork in surprise.

"So you do know how to speak."

He snorted. "Have you been waiting for me to say something in particular?"

He leaned in closer to keep their conversation private, and the heat of him radiated against her arm. Her eyes dropped to his lips and then back up to meet his gaze.

"No, but I was hoping you'd back me up with something."

His eyes narrowed, but he didn't move away. "Back you up with what?"

"With this." She took a bolstering breath and turned toward the table. "I'm going to be leaving Glenmore House."

The buzz of conversation died, and all eyes turned to her. She cast Brogan a sideways glance, but he only frowned.

"I think that would be a mistake," Declan said, drawing her gaze.

"And why is that?"

"Because your family thinks you're dead."

"Exactly," she told him. "Which means I'm free."

Declan scoffed, and she jerked her chin up. "What it means is that the minute he finds out the traitor he thinks is dead is actually alive, he's going to hunt you down and kill you."

The hair stood up on the back of her neck, and her fingers tightened on her fork until her knuckles were white. "You don't know that."

"Yes, I do. Because it's exactly what I would do if I were him. Then again, my men wouldn't have missed their first shot."

"If I can slip away undetected, maybe at night."

"You don't have a car, so you have to take a bus, a train, or a plane. And if you don't think he's got people watching those just in case, you're not as smart as I thought."

Libby glared at Declan, setting her fork down with a snap. "So I'm, what, stuck here forever? My options are to stay in hiding in Philadelphia or be murdered by my own father?"

"That's not what we're saying," Brogan assured her.

Libby whipped her head around to face him. "Then what *are* you saying? Because it sounds like you want to keep me locked up here. Indefinitely."

"We're only offering protection," Evie countered.

"At what cost?"

She thought Declan might have looked impressed for a minute, but it was gone so fast she couldn't be sure.

"In exchange for Callahan protection, you help us."

"You'll have to be more specific."

Declan's lips twitched, but he didn't smile. "You help us take down your father."

Libby's mouth fell open. Of all the things she expected him to say, that had not been one of them.

"You want to take out the entire Italian Mafia?"

"No," Finn replied. "Not exactly. Only your father and the men loyal to him."

"And then?"

"And then we install someone else."

Understanding hit her, and she sat back in her chair. They didn't want to end the Mafia. It served its purpose in the city. It had its place. They didn't want to tear it down so much as they wanted to remake it in their image.

"Choose someone who'd be beholden to you, you mean."

"Exactly," Brogan replied.

She chewed on the inside of her cheek. They wanted her to help them kill her entire family. Not just her father or DiMarco, who she'd gladly see buried for what they'd done to her, but her brothers, since they were certainly a threat, her mother, and probably a dozen or more men beyond that. All so they could play their political games and keep an even tighter stranglehold on this city. She wouldn't do it.

"No."

"No?" Declan's voice was cold.

It wasn't the answer he'd been expecting. He probably didn't hear the word often.

"No," she said again. "My father, yes. DiMarco, definitely. But you're asking me to betray my whole family. My mother, my brothers. I've got half siblings all over this city. Not all of them are loyal to my father, but many are. And I've got a sister to protect. So, no. I won't help you exterminate every Giordano who won't bend the knee to you."

"Not even knowing what he's doing?"

Libby glanced at Aidan, who pinned her with a cool stare. She could tell he didn't think much of her, but the feeling was entirely mutual.

"You've caught them once. You can catch them again. It's not like I'm on the inside to help you anymore, anyway."

"You sh—"

"Let me show you something." Brogan interrupted Declan and pushed away from the table, holding out his hand for her.

"What?"

Brogan shot a look at his brother and then met Libby's gaze again, holding it. "I want to show you something before you decide."

Hesitant but eager to get away from the curious and angry stares that lingered on her from around the table, she pushed to her feet, jerking slightly when he took her hand and led her from the room. She could hear conversation resume in hushed whispers as they made their way down the hall and turned toward the stairs.

"If this is some kind of trick to get me to change my mind—"

"It's not a trick," he said, finally letting go of her hand when they reached the third floor and turning left down a long hallway. "It's a reminder."

She followed him past a big, beautiful library that reminded her of her sister and down a short hallway into a windowless room filled with computers. It looked like some kind of tech center. The space was immaculate, with papers lined up in ruthlessly straight stacks.

"What is this?" she breathed as he crossed the room and sank into a high-backed desk chair.

"I call it my lair. Because"—he gestured to the walls—"no windows."

Her eyebrows shot up. "This is your stuff?"

He shuffled through a stack of papers to find the ones he wanted. "Why does that surprise you?"

She moved to stand on the other side of the desk, facing him, and she could feel her face heating at her assumption. Her first impression of him was that he was strong, but not particularly smart. Looks like she might have made an ass out of herself with that one.

"I don't know." She crossed her arms over her chest. "You seem too...buff to be a computer nerd."

He barked out a laugh and shook his head. "I'm not sure if that's a compliment or not. But here."

He flipped pages out of the stack and set them on the desk, facing her. Pictures of women with a faraway or terrified look in their eyes, some with bruises, all of them haunted.

"What are these?"

"These are the women you helped save."

Libby's head jerked up from her study of the pictures. "These are…"

"They are."

She picked up each photo to study them, setting them down when her fingers began to tremble. She knew the Callahans had successfully rescued them, but it was nice to put faces to victims that had only ever existed in her mind.

"These," he added, laying out newer photos that looked like headshots for driver's licenses, "are what they look like after a week of good food and not being beaten or raped every day. You did that."

Libby shook her head. "I told a story, wrote a note."

"Libby." He waited for her to look up before continuing. "They would be Christ knows where right now if you hadn't risked yourself by coming to Reign or sending us that note. You saved them. You damn sure saved Evie."

She shifted, blinking back tears. Why didn't that make her feel any better?

"You don't know what you're asking," she murmured, setting the picture down when a tear fell on the glossy surface.

"I know there are more women out there like them. DiMarco had dozens of numbers on his encrypted lists. There's no telling how many women. Yes, Declan wants to see the end of the Giordano reign over the Mafia. It hasn't exactly been a banner rule for the Italians."

Libby snorted. "You're asking me to sacrifice the only people that have ever loved me."

Brogan tossed the rest of the photos on the table and stood, leaning against the edge so their faces were level.

"Those people don't love you. People who love you don't beat you. And don't tell me it was the first time, either. Because I saw a bruise on your stomach that first day you came to the club."

"My father has hit me, sure. But my brothers? My mom?"

"Have they ever stopped him?"

She rubbed her forehead. What had her mother said to her at the party after her father backhanded her in front of the entire crowd? *I told you to keep your mouth shut.*

"No," she murmured. "They've never stopped him."

"Then who exactly are you protecting?"

She hung her head. She owed them nothing. They had, all of them, stood by for years while her father vented his frustrations with his fists. Her mother had been more than happy to deflect a beating onto her own child. With Teresa safely at school, who was she protecting?

She started to speak when a photo on the top of the stack Brogan had tossed aside caught her eye. She grabbed for it, her heart dropping into her stomach. No. It couldn't be.

"Where did you get this picture?"

Brogan frowned, clearly thrown off guard by her change in topic, and glanced down at it. "Ah, when we went to the address you gave us, the women we found got loaded into a van. These two were taken out the front door and put into a car. We lost them when they got on the highway. Why? Do you recognize them?"

She looked up at him, and he straightened at the look of horror on her face. "That's my sister. Teresa."

She let the photo drift to the top of the desk and reached out to grip the edge to steady herself. Brogan came around the end of the table and wrapped an arm around her waist when she swayed, but she couldn't hear him over the ringing in her ears.

Everything she'd ever done her entire life, every beating she'd ever taken, every sacrifice she'd ever made. It had all been to make sure that Teresa got a better life. To make sure that Teresa escaped their prison.

She thought she'd done it. Teresa wanted to go to NYU but settled for Villanova, and it was a good school, even if she hated that it was in the same city. Teresa enjoyed college and the friends she'd made. She was supposed to be there right now, doing some work-study program for her senior internship credit.

Libby glanced at the picture again, at her sister's grainy face filled with fear as she was shepherded into a car. Teresa wasn't at school. She was a prisoner, just as Libby was. Held against her will, subjected to untold horrors by DiMarco and his band of thugs.

A sudden, overwhelming urge to make them all pay washed over her, and rage bubbled in her chest. Every last fucking one of them deserved to pay for what they were doing. Anyone who'd ever turned a blind eye to her father's violence or DiMarco's cruelty. She knew now that seeing it and doing nothing was just as bad as committing the sin yourself.

Whatever lengths she had to go to, they would pay. She would make sure of it.

"I'll do it." She looked up at Brogan, whose arm tightened around her waist. "On one condition."

"What's that?"

"We have to find my sister."

"Okay," he agreed after a long moment of silence. "Let's go tell the others."

She gripped his hand tightly on their way down the stairs,

as much for balance as for the feeling of someone anchoring her to the earth. This was no small step she was taking, but it was the right one to take.

When they stepped into the dining room, the conversation died. Libby surveyed each of them. This was a betrayal she could never come back from. But if her father had taught her anything, it was to be ruthless in the pursuit of what she wanted. And now she wanted him to pay.

"I'm going to help you take down the Giordano Mafia," she said into the silence. "When can we get started?"

Chapter Fifteen

I t took two days for Declan to decide how he wanted to hit back at the Italians, and another three for Brogan to run preliminary surveillance on the warehouse her father used to run his drug trade. Libby had never been to the warehouse, but it wasn't exactly a well-guarded secret.

Brogan's surveillance confirmed the information she gave Declan. Tony ran a skeleton crew in the warehouse at night, mostly because he was too cheap to pay for more men. New shipments usually arrived in the morning and could sit for anywhere from twenty-four to forty-eight hours before being packaged and distributed to sellers.

Declan scoffed at her father's lazy approach to his biggest source of income, but Libby could only shrug. It had never made sense to her either. Her father's men complained about it all the time to their wives or girlfriends. If the drugs weren't being sold, they weren't being paid, and sitting drugs didn't sell.

Shipments had been arriving more sporadically in recent weeks. She knew that much from the hours her father kept. He spent more time in his office at the house when a new shipment came in, usually because it meant an influx of cash. Cash always improved his mood.

Her estimate had only been off by a day, and a new shipment arrived this morning. The Callahan men spent the entire day at the club with the soldiers they handpicked for this job to get them ready for tonight. The plan was to get in and out under cover of darkness with no one the wiser.

Evie's suggestion to let Giordano wonder if it was an inside job and he hadn't flushed out the traitor by taking care of Libby was brilliant. Libby took a small measure of satisfaction knowing the wondering would drive her father insane. He deserved that and so much more.

Now she was alone—Evie and Cait were at some function with other syndicate wives—and bored. Itching to get out of this room and keep her brain from running over every way this could go horribly wrong, she pushed off the bed and turned toward the door, barely swallowing the strangled scream that clawed at her throat.

"Jesus Christ, Brogan. You scared the life out of me." How did a man of his size move around so quietly? "What are you doing here?"

He quirked a brow, a grin tugging at the corner of his mouth. "I live here."

"I mean, why aren't you gone with the others?"

"Because I'm the eyes and ears. And you're going to help me."

When he disappeared from the doorway, she was forced to follow him, jogging to catch up with his long strides. He climbed up to the third floor and turned toward his lair, looking back to ensure she was behind him.

The door was closed this time, and he pressed the pad of his thumb against a biometric lock before keying in a numeric code with a series of beeps. The lock opened with a whirring click, and he pushed inside.

The hum of computers and the wall-mounted air conditioning unit that she assumed was to keep the room from overheating washed over her. She hadn't been able to hear that from the hallway. So the room was soundproof too. Interesting.

Brogan rounded the desk and settled in his rolling desk chair, pulling up a second chair that hadn't been there the last time she'd been in this room. Had he brought in a second chair just for her?

He gestured for her to sit, keying in a complicated password. The screens blinked to life with images, video feeds, and what she assumed were live mics with the way the audio bars spiked up and down in bright green.

"How did you learn how to do all this?" she wondered, impressed.

Brogan swiveled in his chair to meet her gaze. "When I was seven, I took apart a DVD player to see how it worked. My father put a video game controller in my hand and told me I wasn't allowed to take shit apart until I learned how to put it back together."

He shrugged when she smiled. "Video games fascinated me, and so did the internet. So I learned how to take it apart and put it back together. I built this computer system from the ground up a few years ago."

She blinked. "You built this?"

"Well, not like how you're probably thinking. But, without getting technical, yes."

"That certainly clears it up," she replied, and he chuckled.

She moved out of the way when he swiveled to face another screen, but he pushed her back into place, his fingers lingering on the arm of her chair. He was close enough that she could smell the woodsy scent of his soap. Too close.

"So what am I doing here? I gave you everything I could remember already."

"If something unexpected comes up, you're our best bet for putting names to new faces or knowing what to anticipate from them. Our men are good, but more data is always better than less. I like to be prepared."

His phone signaled an incoming message and his expression sobered. "Here we go."

She watched as he tapped the keys to unmute the mics, filling the room with voices. He arranged the screens with side-by-side video feeds, and she recognized the main warehouse plus vantages of all the major streets that led there.

"You can hack into traffic cameras?"

The corner of his mouth tilted up into a grin, but he said nothing. Lights flashed in the bottom left of the camera trained on the front of the warehouse just as a voice she didn't recognize announced their arrival. They cut the lights on the truck, and Brogan switched camera angles, alerting them to the three guys inside.

She pointed to one man who sat in a chair, balancing on its two back legs. "Looks like he got a promotion."

Brogan squinted, as if trying to place the man in his mental files. "How do you know that?"

"Because he was driving the van. I heard the other guy say his name. And now he's there."

Brogan stiffened beside her, eyes locked on Tommy's face, and she wondered if he was committing it to memory.

"The big one is married to one of my half sisters," she said, glad when he visibly relaxed. "I've only met her a couple times, but she didn't seem all that excited about it at her wedding."

"And the other one?"

"That's my brother. My dad calls him the spare. Which he hates. Gio considers this type of work beneath him, so he must have said or done something stupid."

Brogan made a noise in the back of his throat, turning

back to the screens as three men dressed in black climbed out of the cab, shouldering duffel bags and disappearing through a side door while two more waited by the truck, guns drawn, bodies alert.

A few taps and Brogan brought up what looked like a body camera that bobbed past closed doors, dusty abandoned furniture, and discarded wooden pallets.

"Fucking bingo," the voice said, stopping in front of a huge pallet stacked with one-kilo bags of cocaine to eye level.

They dropped their duffels with a grunt and made quick work of swapping out bags full of plaster dust with product, careful to disperse them as easily as they could in the pile to keep it from being obvious. They took a dozen more bags than they replaced, arranging the stack to look like nothing was missing.

They worked quickly, perfectly in sync, and Libby was fascinated by their care and precision. Her eyes were fixed on the men who were now loading their bags back up and heading back to the truck, but Brogan's darted from video feed to video feed, constantly alert.

"Brogan," she said, catching movement in the corner of her eye and noticing her brother had gotten up from the desk to poke his head out into the hallway.

"Shit. Rory, freeze for a second. We've got movement."

Her eyes snapped to Brogan's face. "You don't want them to get out of there?"

He clicked the video to enlarge it. "If I tell them to book it, they'll definitely make enough noise to send him looking. Let's give it a second to see if he brushes off whatever noise he heard as his imagination."

Libby held her breath as her brother looked left, then right, seeming to consider going to investigate before thinking better of it and stepping back into the room, dropping into his chair.

"Go," Brogan said. "Quick and quiet."

When the men appeared at the side door, the tension drained from her shoulders, and she exhaled long and slow. They crossed the parking lot, loaded into the truck, and carefully backed out onto the road. Everyone inside the warehouse oblivious to what had just happened.

When celebratory cheers rang out from the mics, Brogan muted them with a tap and turned to her with a grin that twisted her insides. God, he was beautiful. The thought caught her so off guard she didn't hear what he said next.

"What?"

"I said, everyone's going to be in a good fucking mood tonight. I think that calls for a beer. You want a beer? Or maybe wine?"

"Ah…" She glanced at the screens as he cleared them with a few taps, bringing up the screensaver. "Yeah. Wine's good."

He cut off the lights and locked the door behind them, whistling to himself and matching her pace down the stairs.

"Oh, hang on. I need to grab something from my room," he said when they hit the second-floor landing. "It's back this way."

She followed the direction of his finger down the hall. The fact that she so badly wanted to see his bedroom is exactly why she forced herself to take a step back and turn toward the stairs.

"I'll just meet you downstairs."

She didn't wait for him to reply before jogging slowly down and putting some distance between them. What the hell was wrong with her? She was not supposed to want to get cozy with Brogan Callahan, no matter how tempting his lips or his hands or his freaking tattoos might be. Whatever tug she felt toward him was gratitude—nothing more.

Focusing on taking down her father and rescuing her sister had to be her top priority. Tonight she'd witnessed a fraction of the power of the Callahan syndicate. Without a doubt, they could wipe out any faction in the city just because they felt like it.

They had the money, the manpower, and the skills to do it without even breaking a sweat. Hell, they could probably do it without creating so much as a ripple in the real world. No one cared about dead criminals.

She saw her father's hatred for them now for what it was. Fear. And fear was a powerful weapon that made men do stupid things.

Chapter Sixteen

Brogan bolted up in bed, his laptop crashing to the floor so hard he winced. He scrubbed his hands over his face to clear away the lingering images of strawberry blonde hair and freckles and lifeless eyes.

He'd fallen asleep trying to crack DiMarco's goddamn cipher. He hoped that knowing the original date and location of their last exchange would give him enough to extrapolate the jumble of letters and numbers into usable data sets. It hadn't, and that pissed him off.

He prided himself on being able to lay his fingers on a keyboard and dig up any information he wanted. No matter what the info was or how long it took him, he always managed to excavate it. He'd just have to keep digging.

He bent to retrieve his laptop, closing it and setting it carefully on the table by the bed. Almost two in the morning. He thought about taking a shower to wash away the rest of his dream but opted for a beer instead.

Having Libby in the house was dredging up memories he'd rather stay buried, and his attraction to her didn't help. How was he supposed to concentrate on what needed doing if he was constantly thinking about her lips, how they'd taste, and what sounds he could elicit from them? Shoving out of bed, he stalked to the door and yanked it open.

He needed this all to be over so he could shove these memories of a woman long dead back in their box and let Libby and her lips melt into the darkness. He promised himself a long time ago that he would not get caught up with another woman who needed saving. His track record since has been impeccable. He wanted it to stay that way.

When he hit the bottom of the stairs, he was so lost in his own thoughts he almost didn't hear the choked sobs coming from the back of the house. Who the hell else would be up at this hour?

Changing course, Brogan wound his way through the family room, past the parlor, and into a solarium his father added onto the house for his mother as a wedding present. Brogan never really spent much time in this room, but the panoramic view of the grounds was stunning in every season.

She was tucked under a blanket on a chaise lounge in the far corner, a single light shone on the table beside her. Her shoulders shook as she sobbed into her hands, and in an instant, his irritation splintered and fell away, replaced by concern and an overwhelming need to fix whatever had upset her. Which was precisely the problem.

For a moment, he considered leaving her alone with her tears and her pain. She could work out whatever was bothering her without his help. She didn't need a white knight. But he didn't have it in him to turn around and go.

He was only going to offer some words of encouragement. That was it. Maybe also to punch whoever had made her cry because he desperately wanted to punch whoever had made her cry. Christ. Taking a deep breath, he crossed the room and sat on the chair across from hers.

It took her a minute to register his presence, and when she

did, she jumped and shielded her face with her hands like she was afraid he might hit her. That rubbed, but he shoved the insult down because he knew she had good cause to be wary of men.

"Want to talk about it?"

She swiped at the tears that streaked down her cheeks, and he reached for the box of tissues on the side table, plucking one out and handing it to her. He waited while she wiped her eyes and nose.

"I keep having these nightmares."

"About what?"

She twirled her ponytail around the end of her finger, eyes staring out into the night. "All I can see when I close my eyes is Teresa's face. But not her smiling, happy face where she's telling me a story about her life at school."

Libby pursed her lips, clearing her throat before continuing. "It's the face from the picture. The one from outside that house. She looked so…"

Her voice broke. "She looked terrified. I imagine she *is* terrified. And all I see when I close my eyes is her terrified face, and then I can't stop picturing every awful thing they must be doing to her right now."

When she finally met his gaze, her brown eyes were brimming with fresh tears. "Why did he take her, Brogan? And how could I not have known?"

He shifted from the chair to the chaise when she broke down again, wrapping an arm around her shoulders and ignoring the warmth in his chest when she molded perfectly to his side. Words of encouragement, nothing more.

"How could you have?"

"I don't know. Sister's intuition?" She shook her head when he raised a brow. "She wasn't texting me back. It should have worried me, but there was so much going on that I didn't really think about it. I overheard them talking about the girls, and then I agonized for close to a week over whether I should seek you out to tell you about it. Then once I did, my father announced my engagement to DiMarco. Which caught me totally off guard."

"He what?" Brogan demanded, and she flinched. "You didn't mention that," he added, softening his tone.

"Yeah, at the party that night. The one I told you I was expected at. Just announced it right in front of everyone with no warning. He backhanded me when I refused." She rubbed absently at her healing lip.

"That's why you had the split lip in the security tape at the restaurant the next day. With all that going on, how could you blame yourself?"

She sighed. "Because whatever I went through, she's had it ten times worse."

When she laid her head on his shoulder, he froze. He should put some distance between them. That's what a responsible man would do. A responsible man who'd been in a situation like this before and knew how it would end. If Teresa wasn't already dead, she likely would be soon. Libby deserved to know the truth about her sister's odds of survival. But he didn't have the heart.

"It's not a competition, Libby, and none of it is your fault."

"Tell that to the guilt that gnaws at the edge of my mind when I can't sleep. How do I make the guilt go away?"

That was a question he couldn't answer. He still held his in a vise grip. "Time, I guess. Just give it time." It was a lie. Time had not eased his guilt over what had happened to Samantha, but it seemed to pacify Libby, so he let it hang between them. "You look tired."

She rubbed a finger between her eyebrows, sighing. "I haven't been sleeping well. Headaches. I should probably go up and try to get some rest."

"I'll walk you up."

He rose when she did, waiting for her to fold the blanket and drape it over the back of the chaise. They climbed the stairs in silence, and when they paused outside her bedroom door, she fidgeted with her fingers before shoving them behind her back.

"There should be something for your headache in the bathroom."

Her cheeks flushed pink, and he decided it was way sexier than it should have been.

"I took the last one in the bottle a couple days ago. A hot shower helps. Enough to fall asleep, at least."

He frowned. "Why didn't you ask for more?"

She opened her mouth and closed it again. "I don't know."

"Wait here."

He retreated to his room, rummaging around in his own medicine cabinet for the bottle of aspirin he always kept there. She was waiting for him in the hall when he returned, leaning casually against the doorframe, comfortable enough to close her eyes. He liked the look of her there.

Shaking his head, he shoved the shock and stupidity of that thought down, waiting for her eyes to open and focus on him before handing her the bottle of pills. When she smiled, his eyes dropped to her lips and lingered there.

"Brogan, I wanted to say…I wanted to say thank you," she rushed out in a quick breath.

His eyes snapped back to hers. "For the meds?"

She flashed a quick smile before catching her bottom lip between her teeth. "Yes, for the meds, but also for believing me, for saving those girls, and for catching me when I fell."

He dipped his head ever so slightly when she pushed up onto her tiptoes, her hands braced against his chest. Her mouth was inches from his before he came to his senses and stumbled back. He took another step to put more distance between them so he didn't haul her onto her toes and take her mouth in precisely the way he couldn't stop thinking about.

"You're welcome. Sleep well," he murmured, turning on his heel and stalking back to his room.

When he was out of sight, he leaned back against the wall and waited until he heard her bedroom door click closed. Fuck, fuck, fuck.

The shock, embarrassment, and hurt on her face when he stepped away sent daggers through him, but he much preferred it to the anger he knew he'd see there when she realized he wasn't the hero she thought he was.

Chapter Seventeen

Libby successfully avoided Brogan in the days following their almost kiss. Keeping to herself saved her from dying of embarrassment. He'd pulled away so fast from her advance that she was surprised he hadn't fallen over. Nothing made you feel more like an idiot than throwing yourself at a man who clearly didn't want you.

So rather than take the chance of running into him again, she spent most of her time in her room poring over the photos Brogan had slipped under her door. Even after making an ass out of herself, he'd taken her tears to heart, downloaded what seemed like every photo her sister had ever posted to social media, and gifted them to her. It was sweet.

She'd have to see about getting frames for a few of them. Like the one of Teresa after she lost her first tooth, her tongue wiggling through the hole. It amazed Libby how far back some of them went. Teresa bundled up against the snow as a toddler, then her first day of school, all dressed up in her plaid pleated skirt and crisp, white button-down.

With a sigh, Libby slipped the pictures back into the

manila envelope and dropped them into the nightstand drawer. The pictures both soothed and haunted. Even with them, she couldn't get the image of Teresa's scared, tear-stained face out of her head.

Libby had no way of finding her, no way of knowing where she was or if she was okay. She'd called the university and found out not only had Teresa never shown up for her work-study program, but she had been unenrolled entirely. Which meant she hadn't been at school for almost a month. She'd been captive instead.

Did their father know where his youngest daughter was? Even knowing what she knew now about what Tony Giordano was capable of, Libby couldn't fathom that he would approve of his youngest daughter being sold to the highest bidder. At least not outside the confines of a good, Catholic marriage.

If he didn't know, and she couldn't be sure either way, he still shouldered some of the blame for Teresa's fate. If for no other reason than he had been the one to give DiMarco the freedom, the money, and the power to do whatever he wanted. Tony had created this monster, so Teresa's blood was on his hands too.

She tensed at the knock on the door. But no one barged in. No angry voices drifted through the thick wood. She forced herself to relax and reminded herself she was safe here.

"Come in!"

"Oh, good. I thought you were asleep for a second." Evie stood framed in the door, one hand resting on her cocked hip. "Get up. We're kidnapping you."

Libby blinked in surprise when Evie disappeared.

"Admittedly," Evie said, making Libby jump when she reappeared in the doorway, "that was a poor choice of words, all things considered. But we've got a surprise for you, so meet me downstairs in five."

With no further explanation, Evie was gone again. Intrigued and maybe a little bored, Libby slid off the bed and crossed into the bathroom to freshen up her makeup, swiping some mascara across her lashes and blending a bit more concealer over the fading edges of the bruise that still ringed her eye.

The cut on her lip was finally healed, and so were the ones along her arms. The bruises on her stomach and back had faded from an ugly, mottled purple to a sickly green that made her look diseased.

She slipped into a pair of flats and left the room, closing the door behind her out of habit more than anything else. It's not like a closed door would keep out a Callahan in their own house, although she didn't have a reason to suspect they were going through her things. Not that she had many things to go through.

She found Evie waiting for her in the foyer, bag slung over her shoulder.

"Ready?"

"Ready for what?"

"We're going shopping."

Libby crossed her arms over her chest. "I thought I wasn't supposed to leave the house."

"We're only going across the street to Cait and Finn's place. We're even going to drive just in case." Evie held up her keys.

"Does Cait have a shopping mall set up in her basement?"

Evie grinned. "Sort of. Cait loves shopping." Libby hesitated. "You'll hurt her feelings if you don't go."

"I don't have any cash. I have some money in a secret bank account I've been stashing for...I don't even know what." This situation had never been in her plans.

"Look at you," Evie murmured.

"But I haven't been able to access it without a computer. Brogan could maybe…"

Evie gripped Libby's shoulders gently, turning her toward the door. "We'll worry about the money later. For now, let's just have fun."

Libby thought it was a euphemism, but Cait's house was literally across the street. True to Evie's word, they drove over in her Maserati, pulling into an empty space in the three-car garage and closing the door before getting out. They entered through the kitchen, and Evie dropped her bag on the counter. It was smaller than the one at Glenmore House and newer, too, but it had a similar feel with its white countertops and dark green cabinets.

"Caitlin!" Evie called.

"In here!"

They crossed through a two-story foyer with a gorgeous drop chandelier that caught the light from the windows and threw rainbows against the wall and into a living room. Libby stopped short at the archway.

Racks of clothing lined the edge of the room. Dresses, tops, pants, shoes, and even an entire collection of bathing suits filled almost every space.

"Surprise!" Cait threw out her arms.

"What is all this?" Libby glanced at the strange brunette standing in the corner and rubbed her clammy hands on her thighs.

Evie held out a glass of what looked like a champagne cocktail and beckoned Libby forward. "You've been cooped up in that house going on two weeks now. I don't know how you aren't going absolutely batshit crazy. We wanted to get you out of there for something fun."

"Yes, and since you still need to lay low for a while, we thought a private shopping experience made more sense."

"MaryAnne is an O'Connor," Evie said, gesturing to the

brunette as if that explained everything. Libby assumed the O'Connors were a syndicate family.

"She owns one of my favorite boutiques, and when I called with my idea, she happily agreed."

"Anything for family. And our best customer." MaryAnne added, and Cait laughed. She turned to Libby. "You are stunning. Tell me what kind of pieces you're looking for."

"Oh, ah, I'm not really sure." She felt nervous with all eyes on her. "Just some basic tops or whatever. I guess. Keep it simple."

"Why?" Evie wondered, removing a dress from a rack in a beautiful shade of lavender and holding it out to study it.

"Because." Libby scooped up a glass off the table and took a deep drink. "None of this is…I can't…"

Understanding lit Evie's eyes. She closed the distance between them to stand between Libby and MaryAnne, her voice low enough that only Libby could hear. "I know what it means to not trust kindness, especially from people you have no reason to expect kindness from. But we have no ulterior motives here, no hidden agenda. We want you to get whatever you want, no strings."

"Why?"

"Because I was alone and broke and scared once, and someone did something nice for me. And it made all the difference. Let's just say I'm paying it forward for an old friend. Okay?"

Libby bit her lip, nodding. "Okay."

Evie's words still ringing in her ears, Libby let MaryAnne lead her around the racks, collecting dresses and tops and slacks while she went on about cut and fit and shape and patterns. Arms full of clothes, she led Libby to a bathroom just off the living room and hung the items she'd selected on the towel hooks before stepping out and closing the door behind her.

Libby liked clothes just fine, but she'd never really cared about fashion, mainly because it was hard to find her size in off the rack, seasonal collections. When her friends went on about which things they'd seen in magazines that she'd never fit into or wouldn't flatter her broad hips, she'd zone out, indulging them in shopping trips where she'd buy some shoes or a bag.

It was oddly touching that Evie and Cait would take that into account and arrange this for her, racks and racks of beautiful clothes she could actually wear. Evie was right. She didn't really know what to do with such kindness. In her world, kindness had strings.

Shimmying out of her jeans and t-shirt, she tossed them over the sink before pulling the lavender dress over her head, fingers smoothing over the impossibly soft fabric. The A-line shape was flattering, the tight bodice accentuating her small breasts and the skirt flaring out over the ample curve of her hips and ass. She twirled in it a bit, allowing herself a small smile at the way it swished around her knees.

"Let's see something!" Cait called from the other side of the door.

"What?" Libby replied, her eyes still studying her reflection.

"Come show us what you got!"

She cracked the door ever so slightly and poked her head around it. "Aren't we too old for fashion shows?"

"Absolutely not. Oh, is that the purple dress? I want to see." Evie crooked her finger and then pointed to a three-sided mirror set in the corner.

Libby's face heated, but she crossed the room and stepped in front of the mirrors. She wasn't sure if being able to study yourself from every angle was better or worse, but she still liked the dress. That was something.

"That fits beautifully. You should get that."

Libby ran her hands down the front of the dress, making eye contact with Cait in the mirror. "Where would I wear this?"

"Who cares?" Evie said. "Wear it around your bedroom for all we care. It's beautiful, you look great in it, you should have it. Next!"

"Next what?"

Cait smiled indulgently. "Go try on something else."

With one last glance at herself in the mirror, Libby stepped away and disappeared back into the bathroom, exchanging the dress for a black romper. She made a face at herself in the mirror.

"I don't know about this one," she called through the door.

"Let's see it."

Libby didn't even bother to cross to the mirrors. The looks on Evie's and Cait's faces confirmed what she already knew. This was going in the discard pile. She tried on a few blouses, a pair of shorts with an ugly floral print, and two more dresses.

The amount of money she left heaped in an untidy pile on the shelf in the corner made her fingers itch to fold it all neatly before she left, even though MaryAnne kept telling her not to worry about it.

She was collecting her purchases and trying not to look at price tags when Evie knocked on the door and pushed in without waiting for an answer, hand over her eyes.

"Are you decent?"

Libby chuckled. "Yes. I was just coming out."

"Okay, well, hold that thought." Evie dropped her hand. "Because Finn just called."

"Okay?"

"He and Declan won't be home for a few hours yet, and Cait's little one is at her parents' house for the weekend."

"I'm missing something."

"We're going to have tacos and margaritas by the pool."

"Oh. I don't—"

"Try these on," Evie insisted, shoving a handful of bathing suits in her direction and taking the clothes from her hands.

Evie stepped back with a grin and closed the door, leaving Libby alone in the bathroom again. She looked at the colorful fabric Evie handed her and immediately ruled out the two-piece, setting it off to the side.

Undressing again, she stepped into a one-piece and pulled it up over her hips, adjusting the straps at her shoulders. The neckline plunged low, too low for this suit to be meant for anything besides lounging by a pool, sipping a drink with a little umbrella in it, which was exactly what she'd be using it for tonight. It created a deep V that exposed the skin between her breasts. If her breasts were bigger, she imagined it would show off just the right amount of cleavage.

But the part of the suit she really liked was the circular cutouts at either hip that exposed her waist. The cuts gave her the illusion of an hourglass figure and accented the roundness of her hips. Her father would never approve, which made her want it even more.

"We're waiting!" Evie called from the living room.

"I'm not coming out in a bathing suit."

"We are literally going to see you in whatever you pick in less than ten minutes." Libby could practically hear the eye roll in Evie's voice. "Our job is to help you pick the right one."

Libby emerged from the bathroom to total silence. Evie's hand froze with her glass halfway to her lips, and Cait's eyes were wide.

"Yeah, this one is terrible," Libby said in a rush of breath, moving to cover herself.

"No," Cait breathed. "You look stunning."

"Really?"

Evie pointed wordlessly to the mirror, and Libby crossed to it, studying her reflection. The more she stared, the more she loved it. But...

"It's not too revealing?"

"It isn't any more revealing than a bikini, which is what I'll be changing into as soon as we wrap this up," Evie said.

"Me too," Cait added. "Do you feel as sexy as you look?"

Libby studied herself again and nodded.

"Then you should get it."

"Okay," she said to her reflection, smiling at the squeals of approval behind her.

When she turned to go back to strip out of her panties and collect her regular clothes, she caught Brogan standing in the doorway staring at her. The way his eyes raked down her body sent heat skidding along her skin. It was like all the air had been sucked out of the room. He left her breathless.

"Brogan, did you need something?" Cait asked sweetly from the couch, and he jerked ever so slightly before dragging his eyes from Libby to his sister-in-law.

"Finn wanted me to grab something from his office before I meet up with him and Declan at the restaurant for stuff."

"Stuff. So important," Cait agreed. "You know where his office is."

Brogan's gaze drifted over Libby one more time before he turned and headed toward the back of the house.

"Excuse me. What was that?" Evie wondered when Brogan was gone.

"Nothing."

"That look was not nothing."

"Yeah," Evie agreed. "It was definitely something."

"Trust me. He is not interested in something...anything to do with me. He was probably just surprised to see me out of the house," Libby countered.

She slipped back into the bathroom to fix her swimsuit and neatly folded her clothes to give herself extra time to regain her balance. Even from across the room, she'd seen the tension in his body and felt the lust in his gaze when his eyes traveled over her. But he'd made his desire—or lack thereof—abundantly clear.

She shouldn't want Brogan Callahan, but she wasn't entirely sure there was anything she could do about that.

Chapter Eighteen

A wildly successful op with zero shots fired and no sign of retaliation should have made Brogan happy. Instead he found himself working out his frustrations on the wall he was tearing down in one of his rental properties. After everything that had happened over the past few months, first with Evie and now Libby, he hadn't had much free time to get away and work on restoring the house he bought last winter.

He liked to do most of the manual labor himself, work up a good sweat, feel the strain in his muscles, knowing in the end he'd create something that would yield him a handsome profit for decades. Plus, taking a sledgehammer to a wall was very satisfying. Especially when you were pissed off for no reason.

He swung the hammer, enjoying the satisfying crack as it splintered through old drywall. It was mindless work—that's what he liked about it—and his thoughts drifted to Libby. To the tears he dried while she cried over her sister and that top-heavy mouth he wanted to ravish when she tried to kiss him a few nights ago but hadn't. Like an idiot.

She'd kept mostly to herself since, hiding away in her room except for meals where her cheeks would flush when she saw him or her big brown eyes would land on him and dart away too fast. The less he saw of her, the more he wanted to see her.

Then there she'd been, half naked in his brother's living room in that damned bathing suit, the golden hair she usually kept tied back spilling over her shoulders. He'd wanted to peel it off her so he could explore every square inch of smooth skin. It was fucking infuriating.

He didn't want to want her, but damn it all if he didn't find himself wanting her anyway. He itched to run his fingers through that thick curtain of hair and explore every inch of her body with his hands and lips and tongue. He wanted to tease her until she begged for him.

Throwing the hammer to the floor, he pulled off his shirt and used it to wipe the sweat and debris from his face and arms. Fucking Christ. He had to get ahold of himself. Not only was Libby Giordano off limits, but getting close to her was a very bad idea. She was a means to an end, hers and theirs. That was it.

When this was all over, she really would be free, and she'd probably disappear. Although he wasn't sure if that strengthened his argument not to touch her or weakened it. If she wasn't going to be around forever, what harm was there in a little fun between now and then? No. He shook his head and bent to retrieve his sledgehammer. Best to not even go there.

He set a brutal pace to remove the rest of the drywall, piling it up in a wheelbarrow he kept in the center of the room. Sweat poured down his torso in the late August heat, but the hard manual labor felt better than a punishing session at the gym, even if he would relish a cold shower later.

With the wall stripped to the studs and the power off, he cut the old electrical cords that disappeared into the ceiling.

The entire house would need rewiring to get up to code. He used a reciprocating saw to cut through the studs and then yanked each one free from the plates nailed into the floor and ceiling.

Using a pry bar, he released the bottom plate from the floor, tossing it on the pile of wood before climbing on a ladder to do the same with the top plate, tapping flat any protruding nails with his hammer to avoid the hazard of cutting himself on one.

Stepping back, he surveyed his work. He'd taken two large rooms and turned them into one massive space. The ten-foot ceilings made it seem cavernous, but he could picture a huge flat-screen TV mounted on the wall between the fireplaces with room for an oversized sectional and a couple of seating areas for reading or entertaining.

He drank from the water bottle he'd left on the floor, grimacing at the heat of it before dumping the rest on his head. He wanted a shower and a cold beer. But first he needed to get this debris out to the dumpster he was keeping in the side yard.

Tossing the empty water bottle into the wheelbarrow, he rolled it outside and down the makeshift ramp he'd set up after tearing out the rotted porch steps. Releasing the latch and swinging the door open with a metallic groan, he dumped the contents of the wheelbarrow inside.

Turning to go back for the discarded studs, he caught the scent of pears on the breeze from the tree that grew out of control in the backyard. He hadn't decided if he was going to rip it out, but he felt it might be a selling point for the right buyer if he could get it looking a little less wild. The smell reminded him of Libby's shampoo.

Sweet Christ. Was there nowhere he could go to get away from her? He stalked back inside for the studs, angrily launching them into the dumpster while grumbling to himself about peace of mind and how women were too much trouble.

By the time everything was cleared and he was locking the house up behind him, the day was yawning to a close. The setting sun painted the sky in vibrant reds and purples. He drove toward home, the older colonials giving way to new construction on smaller lots which gave way to the stately mansions of the wealthy towns that dotted the Main Line.

This part of Philadelphia was where old money mingled with new. Some families, like his own, had lived here for generations, passing their estates from one heir to the next, assuming they managed to escape the crashes. Then there was new money. Professional athletes and tech CEOs who liked to fly their choppers to NYC for meetings just because they could.

Here the lots weren't big; they were massive, with manicured lawns and landscaped gardens and trees that offered privacy and security. For the most part. Their secure perimeter had been breached when Evie's stalker, Peter, broke into the house and held Evie at gunpoint before Declan killed him.

In the time it took Evie to plan the wedding, they'd installed over a mile of fencing around both Glenmore and Finn's property for good measure and set up trail cameras and sensors to monitor activity. A breach like that would never happen again.

Pulling into the driveway, he hit the button for the gate and angled into the garage, closing the door behind him. Evie's Maserati was gone, and he assumed they were out for the night, probably at Reign being seen. With any luck, he could avoid Libby and that tempting mouth of hers altogether and veg out in front of the TV with a beer and whatever leftovers he could scrounge up from the fridge.

Letting himself in, he made his way back to the kitchen for that beer. The sounds of someone moving around didn't really register as off. It had to be either Marta or Rachel. But when he stepped into the open doorway, his eyes narrowed on Libby, swaying her hips to some song only she could hear. Damn her.

When she looked up to reach for something across the island, she spotted him, slapping a hand over her mouth to muffle the shriek. The knife she was holding clattered to the cutting board.

"What is it with you and sneaking up on people?"

"I wasn't sneaking." He stalked across the kitchen to the fridge, yanking it open and pulling a bottle of beer from the door. "What are you doing?" he asked, twisting off the top and tossing it into the trash.

"Well, ah…" She stepped away from the counter, her cheeks flushing. "Evie and Declan are out, and Evie said I could use the kitchen if I wanted to. I can go or…I can make you something? I was going to watch a movie."

She seemed to be settling in just fine. He watched her over the top of his beer as he took a sip. "What are you making?"

"Alfredo. Cliché for an Italian, I guess, but it's one of the few things I know how to make without messing it up. And you had everything. Plus, a little side salad with some cherry tomatoes that looked nice and ripe." She gestured to the tomatoes she'd been halving. "Oh, and garlic bread."

The oven timer beeped, and she jumped. When she bent to check the bread, he got a good view of the ample curve of her ass and swallowed more beer around the lump in his throat. She carefully rotated the bread, pushing it back into the oven before resetting the timer and turning to face him again.

"Anyway, the pasta doesn't take long, so I could make

enough for two. Or eat in my room if you want the house to yourself."

Before he could stop himself, he closed the distance between them in two strides, yanking her up onto her toes and crushing his mouth down against hers. He dragged his teeth across her upper lip, then soothed it with his tongue.

He expected her to push him away, but instead she leaned into him, all soft curves and eager hands, her fingertips skimming up his chest and gripping his shoulders. Her lips parted, and he slid his tongue against hers, delighting in the groan she rewarded him with and the way she pressed even closer.

With another nibble of her lip, he leaned back but kept his arm tight around her waist. When her eyes finally fluttered open, they were hazy with lust and surprise, her mouth wet and swollen from his kiss. That was a mistake. And one he wanted to repeat as soon as possible.

"Pasta and a movie sound great. I'm going to go grab a shower."

Thinking better of dragging her down to the kitchen floor and fucking her senseless, he turned on his heel and left the way he came. Irritated and horny. He would need a very cold shower to get through an entire movie without doing that again.

Chapter Nineteen

W hat the fuck was that? With Brogan gone, Libby rubbed at her lips, still tingling from his kiss. She should have shoved him away. She meant to, but then his teeth were dragging against her skin, his tongue moving against hers, and electricity coursed through her. Not only did she not pull away, she pressed closer, wanted more.

Angling back to the counter as the timer beeped a one-minute warning, she dumped the tomatoes on top of the salad she'd already prepared. When the timer went off, she checked the bread and, satisfied it was done, put it in the warmer.

Shaking out her hands to keep her fingers from trembling, she set the pasta on to boil, adding some of the water into a pan over low heat and whisking in butter until it was melted and smooth. Then she added finely grated Parmesan, whisking it into a smooth sauce before piling in the pasta and tossing it to coat.

Her grandmother taught her to make this pasta one summer. The last summer they'd ever spent together before she died. Libby hadn't often been allowed to spend time in the kitchen. Still, whenever she could sneak in there, she made this dish. It reminded her of her grandmother, the only person who'd ever loved her without conditions.

Brogan reappeared just as she was plating the pasta, sprinkling it with more cheese and a little freshly cracked pepper. His hair was damp, and he'd changed the dusty jeans for a pair of baggy sweats. The way his t-shirt stretched tight across his broad shoulders made her remember the way his chest felt under her hands, and her fingers flexed on the bowl she was holding.

"Smells good. Need any help?" he asked after a long beat of silence.

The offer to help managed to throw her more off-balance than the kiss. She didn't know a single man who would offer to help a woman in the kitchen.

"You can stir up that dressing and toss the salad with it. Once I cut the bread, we should be good to go." She bent to retrieve the pan from the warmer and slid the loaf onto a cutting board. "And we should probably set the table," she added, watching him.

"Why? I thought you wanted to watch a movie?"

She frowned, eyes narrowing. "Because the couch is white."

He cocked his head, using a fork instead of the salad tongs she'd set by the bowl to coat the salad in the dressing. "It's brown."

"The couch in the front room is white."

A slow grin spread across his face, and she found it both annoying and sexy. Jesus. This man should not be able to twist up her insides with a smile and a kiss.

"We're not going to watch a movie in there."

"It's the only room with a TV other than that tiny thing over there."

She pointed with the knife she was using to slice the garlic bread at a small TV mounted under the cabinet that Marta used more often than anyone else.

"That's because you haven't found the basement yet."

She arranged the bread on a plate and handed it to him to load with everything else onto a large tray. When he set off down the hallway, she followed, past the dining room lit only by the faint glow of the kitchen and the large family room where they liked to gather before dinner, stopping in front of a panel on the wall. Balancing the tray with one big hand, he reached out and pushed on the panel until it gave way with a click, sliding into the wall like a pocket door.

She gaped. She'd walked past that spot dozens of times and never would have known it was a door. Which was probably the point. As he descended the stairs, a series of lights flashed on at his movement, and when she reached the bottom, she couldn't stop staring. Just when she thought Glenmore House couldn't get any bigger, she discovered an entire hidden level underground.

Though not entirely underground. She could glimpse her reflection in a set of wide sliding glass doors. Brogan crossed to a seating area arranged with brown couches and a long coffee table, setting down the tray he carried. Picking up the remote off the table, he used it to turn on the TV.

"Pick something. I'm going to go grab another beer."

He left her there, standing in the middle of the room, looking down at the remote like it was foreign to her. She barely had time to take in the full bar nestled against the back wall, the pool table, or the pinball machines before she heard him jogging down the stairs with a bottle of beer in one hand and a glass of red wine in the other.

"I have no idea what kind of wine goes with pasta. Actually, I don't really know what kind of wine that is other than Declan serves it at the restaurant and Evie likes it."

She smiled. "Red is fine. I have no idea how to work this thing," she admitted, holding up the remote and following him to the couch, sinking into the soft leather with a sigh.

He took a seat beside her, plucking the remote from her hands and expertly flipping to the right streaming service. "Funny? Sexy? Scary?"

"I'll watch pretty much anything except foreign films. The subtitles give me a headache. Oh, that one looks good," she added when he paused on a horror flick about a haunted house and a demon-possessed kid.

"Yeah?"

"You sound surprised." She reached for one of the plates of pasta and twirled the strands around her fork.

"I didn't have you pegged for a demons and hauntings kind of woman." He pressed play, forking up a bite of pasta. "Oh my God," he groaned. "You made this? From scratch?"

She hid a grin. "I did. You didn't have any fettuccine, so I had to use spaghetti. I'm sure my poor grandmother is spinning in her grave."

"No offense to your grandma, but this is delicious. What else do you know how to make?"

"She showed me how to make a few things and taught me the basics, but this is the only one I have memorized."

"Why didn't you just look up a recipe and follow it?"

"Because I don't have a phone," she said around a mouthful of pasta.

His eyebrows shot up as if he realized that for the first time. "No, I guess you don't have one."

He looked like he wanted to say something more, but the credits finished and the movie started, so he lapsed into silence instead. The longer the movie played, the worse it got, and she nearly groaned out loud at a bad bit of dialogue and a plot hole so big you could drive a car through it.

"This is terrible," she murmured when the main character

suggested they try a virgin sacrifice to rid the house of the demon.

"Oh, thank God." Brogan shifted to face her. "I thought you were enjoying it."

"Absolutely not. We all know that no one in that room is a virgin."

Brogan chuckled. "Least of all the blonde."

"Who do you think gets possessed by the end?"

He pursed his lips, considering. "The dude with the sunglasses."

She cocked her head. "Really? Not the redhead?"

"No. He looks stupid enough to do something dumb like invite the demon inside him to prove it's not real."

Not twenty minutes later, Sunglasses was shouting for the demon to show itself, to come into his body and prove it was real. She swatted Brogan on the arm.

"You've seen this one before!"

"I swear I haven't. He's the only one who's been saying since the beginning that it's probably just their imaginations. So it makes sense he'd invite it in if he didn't think it was real."

She frowned. Well, that did make total sense. The movie had some well-timed scares, with things jumping out or sinister shadows passing in the background. But the demon face at the end made her scream, and she reached for Brogan's arm, clutching it as her heart beat wildly in her chest.

"I don't think you should get to pick the movies anymore."

She turned to face him at the exact moment he did the same, and she was suddenly acutely aware of how close they were. His arm pressed between her breasts, his hand on her thigh. His face was so close to hers that she could feel his breath warm against her lips.

123

Without thinking, she gripped his face in her hands, bringing her lips against his in a kiss that heated her blood and vibrated along her skin. He shifted, dragging her onto his lap, and she immediately straddled his hips with her knees.

She may have initiated the kiss, but he took control, angling his mouth against hers to take it deeper, sliding his tongue along her bottom lip before slipping inside. His hands moved up to cup her breasts through her shirt, squeezing roughly until she gasped against his lips.

She nipped his lip hard enough to make him hiss, and he squeezed harder. She didn't want soft and gentle, not with Brogan. She wanted to be greedy about it, to take as much as he would give her.

Breaking the kiss, she skimmed her teeth along his jaw to his earlobe, sucking it between her teeth. His groan reverberated through her, and she shivered. While she explored the muscled column of his throat, his hand slipped under her shirt and into the cup of her bra. Twisting her nipple between his fingers, he pulled her back for another kiss, hungrier, needier.

More. That's all she could think. She wanted more of him. She didn't want to think about what it might mean or what the consequences might be. She could think about that later. Right now she only wanted to get lost in him. In the way his hands felt on her body, the steel of his thighs, or the hard length of him that pressed against her core.

His lips skimmed her jaw and then his teeth. His free hand slid up her back to grip her ponytail, and he tugged it to pull her head back and expose the skin of her throat. She froze.

No, no, no. She didn't want to go back there. Back to the morning DiMarco had yanked her around by her hair, beating her until she lost consciousness, but she couldn't stop the images that flashed in her mind.

Her head snapping back when DiMarco grabbed her ponytail. The shock of being kicked in the stomach, the air whooshing from her lungs. The sharp, stabbing pain as he hit and kicked her until she slid into blissful nothingness. She was living the nightmare all over again, and she couldn't make it stop.

Her body went rigid. She could just make out the faint sensation of Brogan's lips on her throat, but she couldn't make her mouth move to ask him to stop, to let go. Her fingers gripped the front of his t-shirt so hard they ached, and she could hear her own ragged breath, the blood pounding in her ears.

It felt like she was moving underwater, trapped, sluggish, unable to make her body do what her brain was screaming at her. Scream, fight, run.

When his body stilled against hers, she thought for a second she might have passed out again, but he sat back, his hands releasing her hair and her nipple and falling to the couch beside him.

"Libby."

His voice was gentle, but it barely cut through the haze in her brain. Scream, fight, run.

"Libby, look at me. You're safe. You're okay. Come back to me."

He kept his voice soft, his tone even. He didn't rush her, didn't try to shake her out of it. He just whispered her name over and over like a prayer until she felt herself slowly slide back into her body. It was almost painful to feel the sensation coming back after the numbness, but gradually she felt his warmth against her.

She released his shirt, flexing her fingers to relieve the ache from gripping it so tightly. As the numbness receded, the mortification set in and heat rushed to her cheeks, the air in her lungs thickening.

"Breathe." His hands gently stroked the tops of her thighs, and the sensation kept her grounded. "In through your nose, out through your mouth. That's it. Again."

She did as he asked, her heartbeat slowing as her body relaxed. Her breathing returned to normal as tears pricked her eyes.

"You're safe, Libby," he said, wiping a tear from her cheek. "Can you look at me?"

She dragged her gaze up to meet his, realizing that she was still perched atop him, wondering how to get up without falling over or pissing him off.

"What do you need?"

The question threw her off guard. "What?"

"I'm guessing you just had a flashback and a panic attack. What do you need?"

Is that what that was? "I don't know." She shook her head. "I've never had them before."

She had the sudden urge to drop her head onto his shoulder and sleep for days. He swiped his thumb across another tear that wound its way down her cheek.

"I'm so tired."

Without a word, he shifted her to standing, waving her away when she leaned down to stack dishes onto the tray.

"Leave it. I'll get it later."

She didn't protest when he took her hand and led her up the stairs, didn't ask him to leave when he said he'd wait for her to get ready for bed, didn't mind when he sat on the edge of the bed once she crawled under the covers.

"I don't know what happened," she admitted, voice thick with tears. "One minute I was fine, and the next…"

"We don't have to talk about it right now. Get some rest." He leaned forward and brushed a soft kiss against her forehead.

"Brogan?" She waited until he paused at the door and turned to face her. "I'm sorry."

He frowned. "For what?"

"For ruining it. Tonight. The…everything."

His frown only deepened, and she shrank back against the pillows. He would never touch her again, and though it was probably for the best, she couldn't stop the wave of disappointment and embarrassment that washed over her.

"You ruined nothing, and you have nothing to be sorry for." He started to leave and then stopped, poking his head around the door again. "If you need me, for anything, my room is right down the hall. First one on the left when you round the corner."

Without waiting for her to reply, he closed the door. The Callahans constantly surprised her, but Brogan most of all. Leaving the small light on by her bed to fend off her own demons, she closed her eyes and slipped into a fitful sleep.

Chapter Twenty

Feeling Libby go rigid in his arms and the look on her face when he'd pulled away—like she was a prisoner in her own mind—flooded Brogan's mind with every memory he had of Samantha's final months. She had that same faraway look in her eyes. Quick, raspy breaths struggled in and out of her lungs, and she languidly slid out of the cage of the past and into the present.

He'd done what had always worked with Samantha—he talked to her calmly and slowly and didn't push her. It worked, although Libby didn't collapse on him in tears the way Samantha often had.

If he'd known Libby would react like that to his touch, he never would have allowed himself to cross that line. The last thing he wanted was to put her through more pain, more anguish.

That didn't mean he didn't still want her, though. Nothing could erase the taste of her lips or the way she felt on top of him, thighs tight to his side while she rocked against him. Every time her voice drifted from a room, he remembered how her breath hitched when he had her nipple squeezed between his fingers.

He wouldn't be torturing himself with any of that every goddamn minute if he'd gone straight upstairs and taken that cold shower. Instead he'd acted impulsively, and now she was seared into his brain, and no amount of frigid water could wash her out.

Which is why he was avoiding her under the pretense of being busy. Not that he wasn't busy. Reagan, a forensics tech at PPD, let them know of an opening for a clerical assistant at the municipal court that Declan wanted to get Mackenzie into. Mackenzie was spending her time shadowing Helen at Declan's offices while Brogan was busy building her a new squeaky clean record, complete with work history.

He'd been keeping an eye on the identities he created for the other girls. So far, none of them had been arrested for anything, which seemed like a positive sign. Then there was regular, everyday syndicate business to attend to. Cameras to monitor, arrest records to alter, evidence to make disappear.

But he filled in every spare minute trying to follow DiMarco's movements around the city and see if he could locate a house he often went to where he might be keeping Teresa and the other girl. But both DiMarco and Giordano had gone dark. It worried him.

With still no response from the Italians for the op they'd run at the warehouse, it was beginning to feel as if they were sitting around waiting for the other shoe to drop. But life didn't stop while they dealt with this little problem.

They still had legit businesses to run, underground deals to close, palms to grease, and money to move. And Declan was gearing up to close a big deal with a new foreign contact today.

Brogan checked the time on the monitor. In fact, he should be meeting with them any second. While Declan and Finn were closing the deal and Aidan was waiting for word to hand off the product, Brogan was monitoring eight different CCTV cameras and the transactions into the offshore account where the money would land to make sure their guy wasn't trying to stiff them. People weren't often stupid enough to stiff the Callahans, but with newbies, you could never tell.

When the black Lexus rolled up outside Declan's restaurant, Breá, Brogan shook all the Italians who perplexed him from his mind, including the one with big brown eyes and kissable lips, and focused on his work.

With a simple tap, he switched camera angles and watched the driver jog around to open the door for a man in his mid-to-late sixties. Glancing up at the screen where he had a copy of the man's passport, he pegged him for Declan's contact and shot off a quick text to his brother.

Go time. Ruzek and two BGs. All strapped.

He tapped more keys to bring up a split screen, the video feed from the private room inside the restaurant on one half and the idling Lexus on the other, while keeping an eye on other cameras that let him monitor if any other vehicles approached that looked out of place. As Ruzek took his seat, bodyguards flanking him, Brogan dialed up the volume on the listening device Finn had slipped under the candle in the center of the table.

"I'm glad you agreed to meet on such short notice," Ruzek said in a thick Austrian accent. "My man said that you have what I want."

Declan nodded. Leaning back in his chair, he looked relaxed, but Brogan knew better.

"I do. They'll be ready to transfer to your shipping container as soon as your payment goes through." Declan nodded at Finn, who opened the lid of a laptop that sat on the table between them. "In full."

Brogan swiveled to the screen that mirrored the laptop

Finn was holding and watched him key in the access code and bring up the system to transfer untraceable funds from one offshore bank account to another. Finn typed in the account number and then the amount for transfer. Five million dollars.

Brogan watched Ruzek type in his own secure account number, gaze falling to the screen that held the account to watch as the money winged its way from one part of the internet to another. The transfer completed with a satisfying ding, and Brogan smiled. It was always nice to get paid.

He checked that the transfer was finished and scanned the laptop quickly for malicious code or a tripwire in the account number Ruzek used. Finding none, he sent Declan another text.

It's done. He's good for it.

"It was a pleasure doing business with you." Declan rose and extended his hand. "My men will have your shipment loaded within the hour."

Ruzek's smile was warm. You'd never imagine this man just bought five million dollars' worth of illegal arms. "It's been a pleasure doing business with you. Tell me," he said, stopping at the door. "Do you know Tony Giordano?"

Declan's smile faltered briefly, but Ruzek didn't seem to notice. "I know everyone in my city. Why?"

"He approached me yesterday and offered me women and drugs for a bargain."

"Did he?" Declan's voice was tight.

"Mmm," Ruzek confirmed. "I told him I have no need to pay for women and no interest in drugs. And he told me to be careful doing business with the Callahans, to watch my back."

Ruzek waved a hand between them. "But there was something not right about him or his man. Something in the eyes. But then again, can you really trust an Italian?"

Declan offered a tight-lipped smile when Ruzek chuckled. "I think maybe watch your back. I would prefer a long and fruitful partnership with a man of your...discretion."

Ruzek pushed out of the restaurant, and Brogan watched him climb into his Lexus and drive away.

"What the fuck," Declan mumbled while Finn gathered their things from the table. "Well, we're talking about *that* when we get home," he added, glancing up at the camera in the corner as he made his way to the door.

Brogan waited until they cleared the restaurant and were in the car on their way home before shutting down his connection to all the security cameras and making his way downstairs to meet his brothers.

When Declan walked in, he was seething. "I guess we know what they've been up to since the warehouse op. How the fuck's he know about a brand new contact?"

"This was a foreign contact, so it wouldn't be impossible to find if you were willing to put in the work to dig it up," Brogan pointed out.

"That's what worries me. That they're taking the time to dig." Declan paced in front of the big stone fireplace. "I'm done playing games. It's time to up the ante."

"What did you have in mind?"

A slow grin spread over Declan's face. "I want to get the cops involved. But first, let's start with a planning meeting. The whole family together." He checked the time. "Three hours. Brogan, I want Libby there."

Without another word, Declan stalked off in the direction of his office, leaving Finn and Brogan alone in the living room.

"When he says he wants to involve the cops, does he mean—"

"Yeah," Finn interrupted. "Probably."

"Well, that's one way to declare war."

Chapter Twenty-One

They decided to take advantage of the nice weather, gathering on the lower patio while they waited for the last of the family to arrive. Brogan only half listened to Finn and Declan debate the merits of involving the Bratva in their crusade against the Italians. His eyes were drawn to where Libby sat on the far side of the patio.

She was tucked into a corner of the couch, her bare feet propped up on the edge of the low table. At some point, she'd gotten her hands on a bottle of nail polish and painted her toenails bright red. It was ridiculously appealing on her. He imagined what they might look like curled from pleasure at his touch, his fingers sl—

"Earth to Brogan," Finn shouted in his ear, making him jump.

"What?" Brogan looked up to find both of his brothers staring at him.

He noticed Finn follow his gaze and raise an eyebrow. Wisely, his brother said nothing.

"I asked," Declan began, "if you can get me more info on what the Bratva have been up to in recent months. See if they've had any unexplained infusions of cash." He swirled the last of the whiskey in his glass before throwing it back.

Brogan nodded. "See if they might be more in bed with the Italians than we thought."

"See?" Finn clapped Brogan on the shoulder. "He was listening, after all! Be careful, little brother," Finn added, lowering his voice when they were alone.

"Be careful with what?"

"Not everyone wants to be saved."

"Nobody knows that better than me. There's nothing going on between us, so your concern is misplaced. And your nagging is annoying."

Finn didn't look convinced, but Brogan pushed away from the table and moved as close to Libby as he dared, dropping into one of the chairs arranged opposite the long couch. The glass doors to the patio slid open, and Aidan stepped out into the fading light, followed by Sean. When Sean's son James appeared, everyone went silent.

James had largely operated in the background of the family business, if he operated at all since his wife was murdered a few months earlier. Brogan hadn't seen him in person since the funeral.

Shoving his hands into his pockets, James met each gaze in turn before settling on Declan's.

"Dad said there was a family meeting."

"And so there is." Declan nodded, and the tension eased. "Grab some pizza and a beer, and we'll get started."

"Well, that was weird."

Brogan looked over at Libby, alone in the corner of the couch. She hadn't said it to anyone in particular, but he felt compelled to answer her. Taking a deep pull of his beer, he shifted off the chair to sit next to her.

"You've met Sean, my father's half brother. That's his son, James."

"Okay." She drew out the word, brows knitted together.

"A few months ago, the morning after their wedding, James's wife Maura was kidnapped and killed."

"Jesus."

"By Evie's twin sister."

Libby's mouth fell open as she looked from James to Evie and back again. "That's horrible. And he blames her?"

Brogan shrugged. "Hard to say. He hasn't been around much since the funeral. I know that Evie blames herself enough for the both of them, even though it wasn't her fault. Nessa might have hidden it well, but she was fucking deranged."

"Was?"

"Evie shot her."

"It's somehow comforting," she said after a moment.

He paused with his beer halfway to his mouth. "What is?"

"Knowing the Callahans are just as fucked up as the rest of us. Thank you," she added over his snort of laughter. "For telling me. I was beginning to think I had become invisible to you."

Brogan frowned. It was ironic she thought that considering he couldn't get her out of his mind. She'd even started infiltrating his dreams. Dreams that forced him awake, cock stiff and aching. She was anything but invisible, but before he could respond, Declan called the meeting to order.

"I think we may be underestimating the Italians."

Brogan felt Libby shift in her seat.

"What makes you think that?" Sean wondered.

"They got to a brand new contact and could have fucked up a five million dollar deal. The interference is problematic enough and something they would've had to answer for anyway. I'm more concerned about the fact that we've only known this guy for two weeks. How did they find out about him so fast?"

When Aidan glanced at Libby, she stiffened, chin ticking up.

"Well, you do have one of them living right under our roof."

"This is my roof."

"And your roof has a traitor under it."

"A traitor who hasn't left this house in weeks. A traitor," she added when Aidan opened his mouth to speak, "who doesn't have a phone or a computer."

Libby leaned forward to set her glass down on the table with a thud. "You may not agree with what I did—what I am doing—to my own. I genuinely hope you never have to make the choices I've had to make for the reasons I've had to make them."

She cast a sideways glance at Brogan, continuing when no one stopped her. "Not all families are worth dying for. Mine sure as hell isn't. If you're looking for a mole, look somewhere else because I've made my choice. And it's one that almost got me killed."

Brogan pinned Aidan with a hard stare. "Anything else you'd like to add?"

"So if it's not a mole," Aidan replied, jaw clenched, "then how did they know?"

"I'm going to look into the mole angle," Brogan said.

"I have to hope that none of our men are that stupid," Sean countered. "These are all families that have been loyal for decades."

"I agree, but it doesn't hurt to officially rule it out. The Italians could have found the name by asking the right people. We had a mutual with this contact. Maybe someone else ran their mouth. I don't know. I'll look, but…"

"But?" Finn prompted.

"Giordano and DiMarco have been hard to pin down lately. They've changed their patterns, gotten erratic. Almost like they know we're watching and are trying to outsmart us."

"Trying to?" Declan wondered. "Or succeeding?"

"I can pick them up, but often there are big chunks of time missing because they swap cars or some shit."

"Which would make a tracking device useless."

Brogan nodded at Aidan. "Right. I'm writing a better facial recognition program, but it'll take time and still might not be perfect."

"I could tail him."

All eyes turned to James, who suddenly looked uncomfortable being the center of attention.

"It might come down to that. But let Brogan try his facial rec first." Declan leaned forward to rest his elbows on his thighs. "In the meantime, I want to hit back a little harder."

Sean's eyebrows winged up. "What did you have in mind?"

"Just a little drug bust from our loyal men on the force."

The plan, to Brogan's mind, was brilliant. Get the man they had working as a detective in the organized crime unit to run a bust on some of Giordano's top sellers. They'd either roll on their boss and do the work for them or take their lumps and do some time.

Either way, Giordano would lose his top moneymakers, and the message would be clear: fuck with our business and we'll fuck with yours. Libby could give them the names of their best dealers because they probably ranked among his favorites. The rest would be cake.

"And we're not worried that involving the cops will somehow piss them off more? Tony Giordano isn't exactly known for his levelheadedness," Aidan reminded them.

Libby chewed her bottom lip. "On his own, my father would tailspin and be too hyper-focused on damage control to think about much else."

137

"I sense a but," Evie said.

"But DiMarco is a wild card. He's got his fingers in a little bit of everything, and it wouldn't surprise me if he used this as an opportunity to usurp a little more power."

"So you're saying DiMarco is the real threat, and this plan may backfire."

Libby shook her head at Sean. "No. I think it's a good plan. Hitting his wallet is the best way to throw my father off his feet. He'll be scrambling, which will be good for us…you," she corrected quickly.

"What I'm saying is, be prepared for DiMarco to make a move. He wants to be head of Philly's Mafia. I think right now my father is oblivious to that simple truth."

"But he won't be oblivious forever," Brogan finished.

Libby rewarded him with a small smile. "Exactly. And when that happens, they'll be fighting among themselves."

"The faster we can make that happen, the better. And we'll start here. I'll reach out to Holt and set it up. James," Declan added when everyone began to rise, "I want to see you in my office before you go."

"No one actually thinks of you as a traitor, you know." Brogan watched Libby stack plates and glasses as the outdoor light clicked on in the fading light.

"We both know that isn't true," she replied, hefting the plates with a grunt.

He took the heavy stack from her hands, following her into the basement and up the stairs to the kitchen. He set them next to the sink while she opened the dishwasher.

"My presence here is tolerated as a means to an end. A mutually beneficial relationship."

"It's more," he insisted. Something about her tone didn't sit well with him. "You seem to get along great with Evie and Cait."

"Yes," she admitted over the clatter of silverware. "They're very nice. A glitch in the matrix. Declan tolerates me. Finn doesn't really trust me, not all the way. I can tell by the way he glances at me when I'm talking to Cait."

She pulled out the top rack and began loading glasses. "Aidan obviously hates me, and Sean is probably somewhere between Aidan and Finn. I'm sure James wouldn't be far behind, given half a chance. And then there's you."

"Me?"

Silence hung between them while she added soap to the dishwasher and set it to run. When she finally turned to face him, arms crossed over her chest, her eyes were sad.

"You've made it very clear how you feel about me. There's no need to hash it out again. Goodnight, Brogan."

When she moved to leave, he reached for her hand, stopping her short. She looked down at their joined hands and then up at him with those sad eyes. He should let her leave and go up to bed, but he couldn't squash the overwhelming desire to make that sadness disappear.

"Libby, I…"

At the sound of conversation from the hallway, his head jerked up and he dropped her hand, immediately taking a step back. He instantly realized what he'd done as the voices faded.

The look in her eyes when he met her gaze again was a punch to the gut, sharp and painful. He hadn't stripped away the sadness; he'd only added hurt. This time when she walked away, he didn't stop her.

Chapter Twenty-Two

What was happening at home right now? Libby rambled through the big house so often empty of people, torturing herself with that question. It seemed like everyone had somewhere to go or something important to do. Everyone but her.

Her job was to wait to be summoned to offer up information that would help men who reluctantly trusted her kill men who didn't trust her at all. She knew Declan had been in touch with his man on the force when he asked for both names and popular dealing locations, neither of which were difficult to provide. If her father knew just how much information his men shared with the women they were fucking, he'd be livid.

Despite that, she felt utterly useless. She served no other purpose in this house. She had no computer to try and find her sister, though even if she did have one, she had no idea what she would even do to search for her. She wasn't supposed to leave the house, but even if she could, she didn't have a car to drive anywhere.

She spent most of her days wandering from room to room,

getting out of the way of the staff as they cleaned. Like now. Abandoning the library when someone came in to dust, Libby retreated to her bedroom, stopping short when she noticed something in the middle of her bed.

Crossing the room, she paused to look down at it, eyes going wide with surprise. Someone, Brogan no doubt, had left her a phone and a laptop. And they looked brand new.

She reached for the phone and tapped the screen to bring it to life. He'd already run it through setup, so it was ready to use. Checking the laptop next, she flipped up the lid and smiled when it blinked on.

After her exchange with Aidan the other night, this gift felt like a simple message: I trust you. That thought wound its way through her and smoothed out the last of the hurt left over from the way he jumped back from her the other night at the thought of being seen together.

Like it or not, they were both stuck in this situation together. The least they could do was be civil to each other instead of all this tiptoeing around. She was attracted to him, something that seemed like it wasn't going away any time soon, and he clearly felt he made an error in judgment ever putting his hands on her.

That stung, but it was hardly anything she wasn't used to. Any boyfriends she had in the past had never been interested for very long. In any case, she and Brogan would have to make nice, and Libby could start by thanking him for the phone and the laptop.

Storing the computer in the nightstand drawer, Libby tucked the phone into her pocket and went in search of Brogan. He wasn't in his lair, or if he was, he didn't answer the door when she knocked. She didn't find him in the family room or on the deck, where he often liked to work when it wasn't too hot.

Close to giving up, she heard a noise in the living room

and changed course toward the sound. He was just reaching for his keys when he spotted her and paused, a single eyebrow raised in a way she found far sexier than she wanted.

"I'm glad I caught you before you left." She kept distance between them when she stopped, reaching in her pocket for the phone and holding it up. "I wanted to say thank you."

"How do you know that was me?"

"Who else would it be?"

His expression softened ever so slightly, and he grabbed his keys, twirling them around his finger while he studied her.

"I meant what I said the other night."

"Brogan, we don't have to—"

"I don't think of you as a traitor," he said. "I trust you."

Those three simple words warmed her down to her toes. "Thank you. Well, have fun doing"—she waved a hand at his unusual outfit choice of gray sweats and a shirt—"whatever."

"I've got to get out of this house and give my brain a break. Want to come?"

She stopped so quickly mid-turn she nearly fell over, reaching out to steady herself on the edge of a chair. "I thought I wasn't supposed to leave the house?"

His lips curved into a grin. "I'll protect you."

She swallowed hard. He was really going to have to stop saying things like that if this whole platonic thing was going to work out.

"Declan won't mind?"

"If he does, I'll handle him."

Libby chewed her bottom lip. Other than the trip to Cait's, she hadn't been outside these walls in ages. A change in scenery would be a welcome sight, even if all they did was drive around for a bit.

"Okay, I'm in."

The arrival of September brought cooler temperatures and shorter days, signs that summer was loosening its grip on the city. She rolled her window down and let her hair loose from its ponytail so it whipped around her face while Brogan took corners at speeds that made her heart race.

The car smelled like him, like soap and spice, and she breathed it deep into her lungs. When he turned the radio on, she smiled at the bass that pumped through the speakers under the shrill shred of a guitar. She'd expect nothing less from him.

Brogan's fingers tapped the steering wheel as he drove away from the Main Line and Center City toward an area filled with nothing but suburban homes and the occasional shopping mall. He slowed, turning down the music and pulling into a neighborhood of single-family homes set on well-manicured lawns the size of postage stamps.

He turned into an empty driveway in front of a two-story with cheery yellow siding and cut the engine.

"This is a house."

"Wow, nothing gets by you."

She rolled her eyes in his direction. "When you said you wanted to get out of the house, I didn't think you'd just drive to a different one. Who's house even is this?"

"It's mine."

She turned to him, eyebrows raised. "If you own this, why do you live at Glenmore?"

"Because Glenmore is my home. I like to buy fixer-uppers, renovate them, and then rent them out."

She followed him when he climbed out of the car, trailing him up the front walk and onto the porch.

"This one was badly damaged in a house fire. The owners couldn't afford to renovate, so they took the insurance money and ran. I bought it from the bank at a steal, fixed it up."

He unlocked the door and paused, motioning for her to go

ahead of him. It was furnished, and she wondered who his current tenants were. An old dresser turned into a sideboard sat in the entryway with a mirror hung over it and to her left was a cozy living room with a sofa and chairs arranged around a TV mounted on the wall.

She could hear him following behind her as she wandered down the hall to the eat-in kitchen, which was bright and airy from a wall of windows that looked out on a well-kept back-yard. Pots and pans hung from a rack over the center island and gleamed in the mid-afternoon light.

"So who lives here now?"

"No one at the moment. I've got to get it turned over for new tenants."

Libby glanced at the table and chairs in the corner of the kitchen, brows knitting together. "Did they leave all their furniture?"

He chuckled. "No, I keep a couple of them furnished for shorter-term rentals. People moving to the city for a new job or something like that."

"I really never know what you're going to say next most days. So what do you need to do to get it turned over?"

"My property manager said everything looked good except for some scuffs on the wall in one of the spare bedrooms that the cleaning service couldn't get off. So we're going to paint that."

"Oh, that doesn't sound too ba— Wait. We?"

He barely bit back a grin. "Yeah, you wanted to come along."

"You invited me! Can't you hire a service for that?"

"I could, but I like to do it myself. Nice to get lost in the sweaty manual labor of it sometimes."

Well, that was an image she didn't need in her head. Brogan stripped to the waist and covered in sweat and paint.

"I'm going to go grab the paint from the basement, and

then we can get started. It's a small room, so it shouldn't take too long."

He disappeared through a door at the far end of the kitchen and re-emerged with a gallon of paint, a tray, some brushes, a roller, and a neatly folded bundle of plastic sheeting. Libby followed him wordlessly up the stairs and down the hall to a bedroom that was painted a soft blue.

She helped Brogan push the furniture into the center of the room and cover the floor with plastic. When he left to get a ladder, she pulled her phone out of her pocket and checked to see if he'd loaded any music onto it. Smiling, she tapped on the first playlist she found, cutting down the volume so it didn't overwhelm.

"Good song," he said, setting up the ladder at the far end of the wall. "I'll cut in along the ceiling and baseboards, and you can paint the wall with that roller."

He expertly poured paint into the tray without a single wayward drip and handed her the roller. She took it, looking at the paint tray while she chewed her bottom lip.

"Is now the right time to admit I've never painted a wall in my entire life?"

He laughed, and heat flooded her cheeks. "Here, let me show you."

He picked up the roller and dipped it into the paint, running it along the flat textured side of the tray to remove the excess before rolling it along the wall in a W shape, then filling it in with up and down motions.

"Draw a W to distribute the paint more evenly, then you can go up and down to spread it out and get good coverage."

He stepped back, handing her the roller. Gripping the pole, Libby dipped the roller in the paint, rolling off the excess, and drew a misshapen W over the wall before smoothing the lines with shaky up and down motions. She stepped back to survey her work. Not perfect by any means, but it would get the job done.

"Not bad," Brogan said while she dipped the brush in again and moved down the wall. "But spread your hands out a bit more on the pole, and you'll get smoother strokes. Like this."

Before she could anticipate him, he stepped up behind her, chest pressed against her back, arms wrapping around her to cover her hands with his and slide them apart on the pole of the paint roller. She turned to look up at him and saw his eyes dip down to her mouth.

"Maybe next you'll have to show me how to shoot pool."

His Adam's apple bobbed and he stepped away, crossing to the ladder and setting the paint can on the ledge before climbing up with the brush. She rolled the paint onto the wall, wondering how he was going to do that without tape. Weren't you supposed to use tape to keep from getting it all over the ceiling and floor?

Libby paused to watch him dip the brush into the bucket, angling it, so he cut a clean, smooth line across the wall where it met the ceiling. He smoothed the uneven underside of the line with his brush and dipped again, dragging a second perfect line next to the first. Jesus Christ, why was that so sexy?

She really needed to get a grip. He wasn't interested. No matter how often she thought about his lips, his hands, his teeth on her skin, he'd made that very clear. Besides, painting was not a sexy activity, and it pissed her off that he looked so damn good doing it.

He dipped the brush a third time and leaned down the wall, cutting another flawless line in a single stroke. Enough was fucking enough.

"Stop that," she snapped, resuming her work of drawing W's across the wall with her paint roller and filling them in.

He paused, looking at her over his shoulder. He didn't even have a speck of paint on him, and she just felt one land on her cheek. The bastard.

"Stop what?"

"Stop painting so...so..."

He raised a brow. "So...?"

Christ, the man was oblivious. "So sexy! If you're not going to touch me or kiss me or even spare me a glance for more than five seconds, I need you to stop being so damn sexy all the time!"

Embarrassment swamped her, her cheeks burning hot as he carefully set the brush down and climbed down from the ladder. He crossed the room, taking the paint roller from her hands, when she stumbled back and leaning it against the corner. The look he pinned her with had her heart beating a wild rhythm in her chest.

"I didn't mean...I was just—"

"Do you want me to touch you?"

His voice was low, commanding, and it ignited something more than lust inside her. Need. Desperate need. She nodded.

"Say it," he insisted, inching closer.

"I want you to touch me," she whispered.

Without hesitation, he reached for her, pulling her up onto her toes and crushing his mouth against her own. Except this time, she was prepared for the hard plane of his chest against hers, the slide of his tongue as he teased her lips open, the grip of his hand on the back of her neck.

She wasn't prepared for the way he lifted her effortlessly off the ground, hands digging into her ass to hold her firmly against his cock while his lips trailed down the column of her throat. She wrapped her legs around his waist, and he groaned against her skin.

His hand slid up into her hair, and then he froze. When he set her back on the floor, she squeezed her eyes shut, unwilling to see the regret on his face when he reminded them both he didn't want this, didn't want her. That this was all a mistake. God, she was such an idiot.

She felt his fingertips along her jaw, and she clenched it. Could you actually die from embarrassment? She was about to find out.

"Libby," he said, his thumb stroking her cheek. "Look at me."

She tried to put some distance between them, but he kept his arm tight around her waist, forcing her to drag her eyes up to meet his. He leaned down to capture her lips again, softer, sweeter, his tongue tracing along her top lip while his fingertips gently skimmed her jaw.

"I want you," he said, and her heart flip-flopped in her chest. "But I don't want to hurt you. I don't want..." His fingers played in the hair that hung loose around her face, and suddenly she understood.

It wasn't that he didn't want to touch her; he didn't want to send her into another panic attack. Her heart did one long, lazy somersault into her stomach. The problem was, she had no idea what might trigger another episode. But she knew if it happened, she'd be safe with him. She believed that to her core.

"I want you, Brogan. I trust you."

He reached for the hem of her shirt, lifting it up over her head and tossing it behind them. His fingertips slid up over the curve of her stomach to her breasts, circling her nipples through the thin fabric, her breath catching in the back of her throat.

She reached around and undid the clasp, sliding it down her arms and onto the floor, and he immediately filled his hands with her breasts. She'd always felt self-conscious about how small they were, but the look on his face while he squeezed her nipples, dragging his thumbnail over them, washed that away.

Brogan bent to take one into his mouth while his hands moved down her stomach to the button of her jeans, flipping it open and tugging down the zipper. He worked them down her hips just enough to get his hand inside, dragging his finger over her clit until she dropped her head back with a groan.

He walked her backward until the backs of her thighs hit the edge of the bed, and he dropped to his knees. The sight of him there made her mouth water, and she ran her hands through his hair. His eyes never left hers as he hooked his fingers into the waistband of her jeans and tugged them down with her panties, helping her kick off her shoes and step out of them.

Easing her back onto the bed, Brogan hooked his arm under her thigh, pulling it onto his shoulder so he could drag his tongue up her slit, flicking it against her clit. She tunneled her fingers in his hair when he wrapped his lips around her clit and sucked, her hips jerking against his face.

He ran his fingers up and down her slit while teasing her with his tongue and teeth before slipping one inside her. She arched against the bed, gripping his t-shirt in her fist while he slid his finger in and out, matching the rhythm of his thrusts to the slow, steady circling and suckling of his tongue.

"Brogan," Libby begged, her body vibrating under his touch, fingernails raking along the skin of his neck.

He slipped in a second finger, slowly picking up the pace, meeting her hips thrust for thrust while using his thumb to rub and pinch her clit. His teeth scraped across her inner thigh, and when she came undone in his hands, she sobbed his name.

"Good girl," he murmured, pressing a kiss against her inner thigh.

Pleasure, warm and unexpected, coursed through her as the words tumbled from his lips. She wanted to hear him say it again.

"Wh—what did you say?" she stammered, still breathless.

He rose over her, bracing himself on his hands and covering her body with his. She could feel the hard length of his cock through his sweatpants where it pressed against her stomach, and she ached to feel him inside her.

The corners of his mouth tilted up into a lopsided grin, his eyes never leaving hers when he repeated, "Good girl."

She wrapped her arms around his neck and brought his lips down to meet hers, dragging her teeth over his lower lip. She didn't want soft and gentle; she wanted him to make her feel alive. She wanted more of this electric feeling that hummed in her blood.

"I want you inside me. Now," she demanded, skimming her teeth along his jaw while her hands made quick work of his T-shirt, tugging it roughly over his head.

"Wait," he groaned in her ear.

"Brogan." She dragged her nails across his shoulders, arching up against him. "I don't want to wait."

He pushed to his feet, and she practically whimpered at the sight of him. Colorful tattoos swirled from his wrists to his shoulders and across his pecs. His abs were well-defined, leading to a deep V that disappeared into the waistband of his sweats, and the outline of his cock, hard and straining against the fabric, had her dragging her tongue over her bottom lip.

"Brogan, you're killing me," she said, sliding her hands over her stomach and cupping her breasts, squeezing them roughly.

"Fuck," he breathed. "You're perfect. Just…wait here."

She collapsed back on the bed when he darted into the hallway, pushing up onto her elbows when she heard him slamming cabinet drawers and muttering to himself. Moments after she heard a strangled groan, he reappeared in the doorway, toeing off his shoes on his way back to the bed.

It wasn't until he set them on the table that she realized he'd gone searching for condoms. She laughed, sitting up while he wrestled one out of the box.

"What were you going to do if you couldn't find any?"

He grinned, hooking his thumbs in the waistband of his sweats, drawing her eyes to the outline of his cock. "I'm sure we could have found other ways to entertain ourselves."

She bit the inside of her cheek, darting a glance at his face. "We're going to try those other ways later," she said, satisfied when his eyes went cloudy with lust.

He shoved his sweats to the floor, his thick, hard cock bobbing in front of her. She reached for the condom, swirling her tongue around his tip and eliciting a groan from low in his throat before sliding it down his length and stroking him back up.

He eased her back onto the bed, sliding over her, and lifted one of her legs to wrap around his waist. He teased his cock across her slit, grinning when she arched up against him before slowly guiding himself inside her.

He slid his cock in deep, grinding against her before sliding out again until she was breathless from his teasing. She ground against him with each torturously slow thrust. She wanted him hard and fast. She needed him to push her over the edge into madness.

"Brogan," she groaned when he continued his slow, steady pace.

He leaned down to capture her lips, tugging the bottom one between his teeth. "Tell me what you want."

"I want you to fuck me."

"I am fucking you." He thrust inside her as if to prove his point. "Tell me what you want," he said again.

Christ, she couldn't just say it. Why didn't he know? Couldn't he tell how much she wanted him, wanted more?

He dipped his head and captured her nipple between his teeth, biting down until she arched under him and cried out. Yes, more of that. More of him rough against her, using her body until they were both sated and sweaty.

"That's what you want, isn't it?" he murmured, tongue swirling around her throbbing nipple to soothe it. "Say it."

He caught her other nipple, holding it between his teeth and tugging it away from her body until she gasped.

"I want you," she panted. "I want your cock, your teeth, your hands. Hard, rough, fast. Please, Brogan," she all but sobbed.

He leaned up on his hands, looking down at her, eyes filled with desire as he gripped her hip, rearing back and plunging himself inside her in one hard thrust. Her breath caught in the back of her throat, and he pulled back and thrust again.

His fingernails dug into her skin, and she relished in the sting, matching his frenzied pace thrust for thrust. Hard, rough, fast. She'd begged for it, and he gave it to her without hesitation. She'd never wanted anyone like this before, with a burning need that threatened to consume her.

She scored her nails down his chest, making him hiss when she caught his nipple with her thumbnail, hips pistoning faster as pleasure shot through her. Sensing her release, he slowed his pace but drove inside her harder, deeper.

He leaned down to capture her nipple between his teeth, licking, sucking, biting as he thrust relentlessly, and when he took them both over the edge, she saw stars.

"Oh my God," she groaned.

"What?" he murmured against her cheek before sitting up quickly. "Shit, did I hurt you?"

152

"Yeah." She tightened her arms around his neck when he tried to roll off. "In all the good ways."

He grinned and pressed a kiss to her lips, sinking into it as his hands wandered up and down her sides, fingertips brushing against the sides of her breasts.

"I would have told you that you were annoyingly sexy a long time ago if I'd known that's what you would do."

He laughed, pressing a kiss to her shoulder before rolling onto his back and tucking her up against his side. "I don't remember you saying anything about being annoying."

"Didn't I?"

"Mmm," he murmured, tracing circles over her back with his fingertips.

"At least now I know you actually can stand to touch me."

His fingers stilled, and she kicked herself for screwing it up. Again. Why couldn't she just keep her damn mouth shut? He bolted upright, pulling her with him and steadying her with his hands on her arms. Great, this time he was going to reject her when they were both naked.

"You thought I couldn't stand the thought of touching you?"

She smoothed a hand over her hair, suddenly irritated with his surprise. "Well, there was the thing in the basement where I...I freaked out. You ignored me for days after that. And then the thing in the kitchen the other night. You jumped back like you were on fire. What else was I supposed to think?"

He skimmed his fingers across her cheek, cupping the back of her neck while his eyes traveled down her body. She shivered under his direct gaze.

"I haven't stopped thinking about all the ways I want to touch you. Every waking moment—and even in my dreams —I think about touching you. I think about every single thing I want to do to you and with you."

His eyes dragged back up to her face, and the want in them made her tingle. "Show me."

He pulled her forward, arching her back as his hand skimmed up her side and cupped her breast, fingers pinching her nipple hard enough to make her jerk. That delicious shot of pain arrowed straight to her core, and she squirmed in his grip.

"I intend to," he promised, leaning down to whisper into her ear. "I've got so much I want to show you."

Chapter Twenty-Three

I t was barely dawn when Brogan woke, gray light slowly warming as the sun climbed into the sky. He felt Libby's absence at his side and reached for her, frowning when he found the space next to him empty. They'd come up for air at some point, hastily capped the probably ruined paint, and driven home where he'd promptly gotten her naked and begging again. And again and again.

Sometime in the early morning, sated and exhausted, they succumbed to sleep in a tangle of limbs. It felt good to fall asleep next to someone again. He'd existed on meaningless one-night stands for so long that he barely remembered what it felt like. He didn't expect to wake up alone, though.

Pushing out of bed, he tugged on the sweatpants he'd discarded in a heap on the floor and realized Libby's clothes were also missing. Poking his head into the hallway and finding it empty, he padded down to Libby's room and carefully eased the door open.

She slept on her side, facing the door, covers pulled up to her chin and gripped tight in her fist. The bedside lamp was on, and he wondered if she might have had a nightmare or something. Why didn't she wake him?

When he heard a noise from the hallway, he stepped all the way into the room and eased the door closed. Now what? He didn't want to scare her by waking her out of a dead sleep, and she'd obviously left his room for a reason, but damn it all, he wanted to be in bed with her again, if only to feel all those soft curves pressed against him.

He should go, though. Right? If she wanted to still be in bed with him, she would be and not here, in her own room, curled up in the fetal position with the light on. Busy debating with himself, he didn't see her eyes flutter open or the way they widened in surprise.

"Brogan?"

"Hey," he whispered. Jesus. Why was he whispering? She was clearly awake. He cleared his throat. "Hey. Everything okay?"

She pushed up onto her elbow, and the sheet fell to her waist. If she'd put her clothes on to leave his room, she'd taken them off again before getting into bed, and the sight of her made his mouth water.

"Yeah. I had a nightmare and didn't want to wake you, so I came back to my room. What are you doing here?"

He shrugged. "I woke up and you weren't there."

Her face softened, and she scooted toward the center of the bed to make room for him. He stripped down to his skin and crawled in next to her, warming when she laid her head on his chest and draped her arm over his stomach. He was in real trouble.

"What was your nightmare about?"

"They alternate."

"Between what?"

"Between being beaten and left for dead and whatever the hell they might be doing to my sister."

"I'm going to save her. I promise."

He regretted the words as soon as they left his mouth. He couldn't guarantee anything, and he certainly had no business making promises with his track record. If they couldn't crack through the walls the Italians had put up to carefully guard their secrets, they might never find her sister. If her sister was even still alive to be found.

He said none of that, though. What good would it do? If hope is what she needed to get her through this so she could be free, then hope is what he would give her. He'd keep digging, keep looking, keep trying whatever he could think of to pin down DiMarco and Giordano.

The bust from the cops would help. That should happen any day now, but the Philly police moved slowly, and cutting through the red tape was a nightmare exercise in patience. He wanted it done so he could sit back and enjoy the fallout, then prepare for what was next.

"What are you thinking?" she asked, her fingertip tracing the bottom edge of one of his tattoos.

"I'm wondering when PPD is finally going to get their head out of their ass and act on this drug bust."

"The wheels of justice and all that," she murmured. He snorted.

"You know when you have a nightmare, you can wake me. Right?"

Her fingers stilled on his chest, and she was quiet for a long moment. "I didn't know that," she said at last. "But I do now."

She sat up, hands braced on either side of his chest, and leaned down to brush her lips against his. When she sat back, her hair framed her face, and he reached out to tuck the strands behind her ear.

Her gaze traveled down over his chest and lingered where

the sheet rode low on his waist before snapping back to his face. A grin, slow and wicked, spread across her lips.

"What other names should I call you to earn a repeat of last night?"

He sat up quickly, yanking her onto his lap and groaning when she straddled him, the sheet the only thing separating his painfully hard cock from her core.

"I don't think name calling will be necessary ever again."

She slid her hands up his chest and over his shoulders, wrapping her hand around his throat and dragging her thumb over his lower lip. "Good."

She brought her lips down against his, and he hissed when her teeth scraped against his lower lip. He gripped her hips to rock her against him, praying there were condoms somewhere in this damn room.

Two swift knocks on the door had her jerking back, teeth nipping into his lip. The taste of blood was sharp on Brogan's tongue.

"Morning, you two!" Evie called through the door, and Libby's eyes shot to his face.

"How does she know you're in here?" she whispered.

"I've already been by Brogan's room, and it's empty. I'm an intelligent woman. Come downstairs. We have bacon and news. You two must be famished," Evie added, and Brogan could clearly hear the teasing grin in her voice.

"We'll be right down. We're not finished here by a long shot," he whispered to Libby, who chuckled softly.

"I'm sorry about your lip," she said, swiping at a dot of blood with her fingertip.

"I could think of worse reasons to bleed."

He reluctantly eased her off his lap and took several deep breaths before stepping into his sweats again. Crossing to the door, he paused with his hand on the knob.

"Remind me I need to keep some condoms in here. Lots of condoms."

Her silky laugh followed him down the hallway to his room, where he quickly changed into a fresh pair of jeans and tugged a shirt on over his head. Running a hand over his stubble, he decided he'd bother with it later in the shower. Maybe he could convince Libby to join him in that shower.

Until then, he'd go see what news his brother had and figure out how to deal with his family knowing, in no uncertain terms, that he and Libby were now sleeping together. They were bound to have plenty of unsolicited opinions. Especially considering he had just told them a few days ago that nothing was going on between them.

Whatever their reaction, he didn't much care. He wasn't interested in giving his family a say in his private life anymore. It had cost him once, and it wouldn't cost him again. Besides, it's not like he and Libby were doing anything more than scratching mutual itches.

Libby met him at the top of the stairs dressed in a similar ensemble of jeans and a t-shirt, purple this time, her hair swept back in its usual tail. He liked the look of it down much better, the way it hung around her face in a thick curtain, swaying when she moved.

"You know," she said as they started down the stairs. "That tub in my bathroom is big enough for two. Maybe we should make use of it later."

"Funny," he replied, taking her hand at the bottom and walking with her toward the back of the house. "I was thinking the same thing about my shower."

"Add it to the list," she teased as they stepped into the dining room where Declan, Evie, and Aidan were already seated.

Aidan's eyes dropped to their joined hands, and he swept them with a look of disgust before returning to his breakfast.

At Declan's glance and raised brow, Libby tugged her hand free and crossed to the sideboard to fill a plate. Brogan followed her, smacking Aidan across the back of the head as he went.

"Fuck off," Aidan snarled, pushing back from his place. "This family's taste in women turns my stomach."

"You're always welcome to leave. Make your own way in the world," Declan said, the sharpness in his tone at odds with his blank expression.

It was a thinly veiled threat. Very thinly veiled. Brogan knew Declan was at the end of his rope dealing with Aidan and his tantrums. The tension was thick as one brother stared down another.

"I have work to do," Aidan said, tossing his napkin on the table and turning to go.

"Yes," Declan agreed. "My work for my money. Neither of which you are entitled to, brother." He sneered the last word and had Aidan pausing at the door before storming out.

"Wow," Libby said when the door Aidan slammed echoed through the house. "He really hates me."

"Don't feel bad," Evie said, sipping her coffee. "He hates me too."

"He's an idiot," Brogan assured them. "On both counts. Now that I have bacon, what's the news?"

"They ran the bust last night."

"What? I thought we still had days to wait yet."

"So did I. Holt contacted me while they saddled up. I sent you a text, but you were...otherwise engaged." Declan's gaze flicked to Libby, whose cheeks flushed red, and then back to Brogan.

Brogan ignored his brother's subtle dig, forcing himself not to roll his eyes and further darken Declan's mood. "So? What happened?"

"I don't know yet."

"News is reporting three dead," Evie offered.

"But they won't say if they're cop, criminal, or civilian. I'm waiting on word from Holt."

Declan's phone rang as if on cue, and Brogan's eyes slid to Libby, who'd frozen, fork halfway to her mouth, watching Declan intently for any tell.

"What the fuck does that mean?" Declan snapped after listening in silence for what felt like forever.

The tone in his brother's voice had every sense on high alert. Whatever had gone down last night had not gone as planned. Brogan watched his brother's face pinch into a scowl as he grunted and cursed his way through Holt's retelling. When he finally hung up, he ran a hand over his face and through his hair.

"Well?" Brogan prompted.

"Not three dead. Five."

"Five?"

Declan nodded at Evie. "They're keeping two out of the press. All Italians." Declan leveled a searing look at Libby. "You said they only deal in threes."

"They do. Or they did. I swear it."

Libby held Declan's gaze without flinching, and Brogan admired her for that. Many men would refuse to meet his brother's eyes, especially when they were filled with so much anger.

"You also said they tend to either turn themselves in or roll."

"Well, that depends entirely on who's dealing, and I—"

"These men decided to go out in a spray of bullets. Seems they were eager for it, actually. Went down shooting, screaming 'death before dishonor'."

Libby's brows drew together, and she swept a hand over her ponytail. "I don't understand. That isn't...that's not—"

"The deal was that you provide information in exchange

161

for my protection. So either you're fucking with me, or your information is bad. For your sake, I hope it's the latter."

"Declan…" Evie said as Declan rose from the table.

"I have a meeting in the city. Brogan, see what video surveillance you can find from the bust. As many angles as possible. I want to watch it with my own fucking eyes." He pinned Libby with a piercing stare. "Then we'll see what we see."

He strode out, and Evie jumped up to follow him. Brogan's eyes met Libby's across the table, and he noted that her shock was tinged with fear.

"I didn't give him bad information, Brogan. I wouldn't do that."

"Of course you didn't. I'll find the footage, we'll watch it, and we'll figure out what happened. It'll be fine." There he was, saying things he couldn't possibly know again.

"And if it's not fine? If he decides any information I might have is ultimately useless to him? What then? If my father or DiMarco find out I'm still alive, they will kill me. Slowly. And they'll enjoy every second of it."

She pushed away from the table, wrapping her arms around herself. "No," she said when he stood with her. "I need a minute alone."

He watched her go and heard the click of the door that led out onto the back patio. He wouldn't let Declan discard her. He couldn't.

Passing the family room on his way to his lair, he glimpsed her standing on the expanse of stone, hugging herself tightly as she looked out on the rolling stretch of grass that disappeared into the trees. Declan's plan be damned; Brogan would kill the bastards himself if it came to it. If that's what he needed to do to keep her safe.

He powered up his system and dropped into his chair. He'd start with street cameras first. There weren't a ton in the area where they did the bust, but enough that he might be able to get a wide angle on the whole scene.

He typed furiously, eyes darting across the screen as he keyed in the lines of code he needed to hack the city's police-monitored security cameras. He hit enter, and the control panel popped up on his screen, giving him full access to view any camera in the city.

He ran a search for the one he needed, queuing up the footage for the date and time. It was a wider angle than he hoped for, and zooming in blurred the footage too much. He let it run anyway.

Three men clustered on the doorstep of a rundown row house. If you didn't know better, they might look like some guys hanging out, shooting the shit. Occasionally someone would pause to talk to them, slap hands together, and leave. It was subtle, but they were definitely dealing.

Brogan saw the flashing lights of the cop cars before they pulled into frame, and men in bulletproof vests jumped out, guns drawn. He frowned. As soon as the cops showed up, the three on the steps immediately put their hands up in surrender. How did they get from that to five dead men?

He watched the rest of the scene play out, frown deepening. Just before they started shooting, something caught his eye, and he rewound the footage to watch it again. Holy shit.

Bringing up a new window, he hacked into the PPD system and ran a search for footage from either car he could see on the street camera. He found them both and ran them simultaneously, eyes flicking from screen to screen.

These were a much better vantage point, closer to the action and aimed right at the Italians without any obstructions from cops or cars. He watched the cops speed through narrow streets and screech to a halt. The videos didn't have any sound, but he didn't need it. Sound wasn't what he was looking for.

He watched their hands fly up, watched them look at each other as they had in the other video. But then...there. That flash of light in the window before two more men emerged from the house, opened fire on the cops, and got shredded for their trouble. He rewound and watched again in slow motion.

If he had to guess, he'd say that someone had given them an order to go down shooting. And wasn't that an interesting new twist for a group known to roll on their own at the first scent of trouble. Libby was right. DiMarco was itching for a power grab, and that was definitely something they could use to their advantage.

Chapter Twenty-Four

"But why would Giordano order his own men to sacrifice themselves over a drug bust?"

Brogan had insisted they bring the entire family together to discuss this latest development with the Italians, and they'd convened around Finn and Cait's pool to soak up the last of the summer heat. Finn flipped steaks and burgers on the grill while Brogan ran them through what he'd seen on the video footage.

"At the very least, it seems like a stupid move to willingly sacrifice your top moneymakers in a snap decision," Evie said, popping an olive into her mouth.

"I don't think it was Giordano doing the ordering."

Brogan picked up his tablet from the table, pulled up side-by-side images of the three men who'd been actively dealing, and turned it around to show the group.

"Who are these men loyal to?" he asked Libby.

She leaned in to study the photos. "My father. They're all sons of top captains, loyal Giordano men."

"And these?" he tapped the screen and brought up images of the other two. "Are they loyal to your father?"

165

"I don't recognize them, so I would say no. My father keeps his loyal men very close, always inviting them to the house."

"These two were inside the house," Brogan began, tapping on his screen again. "They're the ones that pushed them from surrendering to shooting, and just before they open fire, you can see a flash of light through the window by the door."

"A cell phone," Declan replied, and Brogan nodded. "So the men inside report to someone who orders them to go down shooting."

"Men not loyal to Giordano," Aidan adds.

"DiMarco," Libby breathed, clenching her hands on the table.

Brogan nodded. "I'd bet money on it. I think you're right." He covered Libby's hands with his own and gave them a squeeze. "I think DiMarco is making a power grab, and he's getting less subtle about it by the day."

"This one he can twist, though," Finn pointed out, flipping the last of the burgers. "He can blame it on the cops."

"Even my father would see this as unusual. They're no stranger to busts. He expects them to keep their mouths shut and do their time. They know if they do, they get rewarded—handsomely—when they get out."

"So the relationship could be fracturing?"

"I'm sure it is," Libby replied.

"Then how do we exploit it?" James wondered.

"Did you find me anything on the Bratva angle yet?" Declan asked Brogan.

"Not yet. I managed to dig out their financials thanks to a very helpful mutual contact. Nothing looked off at first glance, but I haven't had time to look too deep."

"You should make time." Declan cast a sidelong glance at Libby.

"See," Brogan began, "that's exactly what we're not going to do. We're not going to question my loyalty to this family because of who I decide to sleep with."

"Brogan, it's fine. I—"

"It isn't fine," Brogan interrupted, lacing his fingers through Libby's and holding on tight when she squirmed. "We aren't doing anything wrong, and you haven't given anyone at this table a reason not to trust you. Unless there's something I'm not aware of?"

He pinned each of them with a hard stare. "I didn't think so," he replied when no one said a word. "Your opinions about my private life are irrelevant."

"You're right," Evie said before Declan could speak. "Our opinions about your love life are irrelevant as long as your love life isn't putting this family in danger. And," she continued, interrupting Aidan, "since that is currently not the case, I think we can table this for now."

She turned to Declan, who searched his wife's face for a long moment before wrapping an arm around her waist with a nod.

"For now," he agreed.

"Perfect," Finn said, sliding the last of the burgers and steaks onto a tray and setting them in the middle of the table. "Food's on."

They slipped easily into comfortable conversation. Libby was always impressed by their ability to effortlessly switch from efficient business to easy banter. In her father's house, it was either business or silence.

They'd smoothed over the rough edges of Brogan's announcement that they were sleeping together. His defense of her wiggled its way into a part of her heart that she wasn't sure was wise to let him into. Whatever this was between them was only temporary.

Declan had made it very clear that his protection had an expiration date and that when that date arrived, she would be on her own. She had some money saved up, enough for a couple of bus tickets somewhere and a cheap rental while she figured out what the hell she was going to do with her life.

She'd never worked a real job before, but she'd have to get one. Nothing about her life was ever going to be the same again. The anxiety of it would swamp her if she let it, so she tucked it away to deal with later. For now, she had the shield of the Callahan syndicate and Brogan in her bed.

He fit there. Far better than she could have anticipated. She wasn't a virgin by any means, but she'd never been with a man who could give her the things she'd always craved but never understood. The sharp stings of pain, the rough but reverent use of her body, the way he wrung every drop of pleasure from her before giving into his own.

It was a heady, powerful experience to both give in to the desires she'd always tried to smother and know she could ask him to stop at any moment, and he would. She wanted to explore more with him, to see what else he could teach and take from and give to her, to know, intimately, every inch of his beautifully sculpted body.

Brogan worshipped her in ways she could only dream of. Rough and passionate and demanding. And until their time was up, she was going to grab onto as much of that as she possibly could and drink it in, drink him in.

"You okay?" he asked her as they cleared out so the staff could clean up and headed for home.

"Yeah," she assured him, smiling when he reached for her hand. "I'm great."

"Wait up!" Evie called, jogging across the driveway to catch up with them. "Declan's right behind me, but I wanted to say that I'm totally team this." She gestured at their joined hands. "Took you both long enough."

Libby wanted to ask Evie what she meant by that but thought better of it when Declan joined them, wrapping an arm around his wife's shoulders and leaning down to press a kiss to her temple. They walked in silence to the end of the driveway and then quickly crossed the road once the gate swung open to let them pass.

"What if, instead of twisting the Bratva angle, you let me kill DiMarco?" Brogan wondered, punching in the code for the gate.

"Brogan, we've been through this before. People know him. They'd notice."

"Well, he's going to die eventually, right?"

"I fucking hope so," Libby muttered, eliciting a quiet chuckle from Declan and a squeeze of her fingers from Brogan.

"Yes, eventually. This won't go unanswered. But—"

"I know exactly how to make him disappear without anyone asking any questions. Or without asking the wrong questions."

Declan frowned as they skirted the gate and started up the drive. "How?"

"I can create whatever paper trail I want. I did it for the new identities for those girls. He's not American. He's an Italian national. All I have to do is make it look like he went back to Italy."

"Hmm," Declan considered. "And his businesses? What about those?"

Brogan shrugged. "He sells them, or he hires a company to run them in his absence."

"Either way, we take ownership of them. Whether outright or by pretense."

"Exactly."

Libby could see the wheels turning in Declan's brain, but she thought both of them were missing an important part of the puzzle here, the part that extended beyond the takedown of the Giordano line and those who were loyal to it.

"And what about the women? The trafficking victims. You said there were dozens, and that's data you have from months ago. I doubt he just stopped when you caught him out. Plus, the bastard still has my sister."

"She's right," Evie agreed. "I like that we have a plan to get rid of DiMarco when the time comes because, Christ, does that sick fuck deserve what's coming to him. But that time isn't here yet. Not until we figure out how to crack open this trafficking ring and free every single woman he's currently holding captive and trying to sell."

Libby looked up into Brogan's eyes. She could see him battling between his desire for revenge, for destruction, and the choice to do what he promised and save Teresa and any other girls suffering under DiMarco's cruelty. He reached up to cup her cheek, brushing the pad of his thumb across it.

"Fine," he agreed. "But once we figure that out, he's dead. At my hands."

"I won't stop you," Libby promised. "So where do we start?"

"The Russians," Declan said simply.

Chapter Twenty-Five

Brogan scrubbed his hands over his face and raked them through his hair. He'd been digging through Bratva financials for two days, and he could find nothing out of the ordinary. Their principal business seemed to be extortion, terrorizing their own neighborhoods and then demanding monthly payments for protection from the very terror they were inflicting.

They also ran a healthy loan shark business out of their strip clubs. Mostly they seemed to enjoy collecting money from people in exchange for not murdering them or threatening their families. Primitive to Brogan's mind, but lucrative, if their books were any indication.

Still, they moved money regularly in small amounts, always below twenty grand. Brogan wasn't sure if the money dripped in that slowly or if they were intentionally spreading out their deposits, but it made it impossible to spot something like an influx of cash from a deal made with the devil.

Standing, he grabbed his laptop and headed downstairs. He had to keep working. Declan was getting impatient, but he needed to get the hell out of this room. He swung through the kitchen for an apple and carried it onto the back patio, surprised to see Libby curled up in the corner of one of the couches with a book propped up on her knees.

He could clearly see the headphones in her ear, so he made sure to slowly move into her line of sight. She looked up at him and her smile arrowed straight to his heart. Christ, not even half a week in his bed, and he was already losing it.

She paused whatever she was listening to and tugged out her headphones. "Hi. Need me to get out of your way?"

He leaned down to kiss her, lingering over it, before sitting next to her and propping his laptop on his knees. "You're not in the way. What are you reading?"

"Oh." She blushed, holding up the book. "I found this in the library. I'm not a great reader. It's hard for me to concentrate, but I borrowed the audiobook, and I listen while I follow along."

"That's smart."

She studied him like she couldn't decide if he was being serious or patronizing. "What are you working on?"

He snorted, gesturing to the screen with disgust. "These fucking Bratva financials."

"Giving you trouble?" she wondered, shifting to lean against his side and peer down at the screen where he pulled up the same documents he'd been looking at upstairs.

"There's no pattern. Or, I guess the problem is that there is a pattern and no deviation from it." He scrolled down the list of deposits, still annoyed that nothing jumped out at him.

"What about the deposits where it's less than normal?" she asked, pointing at one.

"What about them?"

"Why are they so different from the others? Most of them are somewhere in the ballpark of twenty thousand dollars, but then every"—she paused to count them with her fingertip

172

—"seven weeks exactly, they dip down to somewhere between thirteen and fifteen grand."

"Those are probably slower weeks where they didn't have as many payments coming in."

"Maybe, but it seems weird that it happens every seven weeks exactly and not the same week each month or every two months. Doesn't it?"

He considered it, looking at this new pattern with fresh eyes. He hadn't put it together in quite the way she had, breezing over the cyclical seven-week timeline because the numbers were similar enough that it didn't raise any red flags. Because he was too busy looking for large lump sums.

"You said you've been watching DiMarco for a few months, right?"

He nodded. "Yeah, save for the last week or so when he's gone to ground."

"Has he ever met up with any Bratva men?"

His fingers flew over the keyboard, and he brought up the log he kept of DiMarco's comings and goings, including every time he'd been seen in Little Odessa. Isolating the smaller deposits into a single list, he brought the two up side by side.

"Son of a bitch," he murmured.

They matched almost exactly. A few days before a smaller deposit was made, DiMarco would drive up to a Bratva business in his black town car, spend fifteen minutes or less inside, and drive away again. Different businesses each time, but always somewhere in Little Odessa. Ivankov had some fucking explaining to do.

"You think they're buying girls or drugs or something else?"

"I have no idea, but it's still happening, and if they stick to their schedule, their next meet should be within the next few days. You're a fucking genius."

He slid his hand up to cup the back of her neck and yanked her up for a rough kiss, hot and demanding, his tongue sweeping against hers and his fingers digging into her skin. When he let her go, her lips were swollen and her cheeks a sexy flush of color.

"You can thank me later," she murmured.

"All the thanking you can handle for being such a good girl."

He delighted when her eyes darkened with lust, and he kissed her again, quick and intense. He wanted to drag her upstairs and thank her right then and there, but he knew Declan would want this information and would want to act on it quickly.

Reluctantly, he stood and strode back through the house, slamming into the car and heading off to Declan's offices. The sooner he told his brother, the sooner he could have Libby beneath him, wet and begging.

He navigated the snarl of late afternoon traffic with as much patience as he could muster, pulling into the employee parking lot of Breá with muttered curses and parking next to Declan's Range Rover. The kitchen bustled with activity while the staff prepared for the dinner rush, and he bypassed the elevator, taking the stairs up to the offices on the third floor.

It was bright white up here, a different look from the stainless steel gleam of the kitchen or the dark mahogany accents of the dining room and bar. Everything was encased in glass, and it made him realize how much he preferred the windowless haven of his lair.

Mackenzie sat behind Helen's desk, and Declan's assistant was nowhere to be seen. She beamed up at him when she caught him crossing the foyer, her fingers stilling on the keyboard.

"Mackenzie, did you quit your job at the courthouse and get poor Helen fired?"

She laughed, making him smile. "It's Mack, please. Today is a holiday, so the courthouse is closed, even for us lowly assistants. Helen is sick, so I'm filling in since I need the typing practice." She wiggled her fingers on the keys.

"How are you doing?"

Her smile was relaxed, happy. "I'm good. Better than good most days. My roommates are amazing. My job is a little boring, but the intrigue, feeling like an undercover agent, makes it much more exciting, and I'm just..." Her eyes filled with tears. "I'm really grateful. To you, to all the Callahans."

He shifted on his feet, a little uncomfortable with her gratitude and unsure of what to say. He opened his mouth and closed it a few times before simply saying, "You're welcome."

Declan's door opened, and he stepped out with a man who Brogan would clock in his mid-to-late forties, dressed in a cheap navy pinstripe suit that wasn't as expertly tailored as Declan's dark gray one. They shook hands and clapped each other on the back. When Declan spotted Brogan, he raised a single brow.

"Councilman, this is my brother, Brogan."

Ah, a politician. Declan loved those, although by the look of this one, he wasn't on the take. Maybe one of Declan's philanthropic partnerships he nurtured to maintain his public image. His brother was an expert at playing the social game. Brogan, on the other hand, would rather gouge his eye out with a dull knife than schmooze a room full of rich suits.

"Your brother?" The councilman didn't sound convinced, but he reached for Brogan's hand anyway.

"That's what they tell me," Declan replied, and the councilman laughed. "I'll see you in two weeks. Mack, can you make sure the councilman gets put on my schedule?"

"Of course, Mr. Callahan," Mack replied and clacked

away on the keyboard as Declan motioned Brogan to follow him inside his office.

"Unusual to see you at these offices." Declan crossed the room to the window, picking up the stress ball he kept on the edge of his desk and tossing it from hand to hand. "Everything okay at home?"

"Yeah. It's fine. I found that Bratva dirt you were hoping for."

Declan turned quickly, the corner of his mouth tilting up in a grin. "Show me."

Brogan set his laptop down on the edge of the desk and pulled up the lists he'd compared earlier, dragging one of the visitor's chairs up to the desk and dropping into it.

"These numbers," Brogan began once Declan joined him, "are deposits the Russians make into their offshore account like clockwork."

"Just one account?"

"That I've been able to find. It fits with their spending habits, so I don't think we're looking at more. Every few days, deposits of around twenty grand. But then"—he tapped keys to highlight the pattern Libby had spotted—"every seven weeks, they make a deposit that's five to seven grand less than normal."

Declan leaned back in his chair, skeptical. "Maybe those are slow weeks."

"That's what I thought, but then Libby pointed out that it's every seven weeks like clockwork."

"Libby pointed that out?"

"She did." Brogan gave a curt nod at his brother's raised brows. "And then she wondered if they coincided with DiMarco's movements."

"Do they?"

"They do." Brogan hit another key and highlighted the corresponding data sets. "He visits Little Odessa, and a few days later, they make smaller deposits. They're paying him for something."

"For what, though?"

"I'm not sure yet, but it's enough to issue a warning."

Declan got up to pace, tossing the stress ball back and forth. Brogan could see a muscle working in his jaw. "Ivankov seems to have forgotten who put him in place twenty years ago, who allows him to remain there." Declan turned from the window. "Let's remind him."

Chapter Twenty-Six

L ibby attempted to go back to her book once Brogan hurried off, but she found it impossible to focus. All she could think about was his lips and his words and everything he might do to her later. After her third reread of the same chapter, she gave up and closed it with a snap.

Looking for something to distract her, she headed back inside and found Evie in the family room, pouring herself a glass of wine. It was probably close to dinnertime. Evie turned at the noise of the patio door and smiled.

"Red or white?"

"White," Libby replied, taking a seat on the couch while Evie looked through the bottles and pulled out the one she was searching for.

"Why are you okay with me and Brogan sleeping together?"

Evie paused halfway into her seat before sinking all the way down into the soft leather of an overstuffed armchair and curling her legs beneath her. "Well, that wasn't the pre-dinner conversation I was expecting."

"Sorry," Libby replied. "I just figured...I'm the enemy, you know? The necessary evil."

"Brogan obviously doesn't think so," Evie said, studying Libby over the rim of her wineglass.

Libby shrugged. "Maybe he hasn't realized it yet."

"Do you honestly believe that?"

"I...no. I don't know. It would be easier if I did."

"Why?"

Libby could feel Evie's direct gaze, but she refused to make eye contact. "Because it'll make it easier when I have to go."

"On you or on him?"

They both looked up at a sound in the hallway to see Declan stride into the room, crossing quickly to his wife and reaching down to pull her out of the chair. He took the wineglass from her hand and planted a searing kiss on her lips.

"Well, hello to you too," Evie breathed when Declan released her. "Did you have a good day, then?"

"Very. I'm taking you to bed."

"It's barely six o'clock."

"We won't be sleeping," Declan assured her, taking his wife's hand and tugging her toward the doorway.

Libby watched them go and caught sight of Brogan leaning against the doorframe, muscular arms crossed over his broad chest. She wouldn't mind taking him to bed, either.

"A productive meeting, I take it?"

Brogan held out his hand, and she didn't even hesitate to go to him. He kissed her knuckles and led her down the hallway, up the stairs, and around the corner to his room. The soft click of the door behind them heated her blood and twisted her stomach in anticipation.

He turned her, pressing her back against the door, arms boxing her in, and leaned down to capture her lips in a soft and sweet kiss that burned her up with need. He touched her

179

only with his lips, his hands pressed flat to the door on either side of her head, his body angled away from her, and his absence made her impatient. She wanted his heat, his weight, his touch.

He gently sucked her bottom lip, grazing it with his teeth before skimming his lips across her jaw and down the length of her throat. When she reached for him, eager to feel his heat under her fingertips, he took her hands and held them against the door while he resumed his slow assault with his mouth.

He traced the shell of her ear with the tip of his tongue down to her lobe, catching it with his teeth, and a breathy sigh escaped her lips. The man was intent on sexually torturing her into an early grave. But what a way to go.

"I have been thinking about all the ways I want to touch you tonight."

"Have you?"

He nipped at the exposed skin of her shoulder. "I have. It's a long list."

"Good. Let's start at the top and work our way down."

He pulled back to look at her, blue eyes teasing. "I already have. And I'm having so much fun watching you squirm. I wonder how much more you can take before you beg."

"Not much. Experiment over," she said, breath hitching when he dipped his head and dragged his tongue over the outline of her hard nipple.

He closed his teeth around it, and she flexed her fingers in his grip, arching her back off the door. She wanted to feel him against her skin, not through the barrier of her clothes. She craved the pain, the roughness of his hands. She panted with it.

He switched to her other nipple, leaving the first one throbbing, and scraped it with his teeth before biting it and giving it a rough tug. She gasped, arching up against his mouth.

"Brogan," she moaned.

"Hmm?" he murmured, tongue and teeth still teasing her nipple through her shirt and bra.

"I need you to touch me."

He pulled back to look at her. His eyes weren't teasing now; they were dark with desire. "Where?"

"Everywhere," she breathed. "Touch me everywhere, and don't stop."

He didn't hesitate then. His hands left hers, and he gripped the hem of her shirt, tugging it off roughly before making quick work of her bra. Once he tossed it to the floor, he bent his head again and took a nipple into his mouth. This time the feel of his teeth, the way he gripped it and tugged and sucked, shivered through her, and she gripped the back of his head to hold him against her.

He kissed between the valley of her breasts and down her belly to the waistband of her jeans, and she watched him intently as he undid them, yanking them down to her knees and roughly gliding his fingers over her slit.

When he slid one inside her, his thumb circling her clit, she dropped her head against the door with a groan, grateful he was supporting her weight because her legs suddenly felt like Jello. He slipped in a second finger, nothing slow and torturous about his pace now as he pumped them inside her, his finger working frantically over her clit in fast, tight circles.

He urged her closer to the edge, peppering kisses across her thighs and sinking his teeth into her hip. When she finally gave in to her own release, shuddering against him, she sobbed with it.

He stood slowly, leaving her jeans around her knees, and traced his fingers, wet with her orgasm, around her nipple before sucking it into his mouth and licking it clean. He repeated it with the other nipple and then ran them across her lips until she parted them, and he slipped his fingers inside.

"You are exquisite. More?"

When she only nodded, he slid his fingers out with a pop and raised a brow. She knew what he wanted without words, and he wouldn't give it until she asked.

"More," she sighed, reaching up to slide her fingers under the hem of his shirt.

He stripped her jeans off the rest of the way and helped her step out of them. Her eyes fluttered closed as he kissed his way up the length of her body, and when he lifted her into his arms as if she weighed nothing, her heart fluttered.

"I don't know how you do that," she said, wrapping her legs around his waist and cupping his face in her hands.

"Do what?"

"Make me feel delicate. Every time you pick me up like it's nothing, I feel dainty and delicate and..." She felt her cheeks heat and let her words trail off.

"And?"

"And desirable."

He closed the gap between them and captured her lips, fingers digging into her ass as he swept his tongue against hers, nipping it gently.

"You don't think by now that I desire you?"

"No, that's not what I meant." How was she supposed to think straight after a kiss like that with his hands on her ass and his hard cock pressed against her core? "I've just...never had a man pick me up before. It's very sexy. That's all."

God, now she felt so stupid. "I'm sorry, I didn't mean—"

"I know what you meant," he said, voice husky.

He reached down between them, and she wasn't sure exactly what he was doing, wondering if she ruined the entire moment until she felt the hard velvet heat of his cock pressing against her pussy.

"Brogan, I—"

"I'm going to fuck you against this door until you scream my name," he promised, grinning at the moan that escaped her lips. "Because you are dainty and delicate and desirable to me. And because I want to hear you scream."

He slid into her, slow and deep, and she gasped, her fingernails raking across the back of his neck. He held her effortlessly as his cock moved in and out of her tight, wet heat. His lips trailed kisses along her collarbone and up the line of her throat to her lips, where he captured them as he thrust harder, deeper.

She panted against his kiss, and he swallowed her moans, pumping his cock into her, his pelvis grinding against her clit. Christ, she had never felt so on fire with need, desperate for every single inch of him inside her. Each time he pulled out, she felt the absence of him acutely until he thrust in again and filled her completely.

"Brogan," she whimpered, feeling the first stirrings of her orgasm as he continued his frenzied pace, face pressed against the side of her neck, teeth and tongue teasing her skin.

She arched in his arms as he drove into her, her hard, sensitive nipples dragging against the plane of his chest, and she groaned.

"I want to hear you come for me," he panted, punctuating each word with a thrust of his hips. He pulled back, eyes boring into hers and wild with lust. "Be a good girl and come for me, baby," he murmured.

At his command, her pussy clenched around his swollen cock with her orgasm, and as he predicted, she screamed his name. He shuddered as he slammed into her and emptied his cock inside her. Somewhere in the recesses of her mind, she thought she should care about that, but she didn't, and wouldn't that be something fun to unpack later?

All she wanted to do right now was luxuriate in the feel of him still inside her, his breath ragged in her ear, his hands still dug into the skin of her ass. Brogan realized what he'd done a scant moment later and pulled back with a jerk.

"Shit. Fuck. I'm sorry. I didn't mean to... I wasn't thinking."

He tried to pull out, but she wrapped her legs tighter around his waist. "Shut up, Brogan. You're ruining my sex high by freaking out."

He pulled back to look at her, and she saw surprise light his features. God, he was beautiful. Did he know how beautiful he was? Probably not. Men never seemed to notice things like that.

"Why aren't you freaking out?"

"Because it felt good, there's nothing we can do about it right this second anyway, and because I'm clean. Wait," she added after a beat, "are you? Clean, I mean. Ah, disease-free?"

He chuckled, lifting her away from the door and carrying her to the bed. "Yes, I'm clean. So we'll worry about the rest later."

She rolled into him when he joined her on the bed, propping her chin on his chest. "Do you regret it?"

"Making you scream? No," he added with a laugh when she drilled a finger into his belly, "but since neither of us has any business bringing a baby into this world, I'll be more careful next time."

She wanted to ask him what exactly he meant by that but didn't dare. This was casual, temporary. She had to remember that if she wanted to come out the other side without getting her feelings hurt.

Chapter Twenty-Seven

B rogan woke the next morning to the sound of the shower. She wasn't in his bed, but at least she hadn't left the room entirely this time. She'd closed the door, though, presumably to keep from waking him.

He eased out of bed and crossed to the bathroom, pushing the door open and leaning against the frame. Her head was tipped back under the spray, eyes closed as the water cascaded down her face and shoulders and over her breasts.

He felt himself go painfully hard for her, but he waited until her eyes opened and found him. Her smile was genuine, bright, and inviting, and he pulled open the door and stepped in, flicking on the second showerhead on the opposite wall.

"Morning," she said, reaching up to lock her fingers around his neck and pull him down for a kiss.

"One of these days, I'm going to wake up and actually find you in my bed."

"You don't like seeing me in the shower?"

He grinned and nipped her bottom lip. "This is a close second favorite, I have to admit. Another nightmare?"

She shook her head. "No. I was way too tired to dream last night."

"Maybe I should tire you out like that every night." He let his hands skim down over her back to squeeze her ass and pull her in tighter. "Then you'll never have another nightmare again."

"But then I'll end up walking around bowlegged."

He laughed, giving her ass a playful smack when she turned and reached for the soap, squirting some onto a cloth and working it into a lather. She rubbed the cloth across her neck and shoulders, working it across her breasts and catching her bottom lip between her teeth, watching him.

"Here," he said. "Let me help with that."

He took the cloth when she held it out to him and spun her around, pulling her back against his chest and groaning softly against her ear when she pressed against his cock. He swept the cloth over her breasts, taking great care to linger over her nipples, smiling with satisfaction when she moaned for him.

He loved seeing what sounds he could coax from her lips, everything from soft sighs to needy whimpers to the way she sobbed his name when she came on his cock. He craved them like a man starved. Cupping her breast with the suds-filled cloth, he gave it a light squeeze.

She was different from any woman he'd ever been with. More eager, more responsive, more in tune with him. He gave pain as pleasure, and she took every bit of it and begged for more. She was perfect.

She made his blood burn and his heart squeeze, and every moment he spent with her in and out of bed only made him crave more time with her. He would have to let her go eventually, and with each passing second, he found he didn't want to.

Something to think about for another time. When she

wasn't vibrating in his arms and arching against his hands on her breasts as he twisted and pinched her nipples. He slid his hand over her stomach, dropping the cloth and its pretense to the shower floor before cupping her pussy.

When he slid his fingertip against her clit, she sucked in a sharp breath—another sound he loved—and looped her arm around his neck. He moved back and forth over her clit in slow, steady strokes. Up and down until she squirmed against him, her fingernails digging into the skin of his neck.

He wanted her to come undone in his arms, feel her orgasm shudder through her, hear her whimper his name. And when she did, when she rewarded him with her release, he pressed kisses against the side of her neck and slipped a finger inside her.

"You are the sexiest woman I have ever met," he whispered against her ear as he thrust his finger inside her, arm wrapped tight around her waist. "I love watching you come. I love making you come," he added when she groaned.

"You...you don't love making me scream?" her voice was breathy, needy.

He grinned against her ear, slipping a second finger inside her. "I love making you scream most of all."

He quickened his pace, rubbing the palm of his hand against her clit while he fingered her, hard and fast. He coaxed her closer to climax with his fingers, and when she went taught in his arms, pussy clenching around him, he slid his fingers out, rubbing slow, gentle circles over her clit while she floated back to him.

He reached beyond her to cut off the showerhead and then behind him to do the same with the other, smiling when she turned lazily in his arms and tilted her head up for a kiss. He obliged, swallowing her groan when he cupped her breast.

Shoving open the glass door, he grabbed the towel from

the hook and quickly dried them both as best he could before tossing it to the floor and lifting her into his arms.

"I'm not finished with you yet," he said, carrying her back to the bed and covering her body with his.

By the time he did finish with her, it was nearly eleven. He checked his phone to see if there was any update about the warning they sent to Ivankov reminding him where his bread was buttered. So far, nothing. Instead he noticed a notification from their security cameras at the club.

Curious, he tapped it with his thumb and brought up a video recording from a little less than an hour ago according to the time stamp, leaping off the edge of the bed while the footage played.

"Shit," he muttered, crossing the room and yanking open the door.

"What's wrong?" Libby asked, hopping into a pair of jeans.

"Something happened at the club. I have to... Declan," Brogan said, spotting his brother at the top of the stairs and racing to meet him. "You need to see this."

"See what?" Declan led him into the study, leaning against the edge of his desk.

Brogan shoved the phone at him, his brother's frown deepening as he watched the scene unfold.

"When the fuck did this happen?"

"That's from about an hour ago. I don't know when the dump was. I haven't looked back that far yet."

"Son of a bitch. This is the Italians thinking they're being clever. Good thing I'm better at this game than they are."

They both turned when Evie raced into Declan's office,

eyes brimming with worry. "Declan, Marta said that two cops just buzzed the gate. Detectives."

Declan glanced at Brogan and gave a quick nod. "Evie, I want you to stay upstairs with Libby out of sight."

"But—"

"Please, love," Declan interrupted. "They can't question you if they don't know you're here."

"Question me about what? What's going on?" Evie looked from Declan to Brogan and back again.

"About the body they found in the alley beside the club." Brogan shrugged when Declan pinned him with a disapproving stare.

Evie seemed to debate with herself a moment before pushing up onto her tiptoes and brushing a quick kiss across Declan's lips.

"If you get yourself arrested, I'll kill you with my bare hands."

He chuckled softly and pressed his forehead to hers. "I'm not going to get arrested. Now go. Tell Marta to buzz them in, and then she and the rest of the staff can make themselves scarce as well."

Once Evie was gone, Declan turned to Brogan. "Text Finn, clue him in but tell him not to come over. They're going to want to see security tapes, but I want to know what's on them first. The Italians are mine, and I don't want to hand them over to PPD on a silver platter."

"You can stall them on that front. Tell them I have to get into the office to make them a copy. Then we can screen and give them what we want to give them."

Declan nodded when the doorbell rang. "Showtime."

His brother was masterful, from the fake polite smile to the perfectly worded answers. The detective's questions were quick and efficient, and Brogan didn't get the idea they considered them a suspect. They sounded almost sympathetic, like it was a shame a man of Declan's stature had to bother with something as awful as the murder of a prostitute.

Declan promised to be as much help as possible and made an appointment with them to review the surveillance tape later in the afternoon. The whole thing was an ugly business, and he would do whatever he could to get a murderer off the streets. Brogan could barely keep a straight face.

"Does it give you a hard-on?" Brogan wondered once the door was firmly shut behind the police and their car drove through the gate.

"What?"

"Knowing you have so many clueless people in power eating out of your fucking hand?"

Declan rolled his eyes, but his lips quirked up at the corners just as Evie and Libby appeared in the doorway. Evie went straight to Declan, wrapping her arms around his neck when he pulled her down into his lap, and Libby stepped into Brogan's arms, laying her head against his chest and squeezing him tightly around the waist.

"What the fuck was that?" Evie demanded.

"A jogger found a body in the alley beside the club this morning. A prostitute, the cops kept saying. Mostly they wanted to ask about surveillance footage."

"They seemed rather apologetic that Declan would have to get tangled up in such nasty business," Brogan said, and Evie chuckled. "If only they knew."

"But you don't think it's a prostitute."

"I mean, it might be," Declan replied. "But I don't think the dump site was a coincidence."

"The Italians?" Evie wondered.

"My guess," Brogan said.

"Let's find out."

Declan flipped up the lid of his laptop and turned it to face Brogan, who brought up the security camera feed and cycled back through the alerts until he found what he was looking for.

"A white van," Libby whispered as Brogan adjusted the laptop so everyone could see and hit play.

They watched the van pull up to the mouth of the alley, and Brogan wrapped his arm tight around Libby's shoulders. Two men got out wearing ball caps that covered their faces and long sleeves to hide any marks or tattoos despite the heat.

They were at least smart enough to know hiding their identity was the surest way to escape Callahan retribution for leaving a body on their property. The men pulled on black leather gloves and slid open the side door of the van.

The body was loosely wrapped in black garbage bags, her blonde hair hanging out of one end. One of the bags fell to the ground when they lifted her from the trunk, and Brogan could see she was naked. He grit his teeth so hard he thought they'd break.

They carried her to a pair of dumpsters, shoving at the first one with their shoulders to make a space between them, laying her body on the asphalt among the trash but tucking her up out of sight of the street. Then they calmly got back in their van and drove away.

"Brogan, can you get a clearer shot of her face? When the bag comes off?"

Brogan leaned forward to rewind, pausing on the girl's face and tapping a series of keys to enlarge it. It was a little grainy considering the time of day, but he thought she looked vaguely familiar.

"Oh God," Libby breathed, and they all turned to look at her. "That girl. That's the girl from the picture with Teresa. The other girl who was loaded into the car with her at the house."

"Are you sure?"

"That picture is seared into my memory. I'm sure."

"Can you pull a clearer photo of her from police records?"

Brogan nodded at Declan. "I can get anything once they add it to their system. Photos, autopsy report, whatever."

"Good. I want to fill Finn and Aidan in before we head down to the club to meet the cops." Declan stood and led Evie into the hallway.

"I'll be right there," Brogan said. "Libby. Look at me." He gripped her chin, forcing her to tear her eyes away from the screen. "That is not Teresa. We don't know that Teresa is anything other than alive."

"What if she's dead?" Her lip trembled. "What if I never see her again?"

She looked up at him with eyes filled with unshed tears, and his heart ached for her. "We don't know if that's happened. I promised you I would find her, and I'm going to keep that promise. Do you trust me?"

She swallowed, nodding. "I trust you."

"Good." He leaned down to brush a kiss against her lips. "I'll be back soon."

He wanted to look back as he strode from the room, but he didn't. If he did, he might not be able to keep going. He would find the bastards who did this, rescue her sister, and kill Andrea DiMarco with his bare fucking hands.

Chapter Twenty-Eight

Brogan fast-forwarded through another hour of video surveillance footage, scanning for the face he was sure was on one of these tapes. He had a clearer picture of the girl whose body had been dumped next to the club from the crime scene photos, and they confirmed what he already knew—he'd seen her somewhere before. Not from the picture with Teresa, though Libby had been right, but somewhere.

Seeing nothing on this tape, he spun up another one, tapping the keys to play it at double speed. His brothers were saddling up to hit a Bratva stronghold today. The Russians had ignored their missive and met with DiMarco anyway. The smaller deposit had popped like clockwork this morning.

There was no way they could let such a blatant show of disrespect from the Russians slide. Brogan didn't fancy a fight on two fronts, but he wouldn't mind getting his knuckles a little bloody. Roughing up a few Bratva thugs would do him some good, but he'd rather go in with a little more leverage than brute strength.

He was so lost in thought he almost missed it, smashing

the spacebar to pause the video. Setting it to normal speed, he rewound the footage and pressed play. There she was, on Ivankov's arm. The same girl from the photo with Teresa, the dead girl in the morgue.

DiMarco had kidnapped and murdered a Bratva while in bed with them doing whatever the fuck they were doing. And now Brogan had evidence to prove it. He sent the still image he had of the woman's face from the video to his tablet and raced down the stairs with it in hand.

"I'm coming with you."

"Brogan, I—"

"She's Bratva," Brogan interrupted, producing the photo from the surveillance footage. "She's one of them. And since she looks young enough to be Ivankov's only daughter, I can't imagine he sold her to the Italians."

Declan shared a look with Finn. "All right. Call Danny, get him to watch our six on the cameras."

Within the hour, Brogan had Danny set up in the back of the SUV with two laptops displaying multiple security cameras. The kid was a quick study. As much as Brogan hated leaving his expensive equipment in someone else's hands, he was looking forward to staring down these disrespectful fucks. And if he got to break a few bones, all the better.

"Anything looks off, don't hesitate," Brogan reminded Danny, who nodded, eyes on the screens perched on either knee. "And Danny? Break those, and I'll kill you."

Brogan slid out of the backseat and joined his brothers and three other men on the sidewalk. Declan nodded, and Brogan went ahead, shoving his way into the dimly lit restaurant.

Two men scrambled for weapons behind the bar, but Brogan was faster, drawing his sidearm and motioning them to step out. One of them foolishly tried to rush him, and Brogan rammed an elbow into the guy's face, delighting in his strangled scream. He was itching for a fight.

Brogan spotted Ivankov in a corner booth. A young woman in a dress that left absolutely nothing to the imagination was pressed against his side, mouth rounded into a wide O. When Declan stepped in, Ivankov had the decency to blanch and shove his way out of the booth.

"Declan," Ivankov said, spreading his arms wide in greeting. "To what do I owe the pleasure?"

"You can start with why the fuck you're doing business with the Italians."

Ivankov chuckled, clearly nervous, and motioned to his men to leave them.

"No," Brogan said, leveling his gun at the man from behind the bar whose nose he hadn't broken when he sidled toward a back door. "They stay."

Two Callahan men moved to flank the doors to the kitchen, the third blocking the rear exit, and Ivankov offered a reassuring smile.

"Please sit, have a drink."

Declan unbuttoned his suit jacket and sank slowly into a chair, waving away the shot glass the woman offered him. "I'm waiting."

"We are only collaborating on a little project. It's all above-board, I assure you."

"What kind of project?" Brogan wondered.

"A new restaurant. I don't really use this one for anything outside of Bratva business, and DiMarco is working with me on a new one. He has a few successful ones around the city."

Declan nodded. "And so you're giving him capital for what? Consulting services?"

Surprise flitted across Ivankov's features. *Callahan eyes are everywhere, you stupid prick.* The Russian recovered and smiled.

"Yes, that's exactly it."

"See, there's just one little problem with that." Declan leaned his elbows on the table. "I don't believe you. Do you believe him?" Declan asked Finn.

"I can't say that I do. Brogan?"

"Not even a little bit."

"What I really want to know is why you've decided to align yourself with the Italians knowing you'd have me to answer to. Seems pretty stupid, especially since my father is the reason you're even sitting here today. Maybe he should have let them slit your throat after all."

Ivankov swallowed hard, sitting up a little straighter in his chair. "I'm indebted to the Callahans, of course. It really is a simple business deal."

Declan held his hand out, and Finn passed him a tablet. "Ivankov, I'm going to level with you. I hate liars. And I hate stupid people. You appear to be both."

Ivankov bristled, his thin face going red. "I don't know what you mean, I—"

"DiMarco is double-crossing you," Brogan said, and Ivankov's gaze snapped to Brogan's face.

"He wouldn't."

"He would."

Declan turned the tablet around and showed Ivankov the picture of his daughter, alive and well, from the security footage.

"That's your daughter, right? Svetlana, I think?" Declan asked, turning to Brogan to feign interest in the conversation.

Brogan shrugged. "Something like that."

"Yes, that's her. What's this got to do with my daughter?"

"Oh, right. Apologies." Declan swiped his finger across the pad to pull up the grainy image of Svetlana and Teresa being loaded into the car and turned it again. "DiMarco kidnapped her. He's been trafficking women through the city. Through *my* city. But I suspect you already knew that."

"My daughter is at university."

"Your daughter is dead."

"No." Ivankov's face fell, and the woman who stood at his shoulder let out a soft gasp. "No, you're lying."

Declan swiped to the crime scene photo. For a fleeting moment, Brogan felt sorry for the guy. The anguish on his face was real, then he remembered that the greedy bastard brought it on himself.

"You're protecting the people who murdered your only daughter after doing God knows what to her for months." Declan handed the tablet back to Finn. "Feel a little bit more like opening up now?"

"That son of a bitch." Ivankov pounded his fist on the table, making the silverware jump. "We've been renting girls from him for the strip club."

"Renting," Brogan repeated, disgusted.

"Fresh girls mean lots of repeat customers. Every few weeks, he brings us more and takes the others away. We keep them in rooms over the club. They get fed, they dance, it's a fine life."

"It's slavery, you sick fuck," Brogan spat.

"What does he do with them after he picks them up?" Finn asked.

"He takes them to the island."

Brogan frowned, stepping forward to press the muzzle of his gun against Ivankov's temple. "My brother is a patient man. I, however, am not. The truth, or I will put a bullet through your brain and not lose a minute's fucking sleep over it."

"I swear it," Ivankov gritted out. "On my life. He calls it the island."

Brogan glanced at Declan, who nodded, and reluctantly lowered his weapon, taking a step back as Declan rose.

"I suggest you do some serious soul searching about where your loyalties lie. We'll speak soon. And Ivankov?" Declan paused. "We'll be watching."

Brogan signaled to their men and turned for the door, passing Ivankov's two thugs on his way out. The thin one, hand still clutching his broken nose, muttered something in Russian. At the end of his patience, Brogan darted forward, gripping the man by the back of the head and slamming him face-first into the bar. He watched him drop bonelessly to the floor with a satisfied smirk and stepped into the sunshine.

"That seemed unnecessary," Finn said.

"Yeah. But it made me feel better."

"The island," Finn said once they were back in the car and heading home. "You think he's taking them out of the country to sell them? Using Philly as a pass-through?"

"I don't know," Declan admitted. "But if he is, this whole thing just got a lot more fucking complicated."

"Where do you want to start?" Brogan asked.

"Let's start with a round-the-clock tail on Ivankov. If he tries to warn the Italians, I want to know about it."

"Done." Finn agreed. "And this island?"

Brogan met Declan's gaze in the rearview mirror. "I'll do whatever I can to excavate it."

"Good. I also want to talk options for Giordano's replacement. I'm tired of waiting."

Chapter Twenty-Nine

L ibby climbed the stairs to the third floor to return the book she'd borrowed from the library and crested the landing to raised voices. Brogan, definitely— she'd recognize the deep bass of his voice anywhere. Was that Declan? No. She shook her head. Finn.

The voices got louder the closer she got to the library, and she forced herself to turn into the room, the voices muffling. Barely. She'd seen the Callahan brothers exchange some terse words, but she'd never heard a knock-down, drag-out fight before.

Then again, Brogan had been irritated and easy to provoke in the last few days, spending most of his time in his lair or in their bed. Their bed. That still felt weird to roll around in her mind, even if it was the truth.

They'd dropped all pretense and hadn't spent a night apart since coming back from dinner at Finn and Cait's. Not that they were getting much sleep. A small price to pay for how alive he made her feel. Plus, there was always napping. She could learn to be good at napping.

When the raised voices moved into the hall and got

louder, she leaned against the door of the library. She felt a twinge of guilt at eavesdropping, but she wanted to know why Brogan was acting so weird. Maybe he'd finally spew it all on his brother, and then she'd at least know why he was the perfect lover at night and a grump during the day.

"You don't fucking get it!" Brogan yelled, and Libby winced. He was pissed. "If I can't figure this out and those girls are sold, or worse, die, then that's on me. Just because you're okay with that doesn't mean I have to be."

"Oh, come off it, you arrogant prick. You act like you're the only one trying to find them and do anything about it."

"That's because I am," Brogan bit off. "Declan is racing to find Giordano's replacement, and he's going to implement the next part of his plan as soon as he finds them. To hell with these girls."

Libby frowned. She hadn't heard about that part. If the Callahans gave up on finding her sister, then she had nothing. No way to track her or get her back. Teresa would be lost to her forever. If she was even still alive.

With a shake of her head, she shoved that thought down. It wasn't helpful to live in what-ifs and maybes. She needed to believe Teresa was alive. Some days it was the only thing that kept her going. She wanted to hold that hope tight around her for a little longer.

"I thought your hero complex with Samantha was a one time thing, but maybe it's just a really unfortunate part of your personality."

"Don't bring her into this," Brogan spat. "Samantha has nothing to do with any of this!"

"Are you sure about that?" Finn yelled back. "Really sure, little brother? Because from where I'm standing, you've been killing yourself over it for seven years. This is why Libby has always been a bad idea for you."

Libby winced. She knew Finn wasn't totally on her side, but it hurt to hear him say it.

"What if you can't save her? Then what? How long will you punish yourself then?"

When Libby heard Finn sweep around the corner, she jumped back into the library, heart beating wildly in her chest. He didn't even spare a glance in her direction before he raced down the steps. The slam of Brogan's door echoed like a shot, and she jolted at it.

Darting across the hall, she leaned over the banister to make sure she couldn't see Finn on the second set of stairs and then zipped down them to her bedroom.

Who the hell was Samantha? And why did Brogan sound so achingly sad when Finn mentioned her? The Callahans didn't have any sisters, as far as she knew. A lover? The jealousy that ignited in her belly burned white-hot, and she had to force herself to take a calming breath.

She couldn't ask Brogan about it. Could she? No, not with the way he'd been slamming around the house and then insisting nothing was the matter late at night when they were curled around each other. Maybe Evie would know…

"Hey, there you are."

Libby yelped, spinning toward the door and slapping a hand over her heart. Evie stared at her from the door, eyes wide and mouth hanging open.

"Jesus, woman." Evie rubbed at her own chest.

"Sorry, I'm sorry. I was thinking and didn't hear you come up."

"Well, I didn't mean to scare you."

"No." Libby waved a hand in the air between them. "Just caught off guard, that's all. Did you need something?"

"Cait and I are going to tidy up and restock the safe house. In case Brogan finds any more girls. Although it doesn't seem to be going well, considering how sullen and moody he's been. Want to come with?"

"I...yeah. That sounds great." The perfect moment to find out about Samantha had fallen in her lap. Between Cait and Evie, one of them would know the story there.

Libby followed Evie out the door and glanced up to the third floor. She felt more than a little guilty about gossiping about Brogan's private life, but she deserved to know as much as possible about the man she was sleeping with.

After picking up Cait, they drove to a pleasant suburb of single-family homes. They were older than the neighborhood Brogan had taken her to, but fixed up nicely and set on neatly trimmed lawns with sprawling shade trees. They pulled into the garage and let the door swing all the way down before getting out.

Libby helped them carry supplies in the house, separating them by kitchen, bathroom, and cleaning supplies. They restocked the bathrooms with everything the last group of girls used during their stay.

Libby arranged tampons under the sink and lined up bottles of shampoo and conditioner in neat rows. She tucked toilet paper into spare closets and put bars of soap that smelled like jasmine into a basket on the corner shelf.

They'd really thought of everything, and it touched her that they were going to so much trouble to help women they'd never met and would probably never see again. Libby grew up assuming every crime family in the city was as cold and distant as her own. She couldn't have been more wrong.

She would miss these women almost as much as she'd miss Brogan when she had to go. They were sitting at the kitchen table folding towels when she came down from restocking the upstairs bathrooms, and she took a seat next to Cait to help.

"Any news from Declan?" Cait wondered.

Evie pursed her lips and snapped a towel before folding it. "No. I take it Finn has been just as tight-lipped?"

"Man's never been so quiet. Something happened when they met with the Russians, and they don't want to say."

"At least I know it isn't just me," Libby said.

"Brogan has been the surliest of them all. Maybe they got a lead," Cait added, smoothing the corner of a towel and adding it to the stack.

"If they did, it's not a good one."

"I heard Declan is choosing a replacement." Evie's head jerked up. "To take over the Mafia."

"Brogan tell you that?"

Libby felt heat flood her cheeks. "I, ah, overheard it. Brogan and Finn were yelling loud enough for the whole house to hear. I'm surprised I was the only one."

Evie glanced at Cait, whose eyebrows went up.

"I don't like that our men are keeping things from us," Evie said, abandoning the towel she was folding and dropping her chin into her hand.

Libby warmed a bit at being included in that group of Callahan women, even if only for a moment. But she had questions that needed answers and now was as good a time as any. She took a steadying breath.

"Who's Samantha?" She tried to keep her voice light, but it sounded squeaky to her ears.

"Samantha?" Evie's brows drew together.

Libby forced herself to shrug and cleared her throat. "Finn mentioned her when he and Brogan were…having words."

"Screaming at each other, you mean?" Evie replied, and Libby chuckled softly. "I don't know a Samantha. Cait?"

Both women looked at Cait, whose face flashed with apprehension.

"You wouldn't know her," Cait said to Evie. "She was after you left."

Intrigued, Evie leaned both elbows on the table while Libby kept her hands from shaking by folding the last of the towels and carefully rearranging the stacks by color.

"She and Brogan were a thing, I guess you could say. Only they shouldn't have been."

"What do you mean?"

Cait blew out a breath. "She was married."

Libby's eyebrows winged up. She tried to imagine Brogan being with a married woman, being willing to share someone he cared about with another man. It was impossible to picture.

"It wasn't a good marriage. From what I heard, he beat her—and often. I don't even remember how Brogan got caught up with her, but he was head over heels. He went to Patrick and begged him to do something about her husband so Samantha could be free."

"Do what?" Libby wondered.

"I don't know. Have him killed? Have the marriage annulled? He's never said. Whatever he tried, it didn't work. Patrick was such a hard ass. A real scary guy. You didn't really push back when he said no."

Evie snorted. "Understatement."

"I guess Brogan told her his father wouldn't come around, and she killed herself. Her husband found her in the bathtub with her wrists slashed."

"Jesus," Evie breathed. "That's awful."

"Brogan took it so hard." Cait's eyes were sad. "He was a mess for a good long while. I think he blamed himself."

"Why?" Libby asked. "He didn't kill her."

"Yeah, but he didn't see it that way. He thought he could have done more. He was only twenty-one. They both were."

"I don't see how he could have," Evie replied. "Patrick Callahan was the law, and the law was unbending."

"Oh, I know. Brogan knew that too. But he couldn't

forgive himself. Whatever was in the note she left tore him to pieces. I haven't seen him really happy in a long time. Not until recently." Cait turned to look pointedly at Libby.

"He makes me happy too, but…"

"But?" Evie prompted.

Libby picked at the corner of a towel, unraveling a loose thread with her fingertips. "But it's only temporary, right? Declan won't protect me forever. When my father is gone, I'll have to be gone too."

"Why?"

Because she couldn't be in the same city and not be with Brogan. "Even with new leadership, I can't imagine the Italians will welcome a traitor back into their midst," she replied. "Besides, Teresa will probably want to start over somewhere new. This city won't have any good memories for her." She bit back a sigh. "It'll be for the best."

"Do you love him?"

Libby's head jerked up, and she looked at Evie, forcing herself to hold Evie's direct gaze. "What?"

"Do you love him?" Evie repeated.

"Evie, please, I've only known him a few weeks. I couldn't possibly know—"

"Yes, you could."

The truth she'd been avoiding admitting even to herself wound its way around her heart and squeezed tight. She was in love with Brogan Callahan. The plain acknowledgment of it hurt as much as it soothed.

"It doesn't matter," she murmured, standing and scooping the towels off the table. "We knew exactly what this was going to be when we started. We can handle its end like grown-ups."

Libby trudged up the stairs, arms full of towels and tears brimming her eyes. She didn't want to think about being in love with Brogan. Actually being in love with him was hard enough. Especially knowing no matter how much she loved him, their relationship had an expiration date. And with each passing day, it drew closer and closer.

Shoving the towels into the closet, she swiped at her eyes. There was no use crying over the inevitable. Even if it did all seem terribly unfair that she had finally found everything she ever wanted—love, passion, a kind of family, even. She wasn't allowed to keep any of it. The story of her fucking life. Good things never lasted. Not for her.

Chapter Thirty

Brogan sat in bed, back pressed against the headboard and laptop propped on his knees. He couldn't stop scowling at the screen. He'd run every search he could think of looking for this damned island. He pored through records looking for connections to shell companies or foreign corporations that might be the owner of a mysterious island somewhere in the world.

Each time he thought he had a solid lead, a new bit of information popped up that poked holes in his theory. He felt like a kid who couldn't get the last two sides of a Rubik's Cube to match up. Every twist only further complicated the problem.

Libby sat beside him, headphone tucked into one ear while her eyes tracked the words on the page of a new book. He wanted to distract himself with her underneath him. Maybe if he did, it would help him think straight. But the weight of Declan's deadline sat heavy on his shoulders. Muttering to himself, he went back to his work.

On a sigh, Libby shoved back the covers and slid out of bed. He looked up at her, frowning. "Where are you going?"

"I can't sit here and listen to you grumble and mutter to yourself anymore. I'm going to sleep in my room."

"Wait." He slid to the edge of the bed and captured her hand, pulling her between his thighs. "I'm sorry. I'm under pressure from Declan, and I don't have much time left to figure it out."

"Is this about the thing with the Russians?"

He raised a brow. "Where did you hear about that?"

Her shoulder lifted. "Evie and Cait."

"I didn't realize you three were so cozy." He reached up to rest his hands on her hips.

"Well, when our men won't talk to us, we're left to talk to each other."

His fingers flexed on her hips as pleasure, quick and bright, burned through him. Our men. Her man. Hers. *Mine.* He pulled her closer, his arm snaking its way possessively around her waist and tugging her tight against his body.

She dropped the book and her phone onto the bed at his side and cupped his face in her hands, massaging his temples with her thumbs.

"I wish you would tell me what's bothering you. Maybe I could help."

He wanted to tell her, but Declan insisted on keeping the information about the island from all three of them. Declan said he didn't want to get their hopes up in case they didn't find the damn thing, but Brogan wondered if it was more than that. If the women didn't know there was a possible location, they couldn't hound Declan to do the right thing before deposing Giordano.

Brogan didn't want to think about that right now. A distraction was sounding better and better.

"We should go out," he blurted.

"Out...side?"

Her eyes traveled over his shoulder to the windows, and

he followed her gaze. The moon hung full and white over the trees, a few stars barely visible.

He grinned. "No, out on a date."

Surprise flitted across her face, and she dropped her hands to his shoulders. "A date? Declan would hate that."

Part of him had to admit that's why he loved the idea. "Well, I'm not going to tell him."

She chewed on her lip. "What about your deadline?"

"I could use a break. Clear my head. Besides, it's late. We'll go to a midnight movie or something. The place will probably be empty. And dark."

When a slow grin crept across her lips, he knew she'd caught his meaning. Yeah, he wouldn't mind having her alone in a dark theater, the sound of explosions muffling her moans and sighs.

"You get dressed and I'll pick something."

"Why do you get to pick?"

He cocked his head. "Do you really care what it is?"

"No," she replied, capturing her bottom lip between her teeth to bite back a grin.

"Then go get ready." He gave her ass a light smack when she turned for the door.

When he met her at the top of the stairs, she was wearing a pretty lavender sundress and a light touch of makeup. He brushed a quick kiss across her lips. It was impossible to resist her mouth.

He held up his phone, screen out. "Slasher flick. Eleven thirty."

Taking her out wasn't without risks, but he craved a little bit of normal with her. Just a man who loved a woman and wanted to take her out somewhere.

The thought nearly had him tripping down the stairs. Love. Did he love her? He thought he'd been in love with Samantha, but this was more. With Samantha, it had been more of an obsession. Maybe he'd been so caught up in wanting what he couldn't have that he confused it with love.

With Libby, it was steadier, stronger, deeper. In quiet moments he let himself wonder what it might be like if she stayed, if they really got to make a go of it without all this other bullshit hanging over their heads. She didn't need Declan to keep her safe. He would. Always.

As he suspected, the place was practically dead at almost midnight on a weekday, and they grabbed seats at the back of an empty theater, sharing a bag of popcorn between them. She looked so excited to be out of the house doing something as mundane as seeing a movie that Brogan knew he'd take whatever punishment Declan wanted to dole out if he ever found out about their little excursion. The look on her face would be worth it ten times over.

They had the theater to themselves, and when the lights went down, she slipped her hand into his, lacing their fingers together. He gave them a soft squeeze. For a few hours, they could have this quiet between the two of them.

The movie was better than the one she picked out for them in the basement, and when she screamed and practically catapulted herself into his lap, he knew the night was going to end better than that one too.

He wrapped his arms around her waist, anchoring her in his lap while his fingers stroked up and down her sides, occasionally brushing the sides of her breasts. When she finally realized what he was doing, she sent him a flirtatious glance over her shoulder, lip caught between her teeth.

Knowing they were alone, he slid his hands up and cupped her breasts, rubbing circles over her nipples through the fabric of her dress. He heard a soft sigh escape her lips and slid a hand down her belly to the hem of her skirt.

His fingers dragged over her thigh as he slid his hand up to cup her pussy. He moaned into her shoulder when he realized she wasn't wearing any underwear. She was already wet for him.

She rocked her hips gently against his hand, her fingers digging into the tops of his thighs, and he circled her clit with his fingers. He only meant to tease her a bit, have a little fun, but now he ached to be inside her, pumping into her in the darkness of the theater. There was something dangerously thrilling about the possibility they might get caught.

His finger circled faster, applying pressure, and she jerked against him, pressing her back against his chest, her hips rocking in a steady rhythm. He could hear the ragged sound of her breath, feel it against his cheek.

He pressed his lips against the top of her shoulder, one hand working her clit at a punishing pace while his other stroked and pinched her nipple.

"Brogan," she pleaded in a strangled whisper, back arched as he pushed her closer and closer to the edge.

"Yes, baby?" His own desire pulsed through him, but he wanted to feel her release first, wanted to make her come undone in his arms.

"I…I'm going to…" she panted.

"Good," he whispered, his own breath ragged as her ass massaged his cock with each rock of her hips. "Come for me, baby."

At his whispered words in her ear, she cried out, slapping a hand over her mouth when her orgasm ripped through her. He grinned against her neck, peppering it with kisses until she slowly relaxed in his arms.

"Do you even know what you do to me?"

"Me?" she said, half turning her head on his shoulder to look at him. "What about what you do to me?"

The grin he sent her was wicked and full of promise. "I think I got to see exactly what I do to you just now."

Her eyes lit with challenge, and she shifted to wriggle

against him, making him groan. "That's what I thought," she replied, leaning back and sighing when he wrapped an arm around her waist.

They watched the movie in silence for a few more minutes, and he kicked himself for not bringing any condoms with him. He should have known he wouldn't be able to just tease her, that she'd have him craving more. He always seemed to with her.

"Brogan?" she murmured when a woman on screen ran screaming up the stairs.

"Hmm?"

"Let's go home."

"But the movie isn't over."

She was silent for a moment. "I could think of more entertaining things to do at home. In bed. Naked."

He didn't hesitate, setting her on her feet and leaping out of his chair. She laughed when he took her hand and dragged her down the stairs and out the long ramp to the lobby. They slipped out a side door to the parking lot. The evening air was tinged with autumn chill, and she shivered next to him.

He couldn't stop himself from taking a quick minute to back her up against the car door and lean down for a taste of her lips. She pushed onto her tiptoes, wrapping her arms around his neck with a sigh.

He had to force himself to pull away and reach around her for the door, in serious danger of taking her against the car in the middle of a well-lit parking lot. He'd take all the time he could with her tonight, Declan's deadline be damned. His hunt for DiMarco's island would start fresh in the morning.

The sooner he found it, the sooner they could get her sister back and think beyond the next chess move. He meant to have the woman he loved this time. Nothing was going to stand in his way on that. Not even a madman.

Chapter Thirty-One

Time dragged. To Libby, it felt like the whole house moved as if it was underwater while Declan's mysterious deadline approached. They were all suspended in time, holding their breaths, waiting.

Brogan wouldn't tell her what the deadline was for or why, but the closer it got, the more the frown lines on his forehead deepened. She'd catch him looking at her in quiet moments, face filled with regret. Then he'd disappear behind his computer and pretend like nothing had happened. It was starting to worry her.

She looked up at a noise in the doorway and saw Brogan staring at her, that same look etched across his features before he masked it and smiled instead.

"Hey, baby. Busy?"

He always asked her that. As if she had actual things to do. She smiled back at him. "No. What's up?"

"Meet me in the lair in five? Got some questions for you."

"Yeah, of course. Brogan," she said when he turned to go, "is everything okay?"

He smiled again, but this time it was forced. "Yep. Five minutes."

She nodded, and he disappeared from sight. Anxiety settled like a lead weight in her chest, making her heart pound slow and sluggish. This was bad news, and whatever bad news he had he wanted to back up with evidence. Otherwise why else would he want to meet in his lair?

She took some deep breaths, in through her nose, out through her mouth. Brogan had shown her how during one of her panic attacks. It helped, but being near him, his hand warm and comforting on her back, helped more.

She checked the time and took another deep breath before climbing the stairs to the third floor. She stopped at the corner, the door to his lair in sight, and squared her shoulders. Whatever bad news he was about to dish out, she could take it. What other choice did she have?

When she stepped into the doorway, she was surprised to see Declan and Finn there as well. The room seemed tiny with all three of them in it, backs to her as they studied something Declan was holding. She cleared her throat.

"Hey," Brogan said, holding out his hand for her, and she crossed to him.

Finn and Declan's faces were all business. Declan handed the paper to her, and she glanced at it. It was nothing but a list of names with some simple symbols next to each one. So, not bad news then. She glanced up at Brogan, then at Declan, confused.

"This is our shortlist," Declan said. "I want your thoughts."

She looked down at the names scrawled across the page again. Of course. He still needed to choose her father's replacement. She waited for the guilt to wash over her, knowing one of the names on this list meant her father's end, her brothers', probably her mother's too.

When the guilt didn't come, she wasn't surprised. Maybe she was her father's daughter after all, just as cold and heartless as he had always been.

"Bello is a drunk, and his only son is a total moron. DeSantis works for DeSantis. He might agree to a truce to your face, but he'll stab you in the back first chance he gets."

"What about Falcone?"

Adrian Falcone. She was friendly with his youngest daughter, Viv, and had been invited to have dinner with their family a few times. He seemed level-headed, fair, and you could see on his face that he loved his wife and kids. If nothing else, he'd do whatever it took to protect his family. That was certainly a step up from the Mafia's current leadership.

"Of all the names on this list, he's probably your best bet. I went to school with his youngest daughter, and I've been over to their house a few times. He was always nice to me, but he's got no love lost for my father."

"How many kids does he have?"

She handed the list back to Declan. "Three sons. Two daughters."

Declan pursed his lips. "Any of them married?"

"Two of the boys are. And Sofia. The oldest girl."

"Married to loyal families?" Finn wondered.

Libby shook her head. "Not Giordano loyal, if that's what you're asking." She grinned. "Sofia reminds me a lot of Evie. She'd never have stood for a lapdog."

A smile teased the corners of Declan's mouth before he hardened it again. "Solid marriages mean more families on the right side of this. And a single daughter means a potential political match."

"Aidan will love that," Libby murmured, suddenly understanding their meaning.

Brogan wrapped an arm around her waist and pulled her in close. "Marriages bond families."

"We wouldn't normally go for the whole arranged deal," Finn explained.

"But desperate times," Declan added, and Finn nodded. "Falcone then. Let's reach out and set up a meeting."

"Yeah," Brogan agreed. "Maybe he'll know something about this damn island."

It was impossible to miss the warning glare Declan shot at Brogan, who only shrugged. "What island?"

Resigned, Declan waved a hand at Brogan, indicating he should tell her. Finally. Now she'd know why everyone had been in such a somber mood this last week.

"That's where the Russians said he takes the girls. To an island. But of all the privately owned islands in the world that I've been able to locate, I can't find a single one that appears to be connected to DiMarco in any way."

"Island," Libby murmured.

That word pulled at something inside of her. She rolled it around in her head, poking and prodding and examining it, trying to find the loose thread so she could unravel it. It danced just at the edge.

"Does that mean anything to you? The island?"

Her head jerked up. "Is that what they called it exactly? The island?"

Finn nodded. "That's what Ivankov said."

"*L'isola.*" Holy shit.

"*L'isola*? What does that mean?"

"It's Italian. It means the island." Libby looked up at Brogan. "That's what DiMarco calls his estate."

Brogan jerked beside her, and Finn and Declan exchanged another look. Of course Brogan hadn't found it. In his exhaustive search, he'd only been looking for actual, physical islands.

Brogan released her and quickly rounded his desk, tapping keys to bring up a black window, and hacked his way into property records. It didn't take him long to find the property. He pulled up an image of it, with its whitewashed brick and red tile roof. It looked out of place among the surrounding homes, like an Italian villa plopped down amid the gaudy mansions on either side.

It was smaller than Glenmore House, newer too. DiMarco had only finished construction on it a couple of years ago. But she knew the security around it was extensive. They'd have a hell of a time getting in there if that's really where he was keeping the girls he was selling.

"Is that it?" Brogan turned to her, eyes hopeful.

She nodded. "That's it."

Brogan's face broke out into a wide grin, and he swiveled to face Declan. "Bingo. We've got the son of a bitch. With twenty-four hours to spare."

Declan stared at the screen for a long minute before nodding. "I want every single thing you can fucking find on that house. Floor plans, security feeds, guard schedules. Everything."

"Way ahead of you."

"We'll meet at the club tonight to start planning. Nice work," Declan said to Libby before leaving, Finn trailing behind him.

"That's Declan's way of saying thank you."

Libby turned to smile at Brogan as he rounded the desk and stopped in front of her. "I know."

He reached up to cup her face, and warmth spread through her. He wasn't looking at her with regret now. What was that? Respect? Admiration?

"You are incredible." He murmured, leaning down until his lips were inches from hers. "I'll never keep you out of the loop again. We could have had this figured out a week ago."

217

"Lesson learned," she breathed, sighing when his lips came down against hers and his tongue traced a teasing line across her top lip.

He broke the kiss to trail his lips across her jaw to her earlobe, nipping it gently before whispering, "I should thank you properly for your help."

Her knees wobbled as he dipped his head to drag his teeth across the side of her throat. "You have a lot of work to do after all that."

He crossed the room, and she felt his absence in the chill that swept over her skin. He bent to dig something out of a low cabinet and came back, setting a box of condoms on the table beside her.

She laughed. "Are you stashing these all over the house now?"

"I'm like a Boy Scout. Always prepared."

"You are anything but a Boy Scout," she snorted. "Besides, we don't need those."

He raised a single sexy brow. "We don't?"

"No. Evie and Doc helped me get on the pill."

He reached behind him and eased the door closed with his foot, stalking toward her until her back was pressed against the wall. She couldn't tell if that news upset him or turned him on. When he gripped her hips and pulled her in tight against him, mouth capturing hers in a searing kiss, she had her answer.

"This room is soundproof," he whispered against her lips, and she groaned. "Let's make the most of it."

Chapter Thirty-Two

The days grew shorter as fall finally found its footing, but Brogan was too busy planning this raid to notice much. Every move needed to be expertly choreographed, every conceivable outcome planned for. Their men were well trained, but that didn't mean he wanted to send them in blind.

The construction was recent, so floor plans were easy to find. Every level had a detailed layout except for the basement, which, according to the plans, was a big open space. Brogan imagined that's where DiMarco built his dungeon, probably with his own men, once the contractor was finished.

The place was guarded like a fortress, which made sense considering what DiMarco was doing behind closed doors. Brogan had scrapped plan after plan to systematically get them past the perimeter defenses until finally settling on one that would work.

First, he'd hack perimeter cameras and loop a feed that would keep their men hidden from anyone who might be watching live monitors. He'd tested one already to make sure it had no alarm triggers, cementing it as part of his plan after a two-hour loop seemingly raised no red flags.

Next, he'd cut power to perimeter lights in sections so they could move in under cover of darkness, restoring them once they were through so nothing looked amiss if someone happened to glance out a window.

Once they were inside, he'd use DiMarco's considerable collection of cameras to follow the Italians' movements and give their guys a leg up. They'd send in four teams at three entry points. Two together on the south side, closest to the basement door. They'd need as many men in the basement protecting the girls they suspected were down there as possible.

Then they'd send one team in through the north side, closest to the suite where Brogan assumed DiMarco slept, and the other on the east, closest to a cluster of bedrooms that were most likely for staff. Either goons or domestic. Either way, best to be prepared.

Their only blind spot was the number of men DiMarco might have inside at any given moment. Brogan had been monitoring activity through the inside cameras for nearly a week now, and the best he had was that it seemed to fluctuate. And there were no cameras in the basement, so they wouldn't have eyes down there either.

It would be impossible to tell if there were three men or thirty or how many women he might have and what state they were in. Like Glenmore, the basement stretched under the entire house. It was a massive space, and everything about it was a mystery to them.

It was the biggest risk in the entire plan. Hence the two teams instead of one. They could handle it, though. They chose their men well, trained them even better, prepared them for what was coming, and drilled the mission into their heads.

Get in, find the girls, no survivors. McGee and his team were on standby for cleanup. It would be a big job, and a fire-fight in that neighborhood would not go unreported, but Brogan had a plan for that too. He would do his best to reroute all 911 calls in the area to a dead number. He'd never done that before. He hoped it worked.

All of this was why he knew he couldn't go inside. As much as he desperately wanted to, as much as he tried to work his absence into his carefully crafted plan, he couldn't. As quick a study as Danny was, there was no way Brogan could teach him all of this in a few short days. Besides, he didn't trust anyone but himself to handle something this big anyway.

His compromise was a fully equipped black panel van that would be parked at the edge of the property. That way, he could monitor everything just like he would at home and jump out to help if shit got dicey.

He had to trust that Declan would be true to his word and capture DiMarco alive so Brogan could be the one to end him, the one to watch the life drain from his eyes. He wanted to destroy the man who had hurt the woman he loved and make sure DiMarco knew Brogan had brought everything crashing down around him.

He'd get his chance soon. They were saddling up tonight. It would be dark in a few hours, and their plan would be a go.

"You're going to be careful, right?" Libby watched him run final checks on the equipment he'd loaded into the van. "I need you to be careful."

"Baby, I probably won't even get to go inside until after it's all over."

"But if you do," she countered, worry edging her voice. "You'll be careful."

He turned, sliding his hands down her arms to capture her fingers in his. "If I do, I'll be careful. I promise."

She rose on her tiptoes to wrap her arms around his shoulders, pressing her face against his neck and inhaling deeply. He ran a hand down her hair, letting it slip through his fingers, and wrapped his other arm around her waist, holding her close.

"I can't lose you," she murmured so softly he wasn't sure he heard her.

He sank down onto the edge of the van, pulling her into his lap and pressing his cheek against the top of her head. He would move heaven and earth to be by her side again. No matter what, he would always find a way to come back to her.

Easing her back, he reached up to cup her cheek. "You're not going to lose me," he promised. "I'll be back in our bed, in your arms, before the sun comes up. Do you trust me?"

She looked into his eyes for a long moment, fingertips tracing his eyebrows and down the bridge of his nose, across his cheekbones, and around his jawline. She took a deep breath, in through her nose, out through her mouth like he'd taught her, and nodded.

"I trust you."

Declan and Evie stepped into the garage then, arms wrapped tightly around each other's waists, and Libby eased off his lap but kept her hand in his.

"Ready?" Declan asked.

"Nearly," Brogan said. "Going to run one final diagnostic, and then we should be good to go."

Declan checked his watch and nodded. "An hour."

"An hour," Brogan agreed.

Libby sat with him while he ran his tests, asking questions to fill the silence. He knew she was nervous. He could feel the anxiety rolling off her, but he kept her talking because it helped him too. He had no doubt they'd get what they came for tonight, but casualties were always a possibility.

The hour whizzed by impossibly fast, and Libby clung to him when he kissed her goodbye. As they drove away, he watched her disappear in the side mirror and wished he'd told her he loved her. He'd been trying to find the right moment to say it ever since he took her to the movies, but nothing ever felt like it fit.

It didn't matter. He'd have plenty of moments after tonight. Because once DiMarco was dead, Libby would be one step closer to freedom. She'd have her sister and her life back, and he hoped to hell she'd choose to spend it with him.

DiMarco's estate was quiet when they pulled up. It didn't look like there was any more activity there than they were anticipating. As soon as the van parked against a backdrop of trees, Brogan climbed into the back and started booting up his equipment.

He'd set up this mobile command center as close to his lair as possible. The screens weren't as big as he was used to, but they were double stacked and three across to give him as much space to watch everything unfold as possible. Danny joined him as a second set of eyes because they could use all the help they could get tonight.

"ETA two minutes."

Declan's voice crackled in Brogan's earpiece, and he made quick work of gaining access to the video feed of every security camera on the property, keying in a command to run them all on a constant loop. Anyone monitoring video feeds would see nothing but what Brogan wanted them to see until they were done.

Moments later, black SUVs rolled up, and their men climbed out before the vehicles drove away. The houses might be set far apart on big lots, but too much activity would look suspicious. Their men blended into the shadows far better than a line of strange vehicles. Just because DiMarco couldn't see them didn't mean a nosy neighbor wouldn't try to call the cops.

"Cameras are a go," Brogan said into his mic and tapped the keys to cut the power to the perimeter lights, watching their men slip through the dark patch and advance on the house.

His heart raced, and he could hear the men mumbling to each other in his earpiece as they surrounded the house and took their positions. Guns fitted with silencers, they shot out the locks on each point of entry in unison and moved inside.

"Team Alpha, two men in the hall to your left. Armed."

They moved forward quickly as a unit and rounded the corner, dropping both men with one shot each. Stepping over the bodies, they continued on their planned route to sweep that cluster of bedrooms.

"Teams Charlie and Delta entering the basement," Declan said in his ear. "Standby for support."

Almost instantly, Brogan heard a volley of gunfire explode in his ear. Fuck. "Danny, stick your head out there and see if you can hear the shots." Brogan shoved Danny toward the door.

His eyes scanned every screen to see if the exchange was coming from above or below.

"Nothing," the kid said, closing the door and moving back to the monitors. "It's quiet."

"Must be in the basement, then." Damn it. He hated being blind down there.

"Brogan." Danny gripped him on the shoulder and pointed at one of the screens.

Shit, shit, shit. "Team Beta, you've got half a dozen men—no, make that eight, nine—moving in to flank you. Three from the rear, two from the front, and four from the left side." Where the fuck had these guys come from?

No sooner had the words left his mouth than Finn's team spun around to greet their attackers, exchanging gunfire. The close quarters were too much, too many bodies in a tight space, and when guns proved useless, they switched to hand-to-hand combat. Only the Italians had knives.

"Team Alpha, Beta needs back up. They're one floor above you, east side of the house."

Aidan's annoyed voice growled in his earpiece. "We're a little busy ourselves here."

Brogan found them on the monitors and watched them exchanging gunfire with two men who kept peeking around a corner and lobbing wide shots down the hallway. They'd probably make a half-hearted run for it if Aidan's team advanced. Aidan was wasting time.

"Aidan, those fucks have no idea what they're doing, and Finn needs cover. Now! Finish it and get upstairs."

His eyes swiveled back to Finn's position, and he clenched his fists on the keyboard. They were losing ground and outnumbered. Aidan needed to haul ass.

"Basement clear," Declan said in his earpiece. "Ten dead. At least twenty women down here. Still counting. No sign of DiMarco. Status report."

"Declan. Finn's in trouble."

"Where?" Brogan could already hear Declan sprinting up the stairs before he burst into the hallway that led to the basement.

"Second floor, east side. Book it."

Brogan tracked them through the house, cycling through cameras. He wanted to run in there and help, but he had to make sure no one else was in there with them.

"Danny, you see anything else?"

Danny did his own sweep through the exterior cameras. "No. No one's going in, but the garage door is opening. One black sedan, tinted windows so I can't see inside."

"Shit," Brogan mumbled. "Danny, watch those cameras. Triple check that no one else is in that house besides the guys they're engaging on the second floor."

Danny moved into the spot Brogan vacated when he lunged for the door, yanking it open as a car squealed out of the bottom of the driveway. He ran into the middle of the road and fired into the windshield. The glass cracked and splintered but didn't break. Bulletproof.

Changing tactics, he fired at the tires, moving toward the car even as it picked up speed. Forced to dive out of the way at the last minute, he cursed when it disappeared around a corner.

"Brogan. They've cleared the inside. All targets eliminated."

Brogan didn't hesitate before turning on his heel and taking off at a dead run toward the house. He had to make sure his brothers were all right, and he prayed DiMarco was on his knees somewhere inside and not in that fucking car.

He burst through the door and past their men that stood guard at each entrance and raced up the stairs to the east wing, to the last place he knew his brothers had been. Rounding the corner, he saw Declan and Aidan at the end of the hall, neither looking the worse for wear.

"Where's Finn?" Brogan demanded, stopping short beside them.

Aidan frowned. "I haven't seen him. I thought he'd gone downstairs or something."

"No." Brogan's throat was tight. "He was here. I saw him fighting with two guys."

Declan spun around. "Check every room!" he shouted. "Find Finn!"

The men stopped moving bodies and started shoving open doors, calling Finn's name. Brogan pushed into the door closest to him, frowning when it hit resistance. He shoved at

226

it harder until there was a space wide enough for him to fit through and eased into the room, reaching out and slapping on the light.

What he saw had him dropping to his knees. Finn lay in a widening pool of blood on the floor, more trickling from a shallow wound on his forehead. He still had a knife clutched in his hand, and two men were dead at his feet.

"Declan! In here!"

Gritting his teeth, Brogan hooked Finn's arm over his shoulder and lifted him to his feet. He was maneuvering him toward the door when Declan burst in, Aidan right behind him.

"Son of a bitch," Declan swore, swooping in to shoulder Finn's other side. "Stay with me, brother. Aidan," Declan barked as they quickly carried Finn down the stairs and through to the car waiting for them in the drive. "Have Doc meet us at the house."

Chapter Thirty-Three

L ibby paced the living room. She didn't expect word, but not knowing was killing her. They'd been gone for hours; Brogan should be checking in by now.

"I'm sure it's fine," Evie said from her spot on the couch, but her voice was tight. She was just as worried as Libby was.

When Evie's phone rang, they both jumped. "It's Declan," she said, her voice relaxing the tiniest bit. "Dec—what?"

Watching the color drain from Evie's face had Libby's heart beating wildly in her chest. She fought to keep her breathing even, fingers gripping her throat. When Evie ended the call, she stared at her phone in disbelief, eyes wide and shining with tears.

"What happened?"

"Finn is… It's bad," Evie added, voice breaking. "They're on their way back."

Libby spun toward the windows as headlights slashed across the living room wall. Finn would be fine; he had to be. Guilt curled in her belly when relief flooded her that it wasn't Brogan hurt.

Then she remembered. Cait had gone home to check on Evan. "Evie. Go get Cait. Hurry."

Evie took off out the front door at a dead run just as the side door from the garage opened. Libby gasped at the sight of them. Declan spattered with blood, Brogan with some smeared across his cheek and forearm, but Finn. Oh God, Finn. It bloomed bright on the white of his t-shirt.

"The dining room table," Libby said, spinning and jogging toward the back of the house.

She pushed everything onto the floor and raced through to the kitchen to grab as many towels as she could find. It had been a million years ago now, but she'd taken a couple of first aid classes one summer in high school. She hoped she remembered enough to keep Finn alive until Doc got here.

When she stepped back in, Finn was laid out on the table, and he was pale, too pale. Deep breath in through her nose, out through her mouth. She needed to focus. Falling apart wouldn't do any of them any good now. When no one moved, she started barking out orders.

"Get his shirt off. We need to try and stop the bleeding."

Brogan stepped forward and split the hem of Finn's shirt with a knife, shredding it the rest of the way with his hands. Libby gasped at the wound that slashed across Finn's side from mid-chest to the waistband of his pants.

Blood oozed onto the table, thick and dark, and she could already see a deep purple bruise spreading over his stomach. If she remembered correctly, that meant internal bleeding. And internal bleeding was very bad.

She shoved the towels at Declan and pressed one to Finn's side hard enough to make him groan.

"I know," she crooned to Finn. "I'm sorry, but we have to stop the bleeding. "Declan. Declan, look at me," Libby repeated, drawing Declan's pained gaze away from Finn to her face. "Doc should be here any minute, but Finn doesn't have a chance if we don't stop the bleeding."

Declan nodded and stepped up beside her. "I need you to help me press these towels to his side as hard as you can. He'll hate you for it, but don't ease up. If one fills with blood, get a fresh one and start over."

When Declan pressed towels into Finn's side, she tried not to gag at the squelching sound it made and moved around to Finn's head.

"Finn? Can you hear me?"

Finn groaned and then coughed, a trickle of blood dripping from the corner of his mouth. "Did we get him? DiMarco?"

"I think we have more pressing things to worry about right now," Brogan said, voice thick.

"Well, if we didn't, then I'm about to die for nothing." Finn's expression sobered, and Libby had to fight back her own sob. "Tell Cait I've never loved anyone but her."

"You can tell her yourself," Libby said, struggling to keep her voice even. "She'll be here any minute and so will the doctor, so you have to hang on."

God, she felt so helpless watching Declan change bloody towels for clean ones, nothing stopping the bleeding. It was head wounds that bled a lot even if superficial, right? So did that mean that they'd hit an artery or an organ? Fucking hell, where was the doctor?

She looked up at Declan. "I don't know if he's going to make it without blood and surgery."

Libby looked down at Finn when he gripped her hand, leaning down so she could hear him whisper, his voice weak and thin. "You have to tell her, Libby. Please."

Libby nodded, eyes filling with tears. "I'll tell her, Finn. I promise."

He nodded, his head barely moving. "Tell her to take care

of herself. She'll want to give up, but she has to take care of Evan, of the baby."

She jerked back. "The what?" she felt Finn's hand relax in hers, felt the tears slip down her cheeks as he exhaled one last time, then went still. "No, no, no. Finn!"

Libby looked up at the sound of pounding feet in the hallway to see Evie, Cait, and the doctor burst into the room. Doc pushed her out of the way, climbing onto the table to begin CPR. Libby covered her mouth with her hand, eyes blurry with tears. The doctor stopped to feel for a pulse and then hung his head.

"He's gone," he whispered.

With one long, keening wail, Cait collapsed onto Finn's chest, begging, pleading with him not to leave her. Declan pulled Evie to him, and she buried her face in his chest, sobbing while Declan watched Cait cry over his brother's dead body.

Immediately, Libby searched for Brogan, finding him with his back pressed against the wall, eyes locked on Finn. When they finally found her, they were filled with so much anguish she thought her heart would break in two. What should she say to him? What *could* she say? His brother was dead, and he was probably blaming her for it right now. He'd have every right.

Cait's sobs filled the room, and, unable to control her own tears, Libby took a step back, but Brogan closed the distance between them in a single stride and crushed her body to his, arms wrapping around her like a vise.

When he didn't let go, didn't shove her angrily away and tell her none of this would have happened if they'd never met, she finally let herself lean into him so they could prop each other up. When he pressed his cheek against the top of her head, she wept over the destruction she'd caused.

Chapter Thirty-Four

Libby stood at the window of her room, arms wrapped around her torso. It was sunny; the light dappled and swayed through trees that danced in the breeze. Deceptively beautiful weather considering they were burying Finn today. She glanced over her shoulder at the clock on the nightstand. They should be lowering his body into the ground right about now, tossing in handfuls of dirt and flowers.

Brogan asked her to go with him, but it didn't feel right. The family deserved the chance to mourn without having to look at her, without having to remember why Finn was even gone in the first place. Cait, most of all, deserved the space to say goodbye to her husband without the pall that Libby would bring. The day was already hard enough. No need to make it worse.

No one had spoken to her much in the days since Finn's death, and that was fine. What would she say to them anyway? Sorry? It rang hollow to her own ears. It would never be enough.

Brogan was the same as ever. No. That was a lie. He was

bereft, silent, stoic. More so than usual, but he hadn't shoved her away. She kept waiting for it. Waiting for him to realize that she was the catalyst for all of it, kept waiting for that look of disgust to settle onto his face. It hadn't come. Yet.

He was tender. Constantly reaching for her hand, touching her absently to make sure she was still there. She wanted to ask him what happened that night, if DiMarco was dead, when she could see her sister, but she couldn't bring herself to. She knew they'd rescued nearly two dozen women from DiMarco's basement torture chamber. So she pulled that hope around herself even tighter and prayed that Teresa was one of them.

When she heard noises from downstairs, she crossed to her bedroom door to close it. Out of sight, out of mind if anyone came upstairs to change or rest before mourners arrived to offer their condolences. She froze when she saw Brogan watching her from the top of the stairs.

He crossed to her silently, and she stumbled back, holding her breath. Was this the moment? The moment where he realized what she'd done and asked her to leave? He closed the door behind him, and she took another step back, preparing for the blow.

"Why are you afraid of me?" he asked. The weariness in his voice tightened her throat.

"I'm not afraid of you."

He leaned back against the door, crossing his arms over his chest. He clearly didn't believe her.

"Every time I touch you, you flinch. Every time you see me, you back away. You fall asleep against me every night, but by morning you're curled in a ball on the other side of the bed. What would you call it?"

"Guilt." She swallowed around the lump in her throat, blinking back the tears that burned her eyes.

"Guilt about Teresa?" He frowned. "I'm sure DiMarco

took her with him when he escaped. I'm going to find her. I promised you that."

A shudder went through her. So Teresa was alive. Maybe. But still under DiMarco's thumb. That bastard still breathed while Finn…

"Not Teresa. Not only about Teresa." Brogan frowned. "About Finn."

She jerked when he shoved away from the door and quickly closed the distance between them. He stopped, sinking down onto the bench at the end of the bed and dropping his head into his hands.

"What do you want me to say? That I hate you? Because I don't. How could I?"

"How could you not?" she asked, voice breaking.

He looked up at her then, eyes full of pain and sorrow. She'd brought this suffering down on him, and the guilt weighed heavily on her shoulders. When he reached for her again, she went to him, running her fingers through his hair when he rested his forehead against her stomach.

"You are the good in my life right now, Lib. You are the thing keeping me going when everything else feels impossible."

His hands tightened on her waist, and a tear slipped down her cheek.

"If not for me—"

"Thirty women would be someone's sex slave right now. And Christ knows how many more." He sat up, pulling her into his lap. "You did the right thing, and I will tell you as many times as it takes until you believe me."

He cupped her cheek in his hand, swiping his thumb through the tears that coated her skin, and leaned in to press a gentle kiss against her lips. She wanted to believe him, she really did, but a part of her still doubted. A part of her wondered if he would come to his senses and realize what everyone already seemed to. That if she had never come to Reign that day, if they had refused her, Finn would still be alive.

"Come downstairs with me."

"What?"

"I need you with me."

"I don't think that's a good idea." She tried to slide off his lap, but he held her firmly in place. "Brogan, your brothers are down there. You'll have them. And Evie."

"I want you."

Those three simple words wound their way through her and arrowed straight to her heart. How could she refuse him? She would endure whatever faced her. For him.

"Okay," she agreed. "Let me get changed."

He released her, and she crossed to the closet to pull out the black dress she'd bought during her little shopping excursion at Cait's house. This wasn't exactly what she had in mind for when she wore it the first time, but at least she wouldn't have to face all those people in jeans.

Smoothing the A-line skirt with shaky hands, she slipped into a pair of black flats. Gathering her hair into a low bun, she pinned it into place and quickly freshened her makeup. When she walked back into the bedroom, she noticed Brogan had stripped off his suit jacket and rolled his sleeves up to his elbows, exposing some of his tattoos. When he held his hand out, she laid her fingers in his and followed him into the throng.

People fell silent when they passed, but no one dared say anything in front of Brogan. There were more people than she expected, though she shouldn't really be surprised. They would be here for Cait as much as for Finn. Everyone loved Cait. It was hard not to.

Brogan kept a firm grip on her hand, as if he was afraid she might change her mind and bolt up the stairs, and led her to a quiet corner of the family room. She hadn't seen anyone she recognized yet, but people stopped to offer Brogan their condolences, generally preferring to ignore her completely. That was fine; her track record with being noticed at parties wasn't great anyway.

Brogan leaned down to whisper, "Want something to drink?"

"Ah, yeah. A glass of wine would be great. Wait, where are you going?" she asked when he released her hand and started to move away.

He leaned down to kiss the tip of her nose. "Wine for you, beer for me. Save our spot."

Before Libby could argue, he disappeared into the crowd, and she sank back against the wall, acutely aware of the curious or downright angry eyes that glanced her way. When Aidan stepped up beside her, she hugged herself tightly and moved as far away from him as the crowd would allow.

"I'm surprised you had the nerve to show your face."

"Brogan asked me to come."

Aidan watched her over the rim of his glass. "The pussy must be awful good if he can forgive you so fast."

"Fuck you, Aidan. Some people do have hearts, you know. Beating ones. With feelings."

He sneered. "I guess I wouldn't know what that's like. Maybe you don't either, all things considered."

"What things?" she spat. "If you're going to say it, then fucking say it."

"If you had never come to Reign that day, none of this would have happened. Then maybe I'd be standing here having a drink with my brother instead of mourning him."

Her breath hitched at the truth in his words. Someone was

finally admitting what she'd already been beating herself up over for days.

"Everyone in this room knows that you're the reason Finn is dead."

Brogan appeared out of nowhere, flying at Aidan and shoving him against the wall, pressing his forearm against his brother's throat. The look in his eyes was deadly.

"What the fuck are you doing?" Aidan wheezed, several people around them gasping.

"I swear to fucking Christ, Aidan, if I ever hear you say something like that to her again, it'll be your body we bury next. And with far less fanfare."

Aidan clawed at Brogan's arm, his lips turning blue. "The truth is the truth," he choked out.

"What the fuck is going on here?" Declan demanded, shoving through the crowd that gathered to watch. He took in the scene, raking Libby with a disapproving stare before zeroing in on Brogan. "Brogan, what are you doing?"

"Why don't you tell him, Aidan? Tell him why it took so long for you to get to Finn with backup."

Brogan released the pressure on Aidan's neck enough that he could suck in air in greedy breaths.

"I was pinned down by gunfire!"

Brogan increased the pressure again, and Aidan sputtered. "Two men! Two men to your six who couldn't shoot worth a shit."

Declan looked at Aidan. "What is he talking about?"

"I don't know. They were firing at us. What was I supposed to do?"

Brogan pounded the flat of his hand on the wall by Aidan's head and screamed, "You were supposed to help them! Instead, you wasted precious minutes trying to...I don't even fucking know what. Look cool? Play cowboy? And because of that, you were too late. And Finn is dead."

Brogan spat the last words, and Libby flinched. "You want to blame someone? Blame yourself."

When Brogan still didn't release Aidan from his grip, Libby reached up and laid her hand on his shoulder. He turned to her, and the rage she saw in his eyes melted back into grief. He stepped back and Aidan doubled over, sucking air into his lungs with rasping breaths.

"You're a son of a bitch," Aidan wheezed. "I didn't—"

"Shut up, Aidan."

Libby turned to Declan, shrinking back from the cold fury on his face. She clutched at Brogan's arm, and he wrapped it around her, pulling her close.

"Declan, you can't really believe I didn't do everything I could to... That she isn't..." His words trailed off when Brogan took a step forward.

"Get out of my sight," Declan said, voice so low, so murderous, that Libby had to swallow around the lump in her throat.

Aidan hesitated, searing Libby with a hate-filled stare before shoving past her and out of the room. The room remained painfully silent until Declan cast one sideways glance at Brogan and Libby together and then disappeared into the crowd.

"Are you okay?" Brogan whispered in her ear.

"Actually," Libby replied, amazed at how steady her voice was, "I've had worse times at parties."

To her surprise, Brogan chuckled softly, pressing a kiss to her temple. "I still want that beer."

"What happened to the other one?"

"I dropped it when I saw Aidan talking to you. I knew what he was saying. He's been saying it for days. Come on, I bet you need that wine right about now."

"Brogan, I..." She really didn't want to be left alone for someone else to pounce.

"You're coming with me this time."

Relieved, she followed in his wake, people parting for him to pass. They were less inclined to hold their tongues now, wagging them over the scene that had just played out, her role in it all, arguing over whose fault it really was that Finn was dead. If Brogan heard, he didn't let on.

When he finally handed her a glass of white, she took a deep, grateful drink and let the alcohol warm her. The alcohol and Brogan's hand that never left her. Whether it was resting gently on the small of her back, wrapped in hers, or rubbing her shoulders. He touched her to make sure she was still there, to keep him grounded, and without knowing it, he kept her grounded too.

It was hours before the crowd thinned enough that the house didn't feel so stifling, and soon they were left with what she assumed were the heads of the families that made up the syndicate and their wives, plus the Callahans themselves. That was when Libby saw Cait for the first time.

She was seated in a high-backed chair in the family room, holding Evan tight on her lap while he squirmed to get down. Poor Evan. Did he even really know what was happening? Would he remember his father?

When Evan finally wriggled out of his mother's grasp and ran across the room to Declan, burying his face in his uncle's neck when Declan scooped the boy up, Cait splayed her hands over her abdomen. She was pregnant. Finn confessed as much with his last breath, but Libby had kept that to herself. It was Cait's news to share.

Cait looked up and spotted Libby across the room. When she rose from her chair, the room fell silent. Everyone watched with curiosity and disdain as Cait approached Libby. This was the moment Libby had been dreading most. The moment when she heard from Cait's own lips that this was all her fault. She would hardly be able to blame her, but it would hurt all the same.

So when Cait wrapped Libby in a tight hug, Libby was just as surprised as the rest of them. After a moment, she returned it, pouring all the apologies she couldn't get past the tight knot in her throat into the embrace.

When Cait finally released her and pulled back, she had tears spilling down her cheeks and reached up to wipe away Libby's own.

"Cait," Libby whispered, voice hoarse. "I'm so sorry."

Cait nodded as the tears fell. "I know. Libby, I wanted to say thank you."

All the tension flooded out of her, and blood rushed through her ears so loudly she wasn't entirely sure she heard Cait right.

"What?"

"You tried to save him. With the towels. Brogan told me." Her gaze shifted to Brogan and back to Libby's face. "You were there to…" her voice broke, and she fought for composure. "You were there to hold his hand. And I'm grateful someone was. So thank you. Did he…did he say anything?"

"Oh, Cait. He loved you so much." Libby could barely get the words out. "He said he's never loved anyone but you. And—" Her breath shuddered in and out, voice shaking. "He said you might want to give up, but you can't. Because you have to be strong for you and Evan. And for the baby."

Cait's eyes went wide, and then she burst into sobs, doubling over with them, arms clutched around her middle as she sank to her knees. When Brogan bent to help her up, she waved him away, reaching instead for Libby's hand and giving it a squeeze.

Libby knelt on the floor in front of Cait, wrapping her arms around her shoulders while she cried, crying with her. Libby tried to back away when Evie came to kneel next to them, but the woman just wrapped her arms around them both and held on tight.

"Thank you," Cait whispered when her tears finally subsided. "For being there for him, for bringing his last words to me. And Libby," Cait added when Libby moved to stand. "Be easy on yourself."

Tears threatened to overtake her again, and all Libby could do was nod. She let Brogan help her off the floor and leaned into him when he wrapped his arms around her, pressing his cheek to the top of her head.

"I think that's enough for one day," Brogan murmured in her ear when the last of the guests filed out and Evie left to go back across the street with Cait and Evan.

"She doesn't hate me."

"You keep saying that like you expect it."

Libby shrugged as they stepped into Brogan's bedroom, and he closed the door behind them. "That's because I do."

"Would you hate me if tomorrow you found out Teresa was dead?"

Libby whirled around to face him, relieved when he held up a hand and shook his head.

"I'm not saying she is dead. I'm only asking if you would blame me if she was."

"No, of course not. Her blood would be on DiMarco's hands. But—"

"But nothing. Finn's blood is on the hands of DiMarco and the man who stabbed him and no one else's. Least of all yours. We all have choices, Libby. You chose to come to the club that day, Declan chose to help you, to start this war, and Finn chose to fight in it. The only person in this room who blames you for the outcome is you."

"I don't deserve you." She sighed when his fingers gripped the pull of her zipper and dragged it down her side.

"I think you have that the wrong way around. Come to bed with me. I sleep better with you in my arms."

She wanted to say it then, to tell him she loved him in a way that didn't seem possible, but she kept it to herself. If there was a perfect moment to confess your love to a man you might not get to keep, it certainly wasn't today. Tonight they would just be. Tomorrow she'd force herself to look at things with a clearer head.

Chapter Thirty-Five

Brogan rubbed at the dull ache in his temple. It had been a long and bloody week. Since they buried Finn, he'd killed his fair share of Italians, just not the ones he wanted. Decimating the last of their loyal ranks didn't have the same weight of satisfaction, knowing the two he really wanted weren't counted among the dead.

Which is why he'd rather be at home sifting through the mountains of evidence he'd been gathering, looking for any sign of those bastards so he could end this once and for all. Instead, he was stuck at the conference table under the fluorescent lights of Reign's basement, waiting for Falcone to show up for this damn meeting.

This was the kind of shit Finn loved. Holding talks and closing deals. But Finn was…well, Brogan figured he'd be sitting in on a lot more meetings like these going forward. Declan sat at the head of the table, looking as in control as ever. The only thing that gave his brother away was the way he gripped his wife's hand.

"Cait and Evan get off okay?"

Evie turned to Brogan, her smile sad. "Yeah. Her parents

came to pick them up this morning. I hope she gets the rest she needs. I couldn't imagine…" Declan lifted her knuckles to his lips.

Brogan's phone signaled, and he pulled up the live video feed for the club's parking lot. "He's here."

They didn't stand when James let Falcone into the basement, but they did, in a sense, prepare themselves for battle. He was older than Giordano but probably not by much, with hair going gray at the temples and a close-cropped beard to match. He was stocky, and his eyes were shrewd, taking in the scene. His eyebrows dipped quickly at seeing Evie before his features relaxed again.

They shook hands, and then he took a seat on the opposite side of the table, studying them carefully.

"Thanks for meeting with me."

"When the man who's been slowly eliminating my fellow soldiers with barely a blip on the public radar asks for a meeting, it seems in poor taste to turn it down."

He was clever, Libby said as much, but Brogan didn't care about that half as much as he cared about whether the man had the right motivations to change sides. This meeting was crucial. Falcone would either accept or he wouldn't leave this basement alive, and they'd have to start their search all over.

"I have a proposal. Giordano out, and you stepping in to take his place."

Falcone considered for a long moment. "And DiMarco?"

"What about DiMarco?" Brogan asked.

"Giordano thinks he calls the shots, but he doesn't. He hasn't for years. If you're looking to replace leadership, you'll need to take them both out."

Declan glanced at Brogan. "We are."

Falcone nodded. "You're targeting the right families. They're all blindly loyal to one or the other. But I might suggest one more."

"I'm listening."

"DeSantis. They're small but not really loyal to anyone but themselves." Another point for Libby. "They'll challenge whoever ends up replacing Giordano. Whether it's me or someone else. Then you've just got more problems on your hands."

Declan nodded. "Fine. So you're interested?"

Falcone sat forward and leaned his elbows on the table. "I'm interested in discussing terms. But what's the catch?"

"Marriage," Evie said. "Your daughter to a Callahan. To Aidan Callahan," she added when Falcone's eyes slid to Brogan.

"We know you love your wife and kids and that three of your children are married to good families, so you'll have support."

"And if I refuse to sell my daughter for my own political gain?"

Declan shrugged, but Brogan could see the vein working in his temple. "Then I think we both know what happens next."

Falcone sat back, steepling his fingers in front of him. "And what if I say yes to this whole thing to get out of this room and then change my mind?"

A dangerous smile played over Declan's lips, and when he spoke, his voice was low. "Then I will hunt you and every Italian thug in the city down until not a single one is left."

Declan leaned back in his chair. "I'm offering you a gift, Falcone. If you don't want it, if you want to hope and pray that your wife and children make it out of this alive instead of living in the shadow of my good graces, my blessing, then be my guest."

He gestured toward Evie and Brogan. "We certainly don't need this deal. There are other ways of handling this little…infestation."

"I'll need to speak to my daughter first," Falcone said after a long pause.

"No," Declan replied.

"No?" Falcone repeated, face reddening. "And if she refuses?"

"Then make her see reason. A marriage between your daughter and my brother or there is no deal. Forgive me for not implicitly trusting the word of an Italian, but I need you to have a little more skin in the game than a handshake and a promise."

Falcone scrubbed a hand over his face. He was between a rock and a hard place on this. Say no, and he's dead. Double-cross them, and he's dead. Say yes, and he promises his daughter's hand in marriage to a man she's never met and may not even like.

Brogan could clearly see the struggle on the man's face, but Declan wasn't willing to budge on this and get burned like they had with Ivankov. Twenty years from now, he wanted blood ties between the families to keep them loyal. Marriage was the only way to get it.

"Fine," Falcone finally agreed. "I'm in. What's next?"

They spent hours hammering out details and check-in schedules and gathering extra intel from their new inside man. If he was telling the truth, Falcone had no idea where DiMarco and Giordano were either. They might be in contact with someone, but right now, with the way things were running and the whispers Falcone was hearing from other sources inside the Mafia, they had both gone dark.

"Well?" Declan turned to Evie once Falcone finally left.

"He seems trustworthy enough to me. As trustworthy as criminals can be." Her slight grin quickly fell away. "But I don't know. Maybe I'm not as good a judge of character as I used to be."

Declan reached down and pulled Evie to her feet. "It's

hard to see the people who are really close to us. Nessa was good at hiding who she really was. Trust your gut. What's it say?"

"He's our guy, and Aidan is going to hate this."

Brogan pursed his lips. "It's the least he can do. And I agree about Falcone." They climbed the steps and headed for home. "Plus, I'm tracking him. I've got one on his car, and I hacked his phone through Wi-Fi, so I'm tracking him there too. If he does something we don't want him to, I'll know about it."

"Good. Now find me DiMarco and Giordano so I can finish this."

"I'm working on that too," Brogan murmured as they pulled into the driveway.

Libby was not waiting for him in the living room when they walked in like she sometimes did. In fact, she'd spent most of the last week in her bedroom when he wasn't home or busy working. It reminded him of when she first arrived, scared and broken. He didn't like it.

"Son of a bitch," Evie breathed, staring down at a small envelope in her hands. She flipped the envelope over and over as Declan crossed back to her, reaching for the note she was reading.

"Fuck!" his head jerked up, and he met Brogan's eyes.

"What?"

"DiMarco wants to make a deal."

Brogan snatched the note his brother held out, scanning it quickly.

A life for a life. I know that Elizabeth Giordano is alive, and I know you have her. Bring her to me within twenty-four hours, or someone dies. I'll pick you off one by one until I have her in my possession. Maybe I'll start with pretty Evie when she's out for a jog or sweet Cait when she takes little Evan to the park. Better hurry. Time is running out. -AD

"He's bluffing."

"You know he isn't," Declan replied, pulling Evie into his side and pressing a kiss to the top of her head. "I know you know that."

"So, what, I'm supposed to send Libby to the slaughter?"

"I'm supposed to send my wife to it? Cait? Evan? Fuck knows who else?" Declan snapped.

"Libby is just as innocent in this as they are! There has to be another way. I just need time to—"

"You don't have time," Declan countered. "I'm sorry, Brogan, I really am, but I have a duty to protect this family. I need to go make some calls." Declan took the rest of the envelope from Evie's hands, the note from Brogan's. "We'll have to—"

"I'll do it."

"Brogan," Evie said once they were alone. "This is an impossible thing to ask of you, of her. But I'm not thinking of myself when I ask it."

"Aren't you?"

Evie shook her head, eyes bright with tears. "I'm thinking of Cait, of Evan, of Aidan, of you. Of anyone else who might be in his crosshairs if DiMarco doesn't get what he wants. We've already lost Finn."

"So I have to lose her? He's going to kill her, Evie. I need…" His voice broke, and he cleared his throat. "I need time to find an alternative. Give me that much."

The pain in Evie's face was raw when he met her eyes, and she nodded. "Okay. I'll talk to Declan about stalling DiMarco. Think fast, Brogan. I won't be able to buy you much time."

Evie followed Declan out, and Brogan picked up the lamp

from a nearby table, hurling it at the wall with a satisfying shatter of glass and splintering of wood. He would not send Libby into the arms of that deranged psycho without a fight. He'd need a day, maybe two, to figure out where the fuck DiMarco was or where he could take Libby.

He could get them both out and away. They could go on the run. With enough money and the right documents, anyone could become someone else. He would not roll over and give up the woman he loved a second time.

Taking the stairs at a dead run, he rushed into Libby's room, frowning when he found it empty. He was about to backtrack downstairs and check the solarium for her when he heard music from the direction of his room.

She was sitting in the middle of his bed, fingertips tapping a beat on her knee while a voice he didn't recognize serenaded her about mistakes made and second chances given. She was completely lost in it, eyes closed.

His heart thumped in his chest. He wanted to memorize her like this. At peace, without worry lines creasing her brow or tears in her eyes. Fuck that. He wanted one more night with her before he brought their world crashing down around them. It would take some of the precious little time he had to figure out a way to get them out of this mess, but it would be worth it.

She opened her eyes when the song changed and saw him standing in the doorway. She'd stopped jolting when she saw him, which was a relief. He did his best every day to remind her that none of this was her fault, that she was as much a victim to this whole fucking thing as anyone else. She'd lost everything in her quest for justice. But he'd found her.

"What's wrong?"

"What? Nothing."

She cocked her head, reaching down to turn off the music. "It doesn't look like nothing."

He slipped into the room, closing the door behind him. "It is."

"How did the meeting with Falcone go?"

He forced himself to keep his voice light. "It was fine, good. He agreed. To all of it."

Libby's brows lifted. "I didn't expect him to come around that fast."

"Declan didn't give him much of a choice." Brogan moved over to the bed. "Come here," he murmured.

She pushed onto her knees and shuffled toward him on the edge of the bed, wrapping her arms around his neck when he gripped her hips.

"Are you sure you're okay?"

He swallowed hard. "I'm sure. I need to touch you. To feel you beneath my fingertips."

"Well," she replied, a little breathless. "I won't say no to that."

He slid his hand up her back to cradle her head and brought his lips down to meet hers in a kiss that was soft and sweet. He coaxed her lips open and slid his tongue against hers, fingertips digging into her hips when she moaned softly against him.

Tomorrow, whatever happened, their entire lives would be different. Tonight he wanted to etch her into his memory. Every sigh, every gasp, every moan, every curve and dip. He wanted one more night to live in a world where tomorrows weren't fleeting and goodbyes weren't permanent.

"Can I?" he asked, fingers stilling on her ponytail, and she nodded.

He undid the elastic, letting her hair cascade down her back. It was longer now, and he liked the way it swung past her shoulders. He liked the feel of it across his chest when she slept. He ran his fingers through it, his other hand slipping under the hem of her shirt, caressing soft skin.

She was perfect, and he wondered briefly if she was even aware of how perfect she was with her curves and her sass and her kind heart. He pulled back, her lips swollen, eyes curious under the lust. He'd yet to be this gentle with her, but he was determined to take his time. He wanted to drink her in and savor every second.

He gripped the bottom of her shirt, peeling it up and off, and bit back a groan when he realized she wasn't wearing a bra. Dipping his head, he captured her nipple in his mouth, swirling his tongue around it, reveling in the feel of her fingers gripping the back of his head.

Libby dropped her head back on a groan when he dragged his teeth over her hardened nipple and soothed it with his tongue. His hands flipped open the button of her jeans, pulling down the zipper and working them down her hips.

He helped her lean back and slid them off her legs, wrapping an arm around her calf and pulling her slowly to the edge of the bed. Her breath hitched when he dropped to his knees, and her brown eyes fluttered closed when he trailed his tongue across her inner thigh.

She arched, hips rocking as he moved closer to her pussy. Her fingers gripped and tugged the fabric of his shirt as if she was desperate to feel his mouth against her. He blew a warm breath across her skin, and she jerked, moaning his name in a way that would have brought him to his knees if he weren't on them already.

He dragged his tongue up the outside of her slit, and her hips rose to meet it. He smiled, reaching up to run his fingers over where his tongue had been, his thumb catching on her clit and rubbing in quick, tight circles.

"Brogan." Libby's voice was hoarse, desperate with need.

"Hmm?"

"Please."

He grinned, rubbing faster while he watched her. "Please what, baby?"

She gripped his shirt harder as her body vibrated under his touch. "Please," she said through gritted teeth. "Stop teasing me."

Thumb never stilling on her clit, he slipped two fingers inside her, pumping them in and out in rhythm with the circles he was drawing on her clit. Her hips jerked against him, her needy cries strangled as he pushed her closer to climax. When he felt her clench around his fingers, he plunged them inside her, leaning down to drag his tongue over her sensitive clit, eliciting one last shudder.

He sat back to look at her, chest heaving, nipples hard, skin flushed from her orgasm.

"Have I ever told you how much I love to watch you come?"

She let out a throaty laugh. "You've mentioned it once or twice."

He kissed the inside of her thigh before standing and stripping off first his shirt and then his pants and boxers. She slid back into the middle of the bed, and he covered her body with his, luxuriating in how she molded against him, her leg wrapping around his calf, her hand traveling from his hip up to his back and gripping his shoulder.

"I could watch you every day and not get tired of it."

"Yeah, see if you still feel that way fifty years from now."

He saw it, the moment's hesitation in her eyes, but he captured her lips before she could take it back. He liked knowing she was thinking about fifty years from now. Even if it meant they had to be someone else, somewhere else, he wanted those fifty years with her.

He moved a hand between them, teasing over her clit as he slipped inside her. She tightened around him, arching under him, and he groaned, grinding against her. She moved with him, matching him thrust for thrust.

He loved the way her breath caught when he slid all the way inside her, the way her leg tightened on his when he pulled out again. He kept up his steady pace, each thrust hard and deep, his finger keeping constant pressure on her clit.

When she tightened around him with her orgasm, his name a moan falling from her lips, he almost lost himself. But he wasn't finished with her yet. He wanted more from her, wanted to give her more.

Sitting back on his heels, Brogan reached down to flip her onto her stomach and pull her onto her hands and knees, smiling when she arched against the hands he ran up and down her back. Sliding his hands around to cup and squeeze her breasts, he thrust his cock inside her again.

He tried to keep it slow, but she rocked back against him, and he couldn't help but pump his hips a little faster. When he smacked her ass, she whimpered, and the sound drove him to the edges of his control.

She dropped her shoulders toward the bed, leaning her weight on her forearms and rocking back to meet his desperate thrusts. Christ, she was perfection. He reached down to rub her clit, and she gasped, jerking against his fingers and clenching around his cock.

"Brogan," she begged, and he drove into her harder, pushing them both closer to the peak.

When she came around him, his vision blurred, and he drove inside her, giving over to his own orgasm. He eased out of her, afraid he'd collapse and crush her beneath him, and rolled onto his side, tugging her back against him.

He pressed a long kiss to her shoulder, his arm wrapped tight around her waist, and listened to her breathing slowly return to normal. When she turned in his arms, he leaned down to press a kiss to the tip of her nose.

"That was...different."

He leaned back to look at her. "Bad different?"

She kissed his chin. "How could sex with you ever be bad? But you'll have to tell me what brought that on so I can make you do it again sometime." She snuggled closer, unsuccessfully stifling a yawn.

"Later," he said, tucking her up against him. "Sleep first."

He traced his fingertips up and down her spine until he felt her entire body relax and go limp against him. When he was sure she was asleep, he slipped quietly out of bed and turned off all the lights. Taking his laptop to one of the chairs that flanked the fireplace, he sat down and got to work.

Chapter Thirty-Six

Libby woke pressed against him, her face buried in the crook of his neck. She breathed in his scent and snuggled closer, smiling when his arm tightened around her waist. No one had ever made her feel the way Brogan did. She doubted anyone else ever would.

He'd touched her a million different ways. They'd had sex more times than she could count, but never like they had last night. Never slow and sweet, with his hands and lips and tongue gliding over her skin as if he wanted to commit every inch of her body to memory.

She wished it felt like the promise of something instead of goodbye. Their time was almost up. Her father and DiMarco might still be alive, but most of their loyal men were dead, and the syndicate would take care of the rest. They'd met with Falcone, and now life would move on.

Deep down, she thought she should mourn the death of her own, wondered what was wrong with her that she didn't. The truth was they had never been her family. Not in the ways that mattered. She'd never felt seen, felt wanted, felt included. Not until Brogan.

She could feel his steady breaths against her shoulder, his fingers splayed across her back. Leaning away from him, she studied his face. She wanted to soak it in like he had with her body last night. She wanted to imprint it onto her memory so she could keep a part of him with her. It would have to last her a lifetime.

Even in sleep, his forehead creased with worry, and she pressed a careful kiss against it so as not to wake him. She ran her fingertips through the stubble on his cheeks, across his angled jaw. Closing her eyes, she pictured his smile, the one he reserved just for her that was full of joy and the love she hoped he felt but hadn't said.

She rolled away from him when he shifted and got out of bed, leaving him to sleep. He'd worked late into the night on something and woken her up climbing back into bed, gathering her against him and caressing her back to sleep.

She pulled on a pair of leggings and a tank top, sweeping her hair into a messy tail before padding down the stairs. It was early yet, but she heard voices coming from the family room, pausing in the hallway when she heard her name.

"If he means to have her, he'll figure out a way to get her. You're asking me to put your life at risk instead."

"No," Evie replied. "I'm asking you to consider that Brogan feels for her what you feel for me and that he needs more time to figure something out."

Declan sighed. "And if I can't stall him and it's your body we bury next? What then?"

Libby could hear the tightness in Declan's voice. The fear.

"DiMarco can't get to me at Glenmore. If he could, he would have come for her already. I'll be perfectly safe here."

DiMarco? Did they know where he was? Was he coming for her? Libby stepped into the doorway and drew their attention.

"You found DiMarco?"

Declan's eyes traveled over her shoulder. "You didn't tell her?"

Libby followed Declan's gaze to see Brogan standing behind her in the hallway, his eyes locked on his brother's face, expression hard.

"Tell me what?"

"Come upstairs with me, and I'll tell you." Brogan reached for her hand.

"No. You had all night to tell her. You'll do it here and now."

"Tell me what?" Libby looked from Brogan to Declan and back again. "Brogan?"

"DiMarco sent us a demand last night," Brogan began, dragging his eyes to her face. "He wants you. He wants us to deliver you to him."

She stumbled back against the door frame, clutching it for support and inhaling deep through her nose, releasing a shaky breath through her mouth. Panic bubbled up into her throat, and she forced it back down.

"And if you don't?"

Brogan's face fell, and he ran a hand through his hair. He opened his mouth only to close it again, like he couldn't quite figure out how to say it.

"If we don't," Evie said softly, "he's threatened to kill us one by one until he has you."

Stomach lurching, Libby staggered into the room and dropped onto the arm of the couch seconds before her legs gave out. DiMarco hit the Callahans exactly where he knew it would hurt. Declan wouldn't hesitate to hand her over if it meant his own wife, his brothers, his people were in danger. She couldn't blame him, really.

So that's what kept Brogan up until the earliest hours of the morning. One last-ditch effort to find DiMarco and get them out of this mess. Suddenly she understood his tenderness last night, and she was grateful for it. Only…his memory might have to last a lot longer than hers.

"When?" Her voice sounded thin.

"Tonight," Declan replied.

That wasn't much time. Not nearly enough time to say goodbye. "I'll do it."

"No! No."

Brogan gripped her arm and yanked her to her feet so fast she crashed into his chest. The terror in his eyes did nothing to ease her own.

"I can't let you do this. I won't."

"You have to."

He shook his head. "No. We'll leave. We'll go somewhere, anywhere."

She reached up to cup his face in her hands, forcing him to look at her. The desperate plea in his gaze nearly broke her, but she had to do this. She had to keep him safe.

"We can't. He'll never stop. He'll hunt them. You know he will. This is the only way to make sure that never happens. To protect the family. To protect you."

"You don't know what you're asking of me." He leaned his forehead against hers and drew in a ragged breath. "This is suicide by psycho."

"Brogan. I love you." When he jerked back, she pushed up on her toes and pulled him closer to brush her lips against his. "I wish I told you weeks ago when Evie first made me admit it, so I could have said it as many times as possible, but I'm saying it now. I love you, and I have to do this. I have to do whatever I can to protect you."

He leaned his forehead against hers again. "How am I supposed to be okay with this? How am I supposed to live without you?"

"Let's not get ahead of ourselves. I never said I was going to go down without a fight."

He blinked in surprise, but it was Declan who spoke. "How do you mean?"

"Well, I might be willing to wander into the viper's nest, but that doesn't mean I'm going to do it without a sharp stick hidden behind my back. Once he has me, he's going to take me somewhere."

Evie leaned forward, eyes bright. "You're right. He's got to have some kind of endgame. He wants you too bad not to have a plan."

Libby nodded and sank down onto the couch. When Brogan didn't join her, she reached for him and waited until he took her hand and sat before she continued.

"He's not stupid enough to gut me right in front of you."

"Libby..." Brogan gripped her hand in his, voice strained.

"Think, Brogan. Think beyond your fear for me. Pretend it's anyone else. What would he do once he has me?"

Brogan rubbed at his brow. "He'd take you to a secondary location."

"Somewhere private," Declan agreed.

"So he could take his time," Evie added.

Libby nodded. "Right. So how do we make sure you know exactly where that location is?"

"Better yet, how do we take him out before he even leaves with you?" Evie asked.

Brogan shook his head. "There's too much that could go wrong, too many variables. I won't take that chance. I can find another way out. Don't give up on me, Lib."

"I'm not doing this to give up." She laced her fingers through his and squeezed. "You can't ask me not to do what-ever I can to keep you"—she gestured at Evie and Declan—"and them safe. Do you trust me?"

When he cupped her cheek, she leaned against his palm, but the pain in his eyes tore at her. "I trust you. I love you."

Her heart squeezed in her chest. If this all went horribly

wrong, she might never see him again after today. She had those words to carry with her no matter what happened, but she damn sure wouldn't go down without a fight.

Brogan didn't like this. Not a single part of it. But no amount of arguing could convince Libby to wait and let him buy them more time. She was determined to put herself at risk and face down DiMarco. He had to respect that, even if he would rather lock her in her room and not let her out until it was all said and done.

"He won't find that even if he sweeps you with a wand." He ran his fingers over the tracking device he'd slipped into a hole in the waistband of her jeans.

The plan was to place a sniper on an empty floor of a nearby office building with a clear shot of the parking garage where DiMarco requested the exchange. One clean shot and she wouldn't have to get in that bastard's car, wouldn't leave his sight. Barring that, he wanted to be able to track her wherever they went. The tiny GPS chip was smaller than his pinky nail and untraceable if DiMarco tried to search her for wires or bugs. With it, they could find and follow them anywhere in the world.

Men were standing by to stage a rescue wherever they ended up. Brogan's only goal was to get Libby out before any damage was done to her. Her body and her mind had been through enough. The last thing she needed was to be raped by DiMarco and God knows who else. She might be strong, but even she had her limits.

Declan poked his head through the door, and Brogan reached for Libby's hand, squeezing it tightly. "It's time."

Evie was waiting for them in the living room. For obvious reasons, Declan was not allowing her to come. They embraced, Evie murmuring something into Libby's ear that had her eyes filling with tears, a crooked smile forming on her lips.

"You." Evie turned to Brogan and wrapped her arms around his waist. "Stick to the plan and don't do anything stupid. You." She pivoted to Declan, who leaned down to brush a quick kiss across her lips. "Come back to me," she whispered.

They drove to the meeting spot in silence, Libby's fingers gripping his. Brogan ran this thumb over the back of her hand in soothing circles, for himself as much as for her. The parking garage was empty when they pulled in, and he checked for confirmation that their man was already in place, ready to take the shot.

They got out when DiMarco pulled up, Declan flanking Libby's other side. DiMarco's smile was violent when he saw their joined hands, and he felt Libby straighten beside him, chin ticking up in defiance. That a girl.

"Elizabeth." DiMarco reached for her. "Come."

When she stepped forward, Brogan gave her hand a gentle tug, pulling her back against him. He leaned down to taste her lips, his other hand braced on the small of her back, stomach tightening at the idea of letting her go. She pressed against him, and he poured every bit of love he had into that kiss. When he pulled back, he brushed his thumb across her cheek, and she gave the slightest nod. She understood. They didn't need the words.

She crossed the open space to DiMarco, and when she refused to take his hand, he pulled her roughly against his side. Brogan clenched his fists when the man leaned down to press his nose to Libby's hair, inhaling deeply.

"If you follow us, I'll know. And if you try to kill me, Teresa dies."

Libby's head whipped around to stare up at DiMarco. "Teresa is still alive?"

"Of course she is, Elizabeth. I know she's your favorite."

Brogan saw the instant Libby's expression changed, and she took a deliberate step forward into their sniper's line of sight. Son of a bitch. She was going to go with him to try and save her sister.

"Gentlemen," DiMarco sneered, reaching behind him to open the car door and shoving Libby inside.

Declan gripped Brogan's arm when the car sped off in a squeal of tires. "Give it a minute. We've got men watching for a tail. We'll get her."

Brogan shot a glance at his brother. "You wanted to hand her over to be murdered."

Lips thinning, Declan nodded. "It was my own blind spot for Evie that had me ignoring the obvious. The woman's smarter than I gave her credit for. Braver too. We'll do whatever it takes to get her back, brother. My word on that."

"Damn right we will. Time to get started."

Chapter Thirty-Seven

Fear coiled around her as the car sped out of the parking garage. Breathe in through the nose, out through the mouth. Her fingers tapped a nervous rhythm against her knee while they drove in a confusing zig-zag of turns.

"I've missed you, Elizabeth."

Libby snorted. "Why? You don't even know me."

She jerked away when he scooted closer, but he gripped her arm so hard she had to grit her teeth against the pain, his fingers digging into her skin.

"I know everything I need to know. Your sister's been fun to play with these last few months, but now I have what I really want." He traced his finger down over her breast and around her nipple. She swallowed against the wave of nausea that shuddered through her.

"If you wanted me so badly, why did you try to kill me?"

He scowled. "I had to teach you a lesson. If you had behaved yourself, I wouldn't have needed to beat you. You'll do well to remember that in the future." He skimmed his hand up her thigh. "For what it's worth, I did argue against your death, but your father insisted. Such a waste."

He gripped her thigh hard, and she shoved at his hands, making him laugh. "For once I'm grateful for your father's incompetent assholes. I would have been truly sad to see you dead. Although it did make this whole thing so much harder."

"Which thing?"

DiMarco waved a hand in the air absently. "This whole takeover. All Tony had to do was realize who the better man was and step down. But he was so stubborn. You're a lot like him in that regard."

Libby's throat tightened. She didn't miss the way he referred to her father in the past tense. "And he had a change of heart?"

DiMarco smiled, quick and cruel. "In a manner of speaking. It's no longer beating."

At a strangled sound from the driver, Libby glanced toward the front of the car and recognized her brother's eyes in the rearview mirror. Giovanni.

DiMarco tracked her gaze. "Ah, yes. Little Gio. I let him live. He's been quite the asset. Teresa too, of course."

"And my mother?"

DiMarco tsked, and her whole body tensed. "A staunch loyalist to your father after all, I'm afraid. I guess they're together in hell now. With your fuck up of a brother. It shouldn't be that hard to follow directions. All I ask for is competency."

"So you've killed my entire family."

He frowned. "Well, not the entire family, darling. There's this one," he reached forward to clap Gio on the shoulder, making him wince. "Your sister, of course, though she might be a little worse for wear. And then there's you."

He stroked a hand down her cheek, gripping her chin in

his hands and forcing her to look up at him. She wanted to tell him to go fuck himself, but she only needed to hold it together long enough for Brogan to track them. Then she could get Teresa, and they could get the hell out of there.

The minute DiMarco said he had her sister, all that hope Libby had been silently smothering since the raid flooded back in. If there was even the smallest chance that Teresa was alive, she had to know, had to try and save her.

So when DiMarco's lips met hers, Libby didn't pull away, but she refused to open for his tongue even as his hand wandered to grip her breast. There was only so much she could force her body to do.

He pulled away from her with a frustrated growl. "You'll learn. Like your sister learned."

"Why?" She hated the sob that escaped her. "Why did you take her?"

"For the same reason I took the Russian bitch. Leverage. I always get what I want, Elizabeth. Even if I have to secure it by force."

She shuddered at the threat, the car lurching to a stop. DiMarco slid out, reaching in to yank her out of the car when she didn't immediately follow. They were parked beside an old warehouse, around the back and out of sight of the road. The trees that shielded them from the next property had begun to burst into vivid color.

DiMarco rounded the trunk, popping it open and pulling out a bag, dropping it at her feet.

"Strip."

She looked up at him, eyes wide as her blood ran cold. Was he going to rape her right here? In front of her own brother? She took a step back, trying to buy herself time to talk her way out of this.

"I said strip. Everything. And change into the clothes in that bag. Now!" he screamed when she didn't move. "You think I'm stupid enough to let you wear whatever clothes you let *him* touch you in? With whatever tracking device he taped somewhere? Do it."

When she still didn't move, he pulled a gun from the small of his back, and she held her hands up, palms out. There was no way she could dig the tracker out of her waist-band without DiMarco noticing. If she left the device behind, Brogan would never find her. And then she'd be as good as dead. Because she'd kill herself long before she let DiMarco touch her.

With trembling fingers, she undid the buttons on her shirt, slipping it off her shoulders and dropping it on the ground next to her feet, trying to ignore the way his eyes roamed over her and how he dragged his tongue over his lips while he stared. She toed off her shoes and wriggled out of her jeans next, kicking them off. They were her last hope.

"Bra and panties too."

"There's nothing in them. I swear."

"Off," he demanded, waving the gun at her.

She squeezed her eyes shut, imagining herself anywhere but here. She reached behind her to unhook her bra and brought Brogan's face into her mind. The hard lines of it, that sweet smile that was only for her, his bright blue eyes. She bit her lip hard at DiMarco's appreciative grunts when she slipped her panties off. She would not let this bastard see her cry.

"Very good." His voice was husky with desire, and it made her want to vomit. "Now get dressed."

He kicked the bag closer to her, and she bent to retrieve it, pulling out a pair of baggy sweatpants that she had to cinch tight at the waist and a shirt that was one size too big.

"Well, it's not what I prefer to have you dressed in, but it'll do for now. Come on."

"Where are we going?" she asked when he didn't move to push her back into the car.

"Christ, you ask so many questions. Didn't your father ever teach you women should be seen and not heard? We're switching cars."

He swiveled, opening up the driver's side door. "Gio, my boy. Pleasure doing business with you."

Before she could blink, DiMarco leveled the gun at her brother and shot him in the chest. She couldn't stop the scream that escaped her when her brother's blood spattered the windshield. DiMarco leapt at her, slapping his hand over her mouth and jerking her roughly back against him.

"Shh, darling." He pressed a long kiss to her cheek, inhaling her scent. "Someone might hear you. Your brother has outlived his usefulness. A sacrifice for the cause. Time to go."

He shoved her toward the warehouse, pulling open the door and pushing her in ahead of him. It took a minute for her eyes to adjust to the darkness, but she could see a row of vehicles. Her father's prized collection of classic cars.

DiMarco hit a button, and a door opened at the far end, filling the warehouse with light. He gripped her wrist and led her past Corvettes and Camaros to a sleek black Mustang with tinted windows.

"Get in," he snapped when she didn't move.

With one last look over her shoulder, she climbed into the passenger side. This car was too old for Brogan to hack any kind of GPS, even if he did figure out which car was missing. Which was exactly why DiMarco chose it. They peeled out of the warehouse, and Libby prayed Brogan could find her in time.

Chapter Thirty-Eight

They slowed as they drove past the warehouse where the tracking chip had been sitting for nearly fifteen minutes. He couldn't see any cars, but Brogan knew they had to be in there somewhere.

"What are you doing?" he demanded when Declan passed the turn for the parking lot for the second time and did another loop.

"I want to be sure it's not a trap."

"There's no one in the parking lot." Brogan gestured out the window. "Property records say it belongs to one of Giordano's shell companies, and it's heavily insured, so I'm guessing it has something valuable inside."

"That doesn't mean he isn't staging an ambush."

"For Christ's sake, Declan. We're wasting time."

Brogan didn't care how many guys were inside. He wanted blood on his hands. Lots of it. He wanted to shoot DiMarco in his smug fucking face and scoop Libby into his arms and never let her out of his sight again.

Declan finally jerked the car into the lot when more backup arrived. They surrounded the building on three sides, pouring out of vehicles with guns drawn. Brogan rounded the side of the building and saw the hangar door open, a row of classic cars stretching back into the darkness, one clearly missing.

Fuck. DiMarco must have changed cars and taken her somewhere else. But the tracking beacon hadn't moved from this location.

"Back here!" someone shouted, and Brogan raced out the door and around to the back.

The car DiMarco and Libby left the parking garage in was parked haphazardly between the back of the warehouse and the trees, the doors and trunk hanging open. Goddammit. As Brogan drew closer, he saw her clothes in a pile on the ground. All of them. And rage burned hot in his veins. That fucking bastard made her strip naked to change.

He heard a cough from behind him and spun, raising his weapon. A man sat in the front seat of the car, one leg dangling out. Libby's little brother. What had she said his name was? Gio.

The man coughed again, and a trickle of blood dripped from the corner of his mouth. His shirt was sticky with it.

"Where are they?"

"I didn't know," Gio rasped. "I didn't know he was going to..."

Brogan reached up to slap Gio hard across the face when his eyes rolled back in his head. "If you're going to die on me, make yourself useful first and tell me where the fuck he took her."

"Palermo. Home," he added, his voice weak and thin.

"Italy? He's taking her to Italy?"

But Gio didn't answer. His body relaxed back against the seat, head lolling to one side. Goddamn it. If DiMarco left the country with Libby, it would be almost impossible to get her back. Brogan stood and sprinted around the building toward

269

the SUV, grabbing his laptop out of the backseat and propping it on the hood.

"What did you find?" Declan asked.

"He's taking her to Italy. Which means airports."

Brogan brought up a search window to check for registered flight plans. Criminal or not, hostage or not, he'd have to file one to get out of the country. DiMarco had a villa in Palermo, a town on the coast of Sicily. Brogan had seen it in his records search.

"There," Declan said, tapping the screen. "I know the owner of that airport. Get in. I'll call in a favor to ground all outbound traffic."

Declan barked out orders for some men to stay behind and clean up the crime scene and for the rest to load out with them. Brogan slammed the lid on his laptop and jumped into the passenger seat. The flight was scheduled to take off in less than twenty minutes. He'd shoot the fucking thing out of the sky if he had to.

Libby went over her options. There was no way for Brogan to track her, no way for her to get in touch with him. If DiMarco had a phone on him, she had no idea where it was, and he'd probably shoot her before she had much time to find it.

The gun sat on the dashboard, and she gauged whether she could successfully make a grab for it. If she managed to wrestle it from him, then what? She couldn't shoot him. He was driving, and they'd crash.

The likelihood that he would do what she said even if she had control of the gun seemed slim. The man was fucking crazy. Plus, he still had Teresa, and she wanted to at least attempt to get her sister out of this alive too. So she waited.

DiMarco made another turn, and when they cleared a line

of trees, a small private airport came into view. Her whole body went numb, and her heart pounded in her ears. This was it. This was his endgame. To get her out of the country and have her completely at his mercy.

She would not get on a plane with him. He'd have to kill her first.

DiMarco brought the car to a screeching halt next to a jet that idled on the tarmac with its door open and stairs extended. A black SUV sat parked in front of them, but he seemed to expect them. Was Teresa in there?

"Come on, darling." DiMarco reached across her to open her door. "Time to go home."

When he got out, she bolted from the car and sprinted toward the closest hangar, hoping someone in there would hide her and call for help. She was nearly beyond the plane when someone tackled her from behind, knocking the wind out of her.

She gasped for breath while they hauled her to her feet, kicking and hitting and scratching at whatever body parts she could connect with. A big man half carried, half dragged her back to stand in front of DiMarco, who frowned his displeasure.

"You will have to kill me," she spat. "Because I am not getting on that plane with you."

DiMarco raised his gun and pressed it against her forehead. She flinched but didn't back down. She would rather die than go anywhere with him and spend the rest of her life as his prisoner. She'd be dead either way, and at least this way she got to choose.

When he lowered the gun, she wobbled forward, but he brought her to her knees with a sucker punch to the gut that had her coughing out a strangled breath. He crouched down and grabbed a fistful of hair, jerking her head up so hard tears formed in the corner of her eyes.

"You have so much spirit in you. It'll be fun to see how much of it I can kill and how much I can keep alive to entertain myself."

He kissed her, lips rough against hers, and she nearly gagged. When he swept his tongue against her lips, she parted them this time, then bit down hard.

He stumbled back on a muttered curse, falling on his ass, and she shot to her feet, giving him a swift kick to the face that resulted in a satisfying crunch of bone before powerful arms wrapped around her again and hauled her back. She kicked out her legs, screaming for help, but the few people she saw earlier were gone now. Had they left to call the police?

"You stupid bitch," DiMarco snarled, on his feet now. "You're getting on that fucking plane, or I'll—"

"Do it!" she screamed, fury pushing at the edge of her control. "Shoot me, you son of a bitch, because that's the only way you can make me go anywhere with you."

He stalked forward, rage boiling in his eyes. She shrank back as much as her captor would allow, but it didn't prepare her for the backhand across her cheek or the second fist to her jaw.

Pain radiated through her skull, and her head fell forward, her breathing ragged as she willed her muddled thoughts to clear. She heard voices, muffled shouts, and the screech of tires. The arms holding her released her suddenly, and she slid bonelessly to the ground, unable to make her legs work enough to keep her upright.

Blood trickled warm and wet down her temple and into her eye, and she tried to blink it away. She wanted to move her arm to wipe at it, but the limb wouldn't cooperate, so she closed her eyes instead. She heard gunfire, but the sounds were sluggish and distant, like watching a movie in slow motion.

Why the fuck couldn't she *move*? She had to get out of here before DiMarco loaded her onto that plane. And where was Teresa? Was she in the other car? Did DiMarco even have her, or was that another lie to get what he wanted?

Everything felt numb and cold. She really was going to die here on this stretch of asphalt. Brogan probably wouldn't even be able to find her body. Brogan, with his strong hands and crooked smile. The only man she'd ever loved. She felt a tear slip down her nose.

As if she conjured him with her thoughts, his voice broke through the fog. At least he would be the last thing she heard instead of this volley of gunfire and shouting. That was better than she could have hoped for.

"Libby." The sound of his voice eased some of the numbing cold. "Libby, open your eyes. Baby, can you hear me? Declan!"

Declan was in her hallucination too? That seemed weird. He didn't even like her. She felt a warm hand grip her wrist.

"She's got a pulse." The hand released her. "She's not dead."

Not yet anyway.

"Libby, baby. Please. Open your eyes."

Brogan's voice again, desperate. Maybe it wasn't a hallucination. Maybe he was real. Her fingers flexed on the pavement, and she felt a firm hand cover her own and give it a light squeeze. She opened her eyes, squinting through the blood that coated her lashes.

"Brogan," she whispered.

"Oh, thank God." The words were a sob, and he scooted close enough that she could feel the heat of him. His body stretched out on the pavement next to hers.

"Are you real?"

He smiled, and she thought she saw a tear slip down his cheek. "I'm real. Hey," he added when her eyelids drooped.

"Stay awake with me, okay? I don't want to move you until Doc and McGee get here, and they'll be here any minute."

"I'm so tired," she murmured.

"I know. I know you are, baby, but I need you to hang on a little longer."

She nodded, or tried to, but she wasn't sure her head was actually moving. "Okay. I'll hang on for you."

"That's my girl," Brogan whispered. He brushed his lips over hers, whisper-soft.

"Brogan?"

"Yeah?"

"If I die, I want to make sure the last thing I say to you is that I love you."

"You're not going to die, Libby. You're not allowed to."

Her mouth tilted up at the corner. "I don't think that's up to you."

"Like hell it isn't. I need you to keep fighting. For me, for us, for those fifty years you talked about. Here's the doc now."

She felt more hands on her, checking her neck, her back, her legs. They rolled her over, and then she was floating, weightless, fighting against the throbbing in her head that wanted to pull her under.

"I'm going to give her something for the pain."

Yes, please, God. Something for the pain.

"Baby?" Brogan said into her ear, his breath warm and soothing against her skin. "You can go to sleep now."

She felt a prick of pain in her arm and let the tide drag her into the darkness.

Chapter Thirty-Nine

"Need any help in here?" Evie poked her head into the kitchen from the dining room, and Libby smiled.

"I'm almost done with this, but you can take the bread and send in a big, strong man to help with this pot of bolognese."

Evie grabbed the basket of bread off the counter and lifted it to her nose. "God, that smells like heaven. The most I can manage is a pancake that won't kill anyone."

"I hear Declan is pretty good at grilled cheese."

Evie laughed. "Thank God for Marta and you."

She disappeared with the bread, and Libby chuckled, giving the sauce one last stir. When arms wrapped around her from behind, she leaned into them, sighing when his lips came down to brush the top of her head.

"Big, strong man reporting for duty," Brogan murmured against her cheek.

"You can take the sauce out to the table. The pasta is done."

He loosened his grip slightly but didn't let go when she

moved to scoop the pasta out of the pot of boiling water, letting excess water drip back into the pot before adding it to a bowl.

"Is that fettuccine?"

She wrinkled her nose. "This is tagliatelle."

Giving her waist a squeeze, he released her and reached to heft the pot of sauce off the stove. "They look exactly the same."

Libby slapped a hand over her chest in mock offense, and he chuckled. "Every Italian nonna worldwide just died a little."

She followed him through the dining room and family room and out onto the patio. They'd set up little heaters to fend off the autumn chill, and the whole family gathered around the table to eat. Well, almost the whole family.

Cait and Evan were still staying with her parents in upstate New York, and Aidan had made himself more than scarce in the two weeks since Brogan and Declan had come to her rescue. Then there was Teresa.

Her sister had been in the SUV, alive but definitely not well. Teresa barely spoke, never made eye contact, hated to be touched. After her first afternoon with Teresa in months, Libby had come home and collapsed into Brogan's arms in tears. Her sister might never be the same, and she had no idea what to do about it, no idea if anything could be done.

Especially when Teresa had refused to stay with the Callahans. Brogan said he understood and suggested they set her up as a roommate with Mack, one of the women they'd rescued from the first raid. Mack had adjusted well and was holding down a full-time job. Brogan thought it might be a nice way to ease Teresa back into some semblance of a normal life.

It didn't seem to be working, but Libby was willing to give it time. She'd give her sister as much time as she needed if it meant she would come back, if it meant she could watch her laugh and read and enjoy life again.

"You okay?" Brogan asked, pouring her a glass of wine.

"Yeah." She smiled. "Just thinking about Teresa."

"I talked to Mack today," Evie said, ladling sauce over her pasta. "She said Teresa seems to be doing okay, that she's been eating more regularly."

Libby let out a relieved breath. "Good. That's good. I can't get more than two words out of her. I think she blames me for not getting her out sooner or…I don't know."

"She'll heal, and she'll forgive. Mack is still easing her toward therapy too."

"Headache?" Declan asked when he noticed Libby rubbing at her temple.

"They're not as bad now as they were. It'll pass."

"I'll go grab your pills from upstairs."

"No." Libby laid a hand on Brogan's arm when he rose. "I'm fine, really. I probably just need to eat something."

"Sweet God," Evie moaned around a bite of pasta. "This will cure you."

Libby smiled into her wine, letting Brogan add more pasta and sauce to her plate than she would eat.

"Feel free to make this again sometime," Declan said around his own bite.

He met her eyes across the table, and she could see the sincerity in his gaze. He gave a slight nod and went back to eating, and she caught Evie's quick grin. That was as much a stamp of approval as she was likely to get from Declan Callahan.

It would take a long time before things regained a sense of normalcy. There was a huge hole without Finn and Cait and Evan. Even Libby, the newcomer that she was, could sense it. Dinners like this seemed empty without Evie and Cait's steady friendship, without Finn's easy laughter and quick teasing. She had only known Finn for a few short months, and she knew the others felt his loss more acutely.

But like Evie said, they would heal, and now she would be a part of the new normal they pieced back together. For the first time in her life, she finally felt home. Brogan had never made her feel anything else.

As the light faded and the outdoor lights clicked on, they let Marta and Rachel handle cleanup. She curled up on one of the couches with Evie while Brogan and Declan discussed Falcone and his progress and what to do about Ivankov now that they had a little distance from the disaster DiMarco had wrought.

"You're quiet tonight," Evie said, drawing a blanket around her shoulders.

"Am I?"

"Mmm."

Libby sighed. "I still have nightmares sometimes. Where I feel his tongue in my mouth, choking me, or he's running after me, and I can't get away. I can never run fast enough. Those wake me up screaming, and Brogan has to soothe me back to sleep. Like a fucking mental patient."

"I have nightmares too. The screaming ones happen less and less often now. But every time I have one, I feel exactly the same. Weak that I can't handle it, ridiculous that it's been almost six months and they still bother me." She glanced over at her husband. "Worried that one day he'll realize I'm more trouble than I'm worth and come to his senses."

Libby shifted so she could see Brogan more clearly. "So what do you do about it?"

"I remind myself that he's never expected me to be perfect or have all my shit together." Evie's smile was soft. "He's pretty good at reminding me too."

"I feel so broken, though," Libby sighed.

"We're all a little broken. It doesn't mean we don't deserve to be loved. Let him love you, Libby." Evie gave Libby's leg a pat as she stood.

Brogan smiled at his sister-in-law when she passed him and sank onto the couch next to Libby, wrapping his arm around her shoulders when she shifted to lean back against him.

"Brogan?"

He laid his cheek against her head. "Hmm?"

"What are you thinking when I wake up from a nightmare?"

"What?"

She took a deep breath and tried to organize her thoughts so they made sense. "When I wake up and you have to talk me off the ledge like a crazy person and then help me get back to sleep. What are you thinking?"

"Well, first, I don't think you're a crazy person."

"And second?"

"And second, I think about how I want to make you feel so loved and so safe that you never have another nightmare again."

She closed her eyes and inhaled the heady, woodsy scent of him, lacing her fingers with his when he reached for her hand. Christ, how she loved this man.

"How long do you plan on doing that for, exactly?"

He brought her hand up to his lips, and she could feel them curve into a smile against her fingers. "Oh, another fifty years or so."

A Note for the Reader

Dear Reader,

From the very bottom of my heart, thank you. Out of all the billions of books available to read you choose mine. I was enamored with Brogan while writing Declan and Evie's story in Sweet Revenge and I was so happy to get to know him better in this book. The way he loves, protects, and wants Libby totally melted me. I am deeply grateful that you took the time out of your life to come along on Libby and Brogan's journey.

If you enjoyed this book, I would really appreciate a little more of your time in the form of a review on Goodreads or Amazon or wherever you purchased it.

I couldn't do this writing thing I love so much without you. I'm beyond excited to share Aidan's story with you in Book Three of the Callahan Syndicate Series. Look for *Deadly Obsession* coming in August 2022 to Kindle Unlimited, ebook, and paperback.

For sneak peeks, bonus chapters, updates, release dates, and more, sign up for my newsletter at https://meaghanpierce.com/newsletter or follow me on TikTok.

All my love,
Meaghan

tiktok.com/@meaghanpierceauthor

Also by Meaghan Pierce

Callahan Syndicate Series

Sweet Revenge

Acknowledgments

Thank you to The Group Chat for always being there to encourage me to go for it, talk me off the ledge, and send the best GIFs when I'm celebrating a milestone. I'm not sure any of these books would get published without you.

To Caoimhe and Paula, my soul sisters. I couldn't begin to express my thanks for your love, support, opinions, real talk, and screenshot evidence when I get too in my own head.

To my betas: Kate, Ali, Caoimhe, Jill, and Kathryn. You helped me make this book better and for that I am so grateful.

Shout out to to my ex-boyfriend, whose incessant lecturing of how vulnerable our data and systems are to hacking really came in handy in this book.

To my editor, Mo. Thank you times a million for answering all of my stupid questions with grace and a perfectly chosen GIF. And to my proofreader, Holly. Experiencing this book alongside you was the most fun I've had in a long time.

Lastly, thank you to all the readers who kept telling me they were as excited to read Brogan's story as I was to tell it. Your excitement kept me going through long nights of rewrites and edits. I hope I did him justice for you.

Printed in Great Britain
by Amazon